THE FORGOTTEN ISLE

Jim Stein

Digital ISBN: 978-1-7335629-9-7
Print ISBN: 978-1-954788-02-2

First printing, 2021

Jagged Sky Books
P.O. Box #254
Bradford, Pa 16701

Cover art & design by Kris Norris
Edited by Caroline Miller

Magic Trade School

Also by Jim Stein:

Legends Walk Series

Space-Slime Continuum

Acknowledgements

Thank you to all the people who helped.

From cover design to editing and beta readers to developmental assistants, all have been critically important to brining this story to life.

And thank you, the reader, for spending time with Jason, Bethany, and the rest.

A special thanks to those who are able to jot off a quick review online. As you venture along with the characters, think about what you like and don't so you can let others know. A simple headline summarizing your most lasting impression and a sentence or two only takes a minute to post and helps me immensely. So, again, thank you!

Visit **https://JimSteinBooks.com/subscribe** to get a free ebook, join my reader community, and sign up for my infrequent newsletter.

1. Demon Lair

NOTHING, THAT'S WHAT the team turned up. Three more black-clad figures tromped back through the dank basement empty-handed. Regina Williams acknowledged their report with curt nods, auburn curls bobbing. She turned my way, no evidence of the smile and dimples that usually got my blood pumping.

"The data's solid." I kept my voice matter-of-fact, trying to sound encouraging.

"Jason, I know Mike Gonzales is your friend and all." Gina waved away my comment. "But this is the third mission that's gone belly up. Are we sure he's fully recovered? Maybe those leftover memories are simply fragmented dreams."

Mr. Gonzales was more than just a friend. As the head of maintenance for the Attwater School, he'd taken me under his wing first semester. I'd learned a lot about piping, plumbing, and electrical systems from his lessons—very productive right up until the self-proclaimed lord of the shadow demons had possessed him. Once Mr. G. was out from under the Shadow Master's influence, the school's security department had been keen to take advantage of the scraps of memory left behind. But the information hadn't been terribly helpful so far, and interest was waning.

"Dreams wouldn't have pinpointed this place." I sniffed, taking in the aroma of burnt cigars and animal musk. "This is definitely a lurker lair. We're just too late."

Lurker demons excelled at hiding in plain sight despite being ugly brutes. They came in shapes and sizes as diverse as the lower-level shadow demons. But where shadows tended to take the smoky forms of common animals, lurkers could look like just about anything, especially when camouflaged. They were creatures of flesh and blood with claws, fangs, and sometimes magic of their own. Gina's security team had scared up a few left over runts in the old mansion, little four-legged aberrations that looked like raccoons crossed with zombie possums.

"You're right about the fact that there *were* a lot of lurkers here." Gina shook her head and waved another team member toward an unexplored alcove. "But we're stretched too thin to keep chasing shadows—excuse the pun. I think this was our last shot at locating the network the Shadow Master pirated."

The Shadow Master had stolen lurker forces from the mimics. Mimics were the third and most powerful class of demons we had to deal with. I'd never seen one up close, but every student was cautioned to call for backup rather than trying to tackle one on their own.

Mimics wielded powerful magic and acted as the commanding generals for lurker forces. Worst of all, they looked just like humans so could infiltrate industry without being noticed. Although few in number, mimics settled into key positions within the various segments of industry the demons sought to control. Attwater graduates were the last line of defense and committed to rooting them out.

With a smile of apology, Gina slipped on thick leather gloves matching her black commando outfit and moved off to join the final sweep. Hopefully she wouldn't be using her pyromancy talent upstairs. The basement, with its stone walls and exposed piping, resembled the archaic interior of our school, but the stained velvet furniture and moldering bookcases above wouldn't do well if the woman unleashed her fiery salamanders.

She sauntered away with cool confidence to see to the final sweep. At just twenty-three, Gina had come a long way from the nervous teacher's aide who'd helped me through introductory welding. Our acting dean, Mary Eisner, had kept Gina on after graduation. That gave Gina and me extra time together, but more importantly gave the decimated security branch a strong second in command.

I stepped over to where my friend Owen pawed through odd gadgets and tools on a long workbench. The main security team hadn't found any of the magic artifacts demons tended to horde. At six feet, Owen was a couple of inches taller than me and wore the jaded smile of an affable cynic who'd seen too much in his lofty twenty-six years—something he assured me that I'd come to understand. Like the four-year difference in our ages made that big of a difference—jerk.

"Check this out, Jason." He waved me over. The twinkle of mischief in his eye made it hard to hold a grudge. "Small engine parts, wheels, and gears. They were definitely building something."

"By Jove, I think you've cracked the case." I imagined a news headline and splayed my hands wide for emphasis. "Lurkers build weed-whacker to undermine forces of good. Film at eleven."

"Laugh it up, Robo-boy." He peered into the open end of a carburetor as if expecting it to spring to life. "You'll be singing a different tune if I find an overlooked artifact."

We didn't know for certain why the demons collected magic artifacts. Presumably they were searching for one in particular or trying to gather parts from some archaic device that could facilitate their plans of world conquest. My friends and I had wrangled an intact device out from under the nose of a bunch of lurkers last semester. The football-sized gadget with silver and gold hemispheres held apart by telescoping rods currently gathered dust in Attwater's vault. Settling into third semester had left me little time, but I planned to explore its function soon.

The football had been left by a long-dead tinker with the talent to repair things both magic and mundane—the same talent I possessed. Despite Owen's jab, I was a tinker, and getting to be a darn good one thanks to my Attwater training. I only built robots in my spare time.

The bit of verbal banter sobered us both though. Owen was in the business of fixing things too. His magic talent breathed life back into the oldest of combustion engines. Unlike my questionable fit of pursuing a welding certification—a trade loosely related to my tinker ability—Owen was a natural choice to be a mechanic, a motorcycle mechanic in his case. Certification still took plenty of training because his magic talent didn't extend past the combustion chain. Owen still had to repair everything from brakes to clutches the old-fashioned way.

But the sentiment underlying his words hit home. We weren't exactly critical to the mission. Neither of us possessed a talent particularly useful in fighting demons. Sure, we'd both trained with common core spells using basic elemental magic. Owen was better with the five elements, but our talents were another matter. You couldn't exactly fix your way out of a life or death struggle with lurkers and mimics.

Gina could send mythical salamanders to scorch her opponents, our friend Bethany made drawings that came to life and literally devoured shadow demons, and Chad from the wide open plains of Montana could call down lightning in addition to his core talent of predicting the weather. Heck, even my high school nemesis Lars the wannabe-rapper grew monstrous plants to do his bidding.

Owen and I were outcasts in the sense that neither of us could quite figure out how our talent helped fight demons. We didn't talk about it often because the topic was kind of depressing. Here we were, learning magic that most people knew nothing about and working alongside similarly talented students from all over the United States. Magic portals brought us all to the massive, semi-sentient building that was Attwater Trade School. But how on Earth did our talents contribute to the greater good?

The current mission was a prime example. We were stuck by the access portal to keep anything nasty from slipping back to the school—highly unlikely. Intellectually, I knew the security team didn't need newbies underfoot. But damn it, we'd been in tougher situations before, and the rear-guard assignment chafed.

Students got tested out on formal missions early in their last semester. How we handled real-world situations would determine our assignment to student security teams. Those teams trained alongside the pros before picking up some of the easier problems called in by graduates in the field.

"Well, good luck finding something they missed. Gina has a crack team." I avoided Owen's glare and scanned the dark archway beyond the swirling green oval that was our entry point. "That's weird!"

Something had moved in the shadows, a glint of silver. I called up the fire element and crept over. My fireballs were slow and weak compared to some, but most lurkers hated flames. Despite my earlier concerns about the danger of setting the place ablaze, there wasn't all that much flammable material in the cellar. Another flash came from the right, a tall thin glimmer like someone in armor ducking around the corner. They'd looked tall and carried a long stick or cane. I slipped to the pillar, back against the cool stone as sweat beaded on my forehead. The team had scoured this level first and given the all-clear. A deep breath steadied my nerves.

"What's up?" Owen's voice jolted me out of sneak mode and nearly had me jumping out of my skin as he stomped over.

"Keep it down!" I hissed, then dropped any pretense of stealth and whipped around the corner with spell ready.

I nearly shot off the fireball, but managed to ground the magic at the last moment. A young man with a broad nose, pointy chin, and stormy gray eyes set in a narrow face crouched before me. The image seemed to be all legs and arms despite broad shoulders beneath the black shirt. Sandy-blond hair was trimmed close over the ears and blended into a messy style above an all-too-familiar face. I raised my right hand to smooth down a spike of hair, and the image followed suit. I'd managed to corner a mirror.

But where had the stick come from? I looked down at my empty hands as if expecting to find a clue. The mirror image had seemed straight and tall even as I'd crept up on the rectangle bolted to the wall. The shine must have come from the frame, even though the metallic paint had seen better days.

"It feels like I'm missing something." Owen straightened his shirt and smoothed back his hair, which always managed to look more stylish than mine despite being longer and shaggier.

Maybe there was some truth to his claim of being tempered by vast years of experience. Brown eyes glimmered with mischief from their crescent slits above his lopsided grin, but dark little crow's feet radiated from the corners.

"I thought I saw…" I trailed off at his raised eyebrow, feeling silly. It was only a mirror. "Okay, I freaked out. Happy?"

"Immensely."

His knowing little nod brimmed with dry humor, but zero animosity. For Owen it was all about the joke, not the people. That was the guy's saving grace, the thing that made his jabs and observations tolerable if not downright amusing.

"Glad I made your day. Let's get back to the portal."

2. Missing People

"I HEARD THE raid didn't go so well." Bethany sat with her girlfriend, Mon, at our usual table in the commons. "Don't worry, you'll get them next time."

Bethany seemed even more upbeat than usual, her hazel eyes shining above a brilliant smile. As the youngest of our Attwater group, I tended to think of her as baby-faced, but something had changed. Her caramel skin might have a bit more glow, or maybe she wore makeup to make her high cheeks rounder? Something subtle was going on behind the thick black braids framing her face.

"Hey, your hair's longer!" I put my finger on the difference almost immediately and wondered if Mon's magic somehow made hair grow fast. We didn't know the Asian girl's exact talent, but she'd be graduating in cosmetology. "Like, since yesterday."

"Don't sprain your brain, Sherlock, they're called extensions." Bethany swung her head and the braids slapped her shoulders. "Looks good, right?"

Ah, so no magic. That made sense. Mon compressed her lips as if trying hard not to comment and settled for shaking her head. Her own hair was a glistening raven-black match to Bethany's, but fell straight to her shoulders. Mon had a year on Bethany's nineteen and stood an inch taller than the other girl's five-foot-four frame. The height difference was hard to judge without an algebraic equation accounting for heels on any given day.

The two had grown close over the past year, Bethany's bright bubbly personality complementing Mon's quiet introspection. I'd upgraded that last from sullen brooding, but at times Mon could still be off-putting. Her black lipstick, eyeliner, pants, and top didn't help. The sharp contrast between Goth outfit and pale skin tended to amplify moods like her current disgust at my apparent ignorance of advanced hairstyles.

"Yep, hair's awesome," I said carefully before deciding to focus on the botched demon raid. "Security isn't going to be checking out any more leads from Mr. Gonzales."

"Can't blame them, especially if the Shadow Master left bum info behind." Chad strode over and squeezed himself onto the bench alongside Mon.

"Geez, keep it down." I pumped my hands palm down to lower the volume of the cowboy's Midwestern drawl.

Thirty or so students sat scattered around the big room, and a few more loaded up lunch plates in the kitchen area along the back wall. No one seemed to notice or care about Chad's statement, but Mr. Gonzalez's possession was a sensitive topic. Hopefully his words had been lost in the general hubbub and the pipes and ducting high overhead. Mon actually smiled, just an upward tick of her dark lip liner, and squirmed closer to Bethany so the big galoot could settle his butt down and lean back against his favorite column.

Chad Stillman ported in from a barn in Montana each day, so much cooler than the old beer store that was my local Attwater branch-slash-portal. At six-two our cowboy was big as life with an annoyingly square jaw and perpetual tan. He also happened to be a marshmallow who'd formed a special bond with the school building—a fact that was painfully clear by the way one hand caressed the stonework at his back. Attwater responded with a gusty sigh from the vents above. Chad even pulled off the cowboy hat with disturbing ease. Today's was dark brown to match his plaid shirt and boots. I could rock a hat too, but refused to don my new headwear in the commons.

"Sorry." Chad gave an easy smile. "I forget that not everyone's read in on last semester's events."

"But you've got a point, and apparently everyone knows about yesterday's mission," I admitted. "Three nests in a row have been deserted. Each was definitely a demon stronghold, so Mr. G's info is accurate. It's like they knew we were coming and cleared out."

"The mimics must realize the Shadow Master got captured," Bethany said. "By now they've probably pulled their lurkers out of every location he knew about, just as a precaution."

The Shadow Master had done more than just steal lurkers away; he'd tried to carve out a place for himself at the top of the demon hierarchy. We knew that the demon lord had been well connected with several key cells controlled by mimics in high places. Getting the drop on those forces could yield information critical to ending the demon infestation once and for all.

"They're up to something," I said. "Those sites we raided weren't near power stations, water treatment plants, or any of the usual targets demons go after. It's been relatively quiet in the field lately, but the Shadow Master thought the mimics were upping their game. Unfortunately, the demon lord was too intent on grabbing power for himself to pay much attention. I think Mr. G. is out of ideas."

"So what's our next step?" Chad wiggled in his seat, trading elbow jabs with Mon as they vied for more butt space.

"Nothing." I was surprised to find I meant it. "Security will keep doing what they do best, and we focus on getting our certifications, graduating, and landing jobs."

"Don't forget about Dean Gladstone." The big sketchbook on the table in front of Bethany vibrated like a cell phone. She laid a hand on the cover with an apologetic grimace. "Mort's bored. Does anyone mind?"

When no one objected, Bethany flipped open the book, and a charcoal-gray cloud swirled up from the page, graphite and ink twisting into a gruesome foot-tall creature with a flattened snout, tusks, and barbed tail. Mortimer zipped around the table, sniffing at everyone and everything. When the gargoyle drawing pulled a pen from my pack, I swatted him away, which he took as an invitation to parry and thrust with the ball point. I grabbed a candy bar from my stash and dueled the transparent little guy for a few seconds. After a half a dozen good slashes, he lost interest, scurried over to the women, and plopped down on top of the sketchpad.

"Shouldn't we be planning a mission to retrieve Gladstone?" Chad asked. "The school's going nuts. They might not know the specifics, but the fact that demons hijacked the most powerful man in the school has everyone looking over their shoulder."

I pictured the dapper man with his button-up coat, goggles, and cane. His white hair and matching pencil-thin moustache were always neat as a pin. A flash of guilt came with the image. He was the reason I was training at Attwater instead of sitting in jail for a stupid mistake. Dean Gladstone had also helped me control my tinker talent and keep the robots I unwittingly imbued with magic from exploding. Like Mr. Gonzales, the dean was a mentor, maybe even a friend. But that didn't change the facts.

"We've done all we can for the dean," I said. "We tracked down where the demons sent his security team. If we'd found them sooner, they'd be home. But we didn't, and he jumped everyone back in time to get out of the trap. Ms. Eisner has experts from the other schools working on it. They'll come up with something, or Dean Gladstone will figure out how to come back on his own. I've learned a thing or two from three *Back to the Future* movies. The fact that a tattered letter delivered by pony express hasn't shown up is a sure sign they'll make it back."

Dean Gladstone had a rare talent with clocks, not just building them, but manipulating time itself. He and half our security force had been trapped in underground, magic-resistant rock. By the time we'd cracked how the device that ported them there worked, thirst and hunger had forced them to flee using the only means possible.

"Waiting feels...wrong." Chad screwed up his face, laid a hand on his beloved column, and let out a big whoosh of air.

"I feel you." I truly did. "But Gina and security will do everything possible. We'll get to go out on the standard training missions, so there should be plenty of action for you. It's our last semester and time to focus on ourselves. I for one am more than ready to start pulling a salary again. My rent isn't going to pay itself."

Handyman jobs had kept me solvent for the three years after high school, but my savings had dwindled significantly during a year in Attwater. I might still live in the apartment over the garage, but Dad was a stickler for paying rent on time.

"Guess so." Chad's little game of seat expansion had petered out, and now he looked glum. "I'm not so sure I'll get to go on those missions though. My meteorology visits are out of control. It's kind of flattering that they think so much of my weather forecasts, but porting around the world is getting old. You'd think Bashar and Chingyow would have people who can read climate. At least that way, I could stay stateside. As it stands, there just isn't room in my schedule to take on student security missions too. You guys are going to have all the fun."

"I'm with you." Mon broke her silence, seemed to realize that was out of character, and actually blushed. "It's just…I'm getting pulled for side projects too. Security might handle the school's core mission of squashing demons, but the staff definitely has other irons in the fire that need students."

Bethany nodded, but looked worried. "A primer on all that would keep everyone on the same page."

Bethany gripped Mon's hand, and they leaned into each other. Mortimer reached out a transparent claw and laid it over Bethany's other hand, lending his own bit of graphite support that left a smudge of gray on her knuckles.

So Bethany was being tapped for mysterious projects too. That would be why she hadn't been assigned to raids as the semester got going. She, Owen, and I had been inseparable during our first two semesters. I got the feeling we were being groomed as a team. Although how that was supposed to carry on after graduation remained a mystery. With different talents and certifications, we of course had varied course loads, but always landed together in common core, practical magic, and other classes.

"Well, at least Owen gets to work on his project bike." Chad made an effort to lighten the mood. "He's crowing about it to everyone who'll listen."

"That old Indian motorcycle?" I'd thought that was still squirrelled away back at his place in Virginia.

"Not that one," Chad said. "The auto shop found a vintage wartime Harley. You know, the drab green ones with a big white star and side car? Anyway, he's working with another guy to get it patched up and roadworthy as part of their final certification. Our little mechanic's getting all grown up."

He delivered that last statement with hands clutched over his heart and batting eyes. My laugh burst out in a wet explosion, and Bethany laughed until she cried. A giggle even escaped from Mon as she pushed the melodramatic cowboy away.

As the lunch hour wore on, we discussed plans for the semester, the various skills we'd have to master, and the dreaded question of how to keep in touch once the school scattered us to the winds.

"Gina says the placement office really works with students." I'd been happy to hear that. "That's how she landed the security job back here instead of heading out to one of the facilities lobbying for her. Of course, with half of security still missing, maybe that's a special case."

"It's just good to hear they give you options," Bethany said. "And with bonuses for our special talents, you can't beat the money."

"Speaking of talents—" I scanned the room, but hurried on when I saw Mon's face darken. "Has anyone seen Roxy today?"

Mon relaxed at the question, probably relieved I wasn't going to ask about her own talent. She was downright secretive about magic beyond common elemental spells and refused to answer whenever one of us pressed. As far as I knew, even Bethany was in the dark about Mon's special skill. Everyone knew she'd be a great cosmetologist, but information beyond that seemed to fall squarely into the "I'd tell you, but then I'd have to kill you" category.

"You need to stop chasing after that woman and focus on Gina." Bethany glowered at me, having apparently caught the look from Mon.

"Come on. It's nothing like that." I couldn't believe she still stressed over the woman I'd sponsored into Attwater. "Roxy's in her second semester now. I just want to see if they finally settled on a talent."

Roxy had entered my life like a battering ram, showing up in my hometown with robots of her own when I'd faced down my first lurkers. The automata I made were geared more toward service—think mechanical butler—but Roxy had been into battle-bots before Attwater. Like me, she hadn't even known she had magic, but man did that woman rock common core classes. Ms. Schlaza, our icy instructor who'd been birthed in the belly of a glacier, said Roxy was the best student to cross Attwater's threshold in years.

There was a two-fold problem in assessing Roxy's talent. Firstly, she was too accomplished at elemental spells. The magic fingerprint every student developed though studying elemental magic was hard to interpret in her case. Secondly, the dean himself had taken up the gauntlet to determine the woman's core magical talent. If anyone could ferret out the riddle of her magic it was Dean Gladstone, but now he was missing in action.

"Don't give me that." Bethany refused to back down. "A pretty blonde struts onto the scene and all of the sudden you're best of pals and hanging out on weekends."

"That's not fair. We only—"

"Fair or not, it's the truth. Think with your head, not your—" Bethany wagged a warning finger. "Just think with your head."

Sure, I'd hung out with Roxy a couple of occasions, nights that I'd rather have been with Gina. But my would-be girlfriend had been busy—hadn't even been my girlfriend at the time. Roxy and I had played games, talked shop, and watched movies, the same kind of stuff I did with my buddy Billy. Admittedly, she was more attractive than my big Samoan friend—a lot more attractive, with her narrow features, pixie nose, and enchanting smile. It was easy to get lost in those emerald eyes, and my mind did tend to twist into knots because—in spite of her obvious confidence—an undercurrent of vulnerability made me want to protect Roxy from the world.

But it wasn't like we were romantically involved. Attwater was great, but we all needed to deal with learning we weren't "normal." Most of us didn't have someone to commiserate with outside of school. I'd lucked out by finding a kindred soul right there in the suburbs of Philadelphia. Sharing hopes and fears about the fantastical world we'd been thrust into wasn't cheating on Gina.

I opened my mouth to argue my point, but a hard glint in Bethany's eyes told me it was a lost cause. Discretion was the better part of valor. She'd come around eventually— I hoped.

3. Geopolitical Studies

I RAN INTO Roxy right after lunch, almost as if she'd been summoned by the use of her name. A goofy thought, especially given she rounded the corner with Mary Eisner in tow.

"There you are!" Roxy wore a pink sweater and a brilliant smile framed by lustrous blond hair that spilled over both shoulders. "We haven't talked in ages."

"Hey, Roxy."

I sensed Bethany watching from the commons as I stammered out a greeting. A silver chain belted Roxy's waist, separating pink top from tight stone-washed jeans. Slim fingers drummed her hip, and she smiled broadly when I realized she'd caught me taking inventory. But my brain had just been trying to work out why my friends thought I was bananas over the woman.

Green eyes flashed above the dazzling smile and pert little nose. A melodic giggle passed her thin lips as our eyes met. The intimate look didn't spark lust. But I liked Roxy, and the protective instinct that uncurled within me rose fast, ready to strike at those who threatened her. Bethany was my friend too, but needed to mind her own business and keep her unfounded rumors to herself.

"You're looking well, Jason." Ms. Eisner's tone was brisk but pleasant.

"Hi, Dean." I'd kind of forgotten the other woman was there.

Ms. Eisner was a short, round Hispanic woman in her thirties and as bubbly and helpful as they came. She'd pulled her dark hair into a bun and rocked a midnight-blue pantsuit trimmed with white piping. As our Common Core instructor, Ms. Eisner had helped bolster my lagging performance first semester—an impressive feat while under the thumb of the militant Annette Schlaza. It was nice to see her rewarded, assuming the headaches of running the place weren't too bad.

"Please, just Mary. Save the honorary for when Dean Gladstone returns."

"No offense, but I hope that's soon," I said.

"Don't we all," Roxy cut in over whatever the acting dean was about to say. Ms. Eisner closed her mouth and waited patiently, but I must have made a face because Roxy threw an apology over her shoulder before turning back to me. "Sorry. So anyway, I'm helping out in the front office between classes. You know filing, answering the phone, taking notes. It's a perfect arrangement. Isn't it, Mary?"

"Yes, quite helpful." Ms. Eisner blinked as if struggling to remember something. "I should get back to my office and let you two love-birds catch up."

"Oh, we're not..." I didn't finish because Mary hustled off toward the admin wing. "I need to get moving myself. Geopolitical Studies starts in a few."

"No problem. We can catch up while we walk." Roxy slipped her arm through mine and steered me down the hall.

"So what's new in your world? The buzz in the front office is that those demon raids aren't very useful."

"That's an understatement."

I gave her the rough outline of how we'd come up empty-handed, told her how I didn't think Mr. G. had much more insight to offer, and finished with my newfound resolution to focus on graduation and leave security to do their job. She nodded, smiled, and held my gaze as we walked. It was a wonder that I didn't trip over my own feet. As it was, she'd just run out of questions as the classroom door loomed close, a good thing considering Bethany and the others were probably already inside. I didn't want to subject Roxy to any nastiness.

A moment of déjà vu had me reeling as I tried to untangle my arm from hers, but I managed in short order, gave her a wave, and bumped into the doorframe as I moved off to find my seat. *Klutz!*

As we closed in on graduation, most of our instruction was geared toward refining our magic talent or completing the technical certification required for our career field. Continuous learning was part of the package when graduating from Attwater, so both would persist in some form after graduation. But the focus left few open timeslots. We'd largely completed the little bit of theory needed, common core magic, and required electives. Geopolitical Studies was the exception.

I was sure the curriculum would've been vastly different at a university. We'd already touched lightly on the various regions, countries, and political groups in charge around the globe. But the bulk of the class was skewed toward laying out the array of magical defenses employed against the demons. Annual supplemental modules would keep us abreast of the changing landscape and impacts to our career field's niche in the protective network.

After bouncing off the doorway, I broke eye contact with Roxy and sheepishly shuffled down the row of desks to my seat between Bethany and Owen. The arrangement was claustrophobic, especially with Chad and Mon behind me. If they'd spotted Roxy outside the doorway, I'd never hear the end of it.

"Smooth move, Ex-lax." Owen grinned and shook his head, clearly amused by my stumble at the door.

"What's today's lecture?" I ignored the insult and turned to Bethany as our instructor, Mr. Grawpin, stepped to the front of the room.

Bethany looked on coolly, as if thinking. Or perhaps she'd spotted Roxy and was about to give me an earful.

"Defensive layers, the monastery barrier, trade schools and point defense." She looked through me like I wasn't even there. "You know, you could read the board yourself."

"What?" I turned to follow her gaze. Sure enough, the lesson was penned on the whiteboard in broad flowing script.

"Let's settle down." Harold Grawpin spoke in a low drawl that rounded off his vowels into a near croak.

Grawpin was a decent teacher who kept things interesting—once you got used to his slow speech. He was round, pudgy, and balding prematurely. A few gray hairs still clung to his shiny scalp, doing nothing to covered dozens of premature age spots. He'd taught our Magical Creatures class, and it had taken real effort to not think of him as a toad. Whispers spread through the few students who hadn't had Grawpin before, but everyone settled down after the initial flurry. Once I'd gotten used to it, Grawpin's voice came across as soothing and didn't even put me to sleep.

"Layered defense is what keeps the demons at bay." Mr. Grawpin launched into the lecture after checking the student rolls. "We will get into the nuances and variations later in the course, but three fundamental layers repel the ongoing demon invasion.

"Monasteries at the edge of the world maintain the outer layer, security forces from the three schools—Attwater, Bashar, and Chingyow—provide the middle layer, and you are the final inner layer. Once you enter the work force, demon activity in your assigned area becomes your responsibility. Each situation must be analyzed. Is it something you can handle, or do you need backup from security? Making that decision quickly and accurately is critical to your continued good health. Dealing with a low level lurker or shadow yourself is point defense for your assigned installation.

"You've all learned about the demon hierarchy of mimics, lurkers, and shadows. Next to perfecting your craft and spells, knowing when to call in backup is the most valuable skill you'll take away from your time at the school. Fight the natural tendency to grow complacent, and never assume your enemies are insignificant. The demon population continues to evolve new forms, powers, and behaviors. It's important to report anything that doesn't fit cleanly into categories you've learned."

"Are the Chrono-monks part of the monastic defenses?" Owen asked.

Oh, someone's been paying attention!

Even though I'd sworn off chasing after the dean, the idea that he might be linked to a group that manipulated time remained fascinating. I couldn't fault Owen for his interest. Before he'd disappeared, I'd tried to pump Gladstone for information, but the dean had proven adept at sidestepping that particular topic. I leaned forward, thirsty to know more.

"Indeed they are, and that's an excellent place to start." Grawpin splayed his flat fingers wide and launched into more detail. "Nearly two thousand years ago, monks devoted to sacrifice and desperate to defend the world from darkness claimed a small island off the coast of Ireland. Their scarlet robes represented the blood spilt to protect the unsuspecting people of the mainland. They built stone huts along the desolate cliffs and carved stairways into the jagged rocks stretching up from wind-battered shores. Many thought their hermitage and austere existence to be simple religious fervor, but in addition to dogged faith, these men brought true power.

"The darkness spreading across the land at the time was not simply the wild imaginings of people driven to their winter fires by snow and ice. For creatures of the void had discovered our reality and locked their drifting realm to our own with grapples of dark magic like plundering pirates.

"Some say the world was lost in those desperate years, that the monks had been too late, were wiped out by Vikings, or had simply abandoned their fortifications to the demon hordes. To this day, wild theories still make the rounds at the fringe of academic society, claiming the Chrono-monks jumped back in time and saved the world after the demons took control. The red-robed monks of Skellig Michael guarded the extent of their power closely, but I think it's safe to say such a feat would have been beyond their ability. The hypothesis remains because it is of course impossible to prove or disprove.

"But the reality is likely simpler. The monks of Skellig Michael were crafty and wise. They had ways of communicating with brethren orders at two other points around the globe—remember, this is well before the internet and cell phones. A vast net of power spread across the edge of our world, stemming from Skellig Michael and the monasteries to the far south and east. The barrier denied access to our lands from the void and remains in place to this day. But many demons had already crossed, and the monks were too few. To deal with the problem, a school was commissioned to train those gifted in magic, creating a formidable force to defend society. But still the threat spread across the globe. One school became two, then three, leaving us with our current arrangement."

"So why haven't we wiped them out? Do the demons breed?" a dark-haired woman in the back asked.

"Not in the traditional sense." Mr. Grawpin scratched at his bald head. "Prevailing wisdom says they don't procreate, although shadows may have the ability to multiply through a kind of mitosis by simply splitting apart when conditions are right. The main reason our fight continues is that the world barrier is powerful but flawed. Think of it more as a net than a wall. Lesser creatures can slip through the gaps; these are the classes we defend against. As difficult as mimics are to defeat, you do not want to meet the demon overlords who set their sights on us back in the day."

Though riveting, the lecture offered little additional information about the Chrono-monks. Mr. Grawpin went on to explain how the barrier spell tended to weaken over time, requiring constant upkeep. The red-robed monks used their powers to mask the fact they'd actually stayed on Skellig

Michael. At least, that had been the case until about a ten years ago.

"An unprecedented event occurred just over a decade ago," Grawpin said. "An explosion seems to have originated on Skellig Michael, releasing vast magical and temporal energy with far-reaching impacts. Although there's no evidence of physical damage to the island, the Monks themselves abruptly vanished. The event damaged and weakened the world barrier, leaving gaps that allow more demons through. The two remaining orders do what they can to bolster the barrier with wards, but the Chrono-monks never shared the secret of how to refresh the original spell." He clapped his hands, startling several out of their rapt attention. "Enough gloom and doom and history. Things are stable for now. The important thing is to keep your head when in the field. Attwater's given you the tools to cope, use them."

"Cool about the Chrono-monks," Owen said as the class broke up. "Think they really went back and changed the past?"

Bethany linked arms with Mon and waved as the pair headed off to their afternoon talent sessions. Chad had slipped out just before the end of the lecture so must have had another of his weather forecasting jaunts lined up. I stuffed the notebook into my string bag, pulled out my leather hat, and settled it on my head with the narrow brim at a jaunty angle.

"I doubt it. The time paradox would be too great." I led the way to the door. "Think about it. Without even digging too deep, going back to stop an event takes away the reason for going back. Unless you subscribe to the theory of new realities being spawned off the timeline at every turn, a single time continuum just can't be modified after the fact."

Owen walked along in silence as we passed under dangling lights resembling Edison bulbs. I'd grown accustomed to the pulsing yellow lights, a result of the living filaments within each glass sphere. My last class of the day would usually have been for honing my tinker skills, but Mr. Girardi had left the hour free to research my final project. I had an appointment down at the school's vault that hopefully would yield some ideas.

Owen must have had a class of his own to get to, but kept pace and swiped into the inner ring after I did. Something was definitely on his mind. At the risk of being late, I slowed to give him time to think.

"It's still possible," he finally said. "Grawpin's right; we'd never know if the past got changed. There's just no way to observe things like that. People like the monks and Gladstone could be going back to fix issues all the time. Hell, the dean's still in the past, and we haven't all winked out of existence."

"Maybe…" I wasn't sure where this was going. "So what's your point?"

"My point is—" Owen sucked in a big breath, a kind of fervor lighting his face. "Fear's an illusion. Mistakes can be fixed."

The declaration made him smile, a relieved expression like when you pass a questionable test.

"Probably better to never make them, but it's good to have goals. As for me, I've got a date down at the vault."

4. The Vault

"**T**HIS IS *not* a date, tiger." Gina pushed me away before the kiss I planted on her could get too involved. "I don't mind letting you into the vault occasionally, but a girl deserves to be wined and dined too. And don't get too frisky. Who knows what kind of recording devices or spells they have in here?"

A massive titanium door blocked the passage from floor to ceiling. An array of gears drove home bolts as thick as my biceps, but the door lacked the giant hand wheel an old-style bank vault would have. There wasn't so much as a keypad.

Gina placed her palm on the burnished metal surface. Magic flared, and the glow of power sank into the metal as the warding spell recognized her access privileges. Large gears turned smaller ones, the bolts retracted, and the door swung outward.

Power slipped across my skin as we entered. That would be a combination of the warding spell that kept out intruders and a powerful dampening spell to ensure the magical artifacts within didn't misbehave.

"So what do you need for this mysterious project?" Gina ran a hand along the racks of swords, spears, and less identifiable weapons that lined the entrance.

"None of these. It's got to be a magic artifact. Mr. Girardi has seen enough of my basic tinker skills. I have to pitch my idea along with a progress plan for approval next week. Since he's asking for that kind of detail, it's got to be something that's going to take more than a few minutes of probing to troubleshoot and repair."

The room opened to a great cavern filled with a disorganized array of shelves, lockers, and bins. Gina made suggestions as we circled the room, pointing to everything from an antique spinning wheel to what looked like a dismantled electric chair. I dutifully inspected her offerings, my tinker ability zeroing in on each item's state of repair.

It turned out that most of the stuff in the vault was broken. Sometimes it was a failed magic binding, other times a mechanical break. To be honest, the treasure trove wasn't nearly as impressive as it had originally appeared. There were ample projects to select from, but I shook my head as we pressed on through the junk. I had my sights set on one device in particular.

"I don't think you're serious!" Exasperation made Gina's statement come out harshly when I turned down an enchanted ice cream maker with a dark aura.

"Sorry." I'd gotten lost in my talent like a teenager on the internet and failed to notice her growing frustration. "I need a real challenge, a mystery, and I know just the item." Her face darkened, so I hurried to add, "it's been really useful looking through this stuff. As part of the proposal Mr. Girardi wants to know what else I considered."

"Well, I'm glad the last half hour wasn't a total waste." Her fury dropped a notch, replaced by sarcasm. "But maybe you should have just told me up front. I'm guessing it's either those egg shards, the globe thingy, or that metal contraption you stole from the owner of that…hat."

I heard the unspoken word 'stupid' in there and clutched the brim with a protective hand.

"Hey, it's a classic. And I didn't steal anything. He would have wanted me to have it."

I'd felt it in the dead man's magic. He'd been a tinker like me and with his dying breath had kept the metal football with its opposing hemispheres safe from the demons. His lingering magic had responded to my own, letting me rescue the device—and the awesome bush hat with its smart leather brim. Okay, so the hat had been an afterthought, but he certainly didn't need it anymore.

"Well, you're on the right trail," I admitted as we strolled over to the far side of the room. Two black eggs about a yard across rose to waist-high where each had been chopped off in a ragged line. "The dragon eggs definitely are broken and had magic at one point, but they really aren't something I can fix. As for the 'globe thingy'…"

My air quotes made her giggle, so I wasn't in all that much hot water. We moved over to an empty nook along the wall. Outlines on the dusty floor showed where a big rolling globe and tall mirror had been stored. Both items would still be in Dean Gladstone's office. I didn't know the backstory on the Gate of Heritiese, but when the globe and mirror were linked to a magic tracking device, the system could pinpoint the source of a magical signature and open a portal to it through the mirror.

I thumped the hinged lid of the ornately carved wooden box standing near where the globe had been stored. Rosewood inlaid with concentric rings of gems at odd intervals made the domed piece look like a cross between a hatbox and a jewelry cabinet. It sat on three curled feet that each looked much like the fancy scrollwork on a violin's neck. The feet would fit into matching brackets on top of the globe's wooden framework. But the dean had been using a newer component shaped like a model rocket made of aluminum and steel to direct the entire arrangement.

"I've got to admit that this tracker is shot." I'd checked the unit out before, but slipped a thread of magic under the lid to confirm that it was broken in a big way, a complex way, a way—now that I thought about it—that would indeed be a challenge to repair. But I stuck to my guns. "But someone already made a replacement that works just fine."

"Discounting the fact that the mirror portal sent Dean Gladstone's security team off into oblivion."

"You know that was because of the spider devices redirecting the gateway, not the tracker." I bit my lip and tried for diplomacy when I realized she'd been teasing. "But I'll keep this as a backup option. Now, let's look at that football."

The dead tinker's device sat inside the cabinet exactly as I'd remembered, opposing gold and silver hemispheres held apart by telescoping rods. Gina had been the one to realize the ends rotated around an inset ring set flush in each hemisphere. The craftsmanship was such that you almost needed a jeweler's loupe to see the seam.

"Does this really qualify as broken?" Gina asked. "We don't even know what it does."

"We do know it has power and that an ancient tinker gave his life to keep it out of the hands of demons. Demons love collecting broken stuff."

I slid my tinker senses into the device. Simple artifacts like enchanted pens or basic machines read like an open book.

Broken parts and problem areas lit up like Christmas lights in my mind's eye. More complex items took more work. It could be quite exhausting to push through and catalogue the various interdependencies of mechanisms and magic. The football was definitely of the latter variety, with such a dense complexity that it seemed a solid mass. But I did catch glimmers of daylight. Unraveling the intent of this design would take a lot of time, but I was relatively certain it could be done. I was less certain whether the football was in fact in need of repair.

I put a palm on each hemisphere and pressed them toward each other a millimeter or so. As before power surged, and I hastily let the rods spring back to full extension. I'd tried the trick before and found the closer together the halves got, the larger the energy surge. The fact that it was able to activate here inside the vault's dampening field led me to believe it wasn't a dangerous artifact.

Fully collapsing the halves into a sphere would make it the size of a bowling ball. But by that point there'd be an awful lot of energy built up, which brought us back to inherently dangerous. In addition to untangling the mess my talent saw inside, a carefully designed experiment could map the thing's power profile. From there I might be able to determine its function and state of repair.

I saw a lot of research in my future. I'd be living in the library, digging through manuals for matching technical specifications and a clue as to the football's nature. The dead tinker knew this was important, and I had to believe Attwater needed to know why.

"Conclusions, Sherlock?" Gina's question pulled me out of my musings.

"It won't be easy, but I think I can work with this." I patted the gold end of the device, but jerked my hand away because I felt like Chad communing with the school. "I'll have to come up with a catchy title for my proposal so the abbreviation is NFL."

"You do realize that it doesn't even look like a football, right?"

"I know, but it carries like one, so I'm sticking with the theme."

5. Mon's Power

M ON MADE HER way down a drab corridor, following the tall figure draped in lacy black layers deeper into the special training wing. Quiet footfalls and a tug of magic told her that Jane followed close. Harsh white lights that somehow left the way shadowed replaced Attwater's cheery glow-bulbs as they passed classroom doors set far apart.

Bethany would be training with her own instructor behind one of those doors. The thought of that sweet face and those kind eyes brought a sad smile. Bethany deserved better, someone without a dark streak. But being with Bethany made the darkness easier to forget, and Mon was determined to hold her girlfriend tight.

"We are here." The woman in black opened a metal door on the right. "Bring her."

Mon cast one last look at the empty hallway. The feeling of sneaking around was an illusion. Only a select handful of students trained in this forgotten section of the school. Her schedule didn't even list a room number or instructor name. The hooded woman with piercing gray eyes that taught Mon cosmetology and so much more never used a name. Mistress beckoned with bony white fingers for Mon to follow and disappeared through the door.

Mon smoothed her skirt flat, suddenly self-conscious of how her black outfit mimicked her instructor's. She waved the other woman forward and cursed as the motion imitated Mistress's imperious wave.

But Jane didn't mind. The middle-aged woman with dazzling blue eyes followed without question. *This* Jane had started with mousy brown hair and a weathered complexion, not lovely in the traditional sense. But despite the issues with her own soul, Mon had grown skilled at spotting the inner beauty of others. Autumnal tones and judicious blending had transformed Jane's drab features. Mon had built the face of a movie star around her gorgeous eyes. Getting the brilliant blue was the tricky part, but specially formulated drops helped return them to ice-clear.

Although it wasn't strictly part of her magic, that ability to recognize beautiful souls was probably what drew her to Bethany, a caring, steadfast lifeline that kept her head above water—barely.

"Send her in alone." Mistress said, her voice a dry wind.

A dingy metal wall partitioned off an entry area. Thick glass windows riveted at eye level allowed viewing of the main room. The arrangement smacked of old cop movies where detectives watched interrogations from concealment, except this glass looked to be two-way. Instead of the iconic desk and chair, the room beyond was empty, the right-hand wall lined with a half dozen doors, each with their own observation ports. Mistress waved impatiently at the open door into the room beyond. Worry fluttered in Mon's belly as she sent her charge in.

Jane swished quietly past without a word of complaint, her blue chiffon dress whispering with each step. Mon could make the other woman beautiful again, but she couldn't make her speak. It was difficult enough overcoming the rigor mortis that set into major muscles just hours after death.

Maybe with more practice she'd be able to unfreeze the vocal cords too, but it wasn't as if Jane Doe was truly alive. She only moved at Mon's command, through the magic of Mon's special talent. Anything the poor woman who'd met her end under a noisy overpass might say would simply be parroting thoughts Mon planted.

Mistress closed the door and fingered the controls on a narrow panel beneath the glass. The door at the far end of the line of cells slid open.

Mon staggered as a furry brown mass blurred through the open door and slammed into Jane. Blue material ripped, and phantom claws sliced underneath Mon's sternum as the lurker demon disemboweled the corpse she'd animated. Her magic broadcast the pain Jane couldn't feel, the sensation startling—surely not as bad as being gutted yourself, but unpleasant nonetheless.

The killing blow meant nothing to Jane, but Mon had her spin away, narrowly dodging the next claw swipe and saving herself the feel of talons raking her neck. The demon moved like an ape, planting its knuckles to execute swift turns. The attacker stood only four feet tall with a hairless front, tusked mouth, and narrow face that swiveled on a dexterous neck to keep Jane in its sights as she danced back, staying just out of reach.

"Close and dispatch the demon," Mistress commanded. "Now!"

She added that last when Mon blinked in confusion. Bethany and Jason had mentioned the pain of losing one of their magical constructs. But neither had said *how* much it hurt, and hers had only been injured, not…killed—for the lack of a better term. Plus, your average housewife didn't take on lurker demons bare handed. But then, your average housewife felt things like fear and pain. Jane was immune to both even if Mon wasn't.

Here goes nothing.

A mental command sent Jane in high with a brutal right jab to the demon's face. The idea was to take advantage of the woman's reach, but agony exploded across Mon's knuckles as the punch sawed across serrated tusks. A brutal kick from the beast crushed a couple of ribs on the right side judging by the white hot poker that pierced her own. She needed to finish this fast. If the lurker had a weak point, it had to be that delicate neck. Lacking weapons, Jane's one advantage was she could take whatever the monster dished out, assuming Mon herself didn't faint.

Mon gritted her teeth, and the woman in chiffon strode forward. Jane ignored the foot that drove into her knee, stumbled forward absorbing a flurry of slashes from razor claws, and wrapped the lurker in a motherly hug. She cradled the creature's head to her bosom, ignoring the gnashing teeth shredding her front and twisted left, hard. With a sharp snap the demon went still.

Mon sagged to the floor, hands flying to her chest to stop the bleeding—only to find she remained physically unharmed. She gingerly probed her stomach, legs, and arms, but the pain that had been so real receded quickly, leaving her gasping as though she'd run a marathon. For once Mistress gave Mon a minute to compose herself. Heaviness still pressed her arms, and with a flash of insight she directed Jane to drop the dead lurker.

"Let us go inspect the results." Mistress entered the chamber leaving Mon to hurry after.

No words of praise passed her instructor's lips, no conciliatory gesture to ensure Mon was well, and certainly no apology for not even bothering to give her a shred of warning about the incredible pain coming her way. Sometimes she envied her friends. Even at the best of times, things in the special studies wing were never pleasant.

Mistress led her toward the gruesome scene slowly. The room smelled like a sewer. Mon's eyes streamed as she peeked into each door they passed like a warden inspecting her inmates. There was no doubt about it, these were cells, and each held a lurker. The demons ranged from simple brutes like the one Jane had bested to busy-looking creatures with too many arms, legs, and eyes. Someone not trained in the varied demon forms would think Attwater was collecting aliens.

The creatures were not in the best of health. Some had clearly been injured during their capture. Others had undergone experiments, judging by the surgically stitched wounds and odd bits of metal protruding from their bodies. It didn't exactly look like torture, but she doubted the demons would agree.

Jane stood over the lurker ape, eyes downcast and bleeding all over the floor. It wasn't exactly blood, just pungent pinkish-green fluid that served to keep the body preserved and supple. Without a pumping heart, the embalming fluid simply oozed from the woman's many wounds.

The lurker didn't bleed at all, but with its neck wrenched off at that angle, was definitely dead. Numb satisfaction came with the realization of how her necromancy training fit into the school's defenses. Her career path had never included dolling up rich girls for their proms. Mon had no beef with preparing those who no longer cared about their appearance for teary goodbyes. Closure was important.

But this little exercise told the rest of the story. Attwater wanted her on the front line of the demon war in hand-to-hand combat—albeit with her reanimated surrogates. Mon hadn't told any of her friends about her dark "gift," hadn't wanted them—especially Bethany—to think worse of her.

"The lurker is dead." Gray eyes sharp with interest shone from the shadows of the instructor's ragged hood.

"Its neck looked fragile." Mon moved to Jane, pulled the tattered dress closed, and tied a makeshift knot around her middle. The woman was going to be at least a quart low, not to mention in need of major stitching.

"Leave the woman be and come here." The whip of command was back.

"Yes, Mistress." Mon hurried to obey.

"Can you handle more than one?"

Could she? The real work was in constructing the bond, of infusing the body with her consciousness until it became a ghostly shadow of her own. The unsettling process bordered on revolting, but was also fascinating. Her magic wanted to flow. Once she'd tucked away the bit of herself that rebelled at the violation, that wanted to shriek and hurl its lunch, the work became infinitely easier. After that initial session tuned her talent to the corpse and brought it to life, control was as natural as breathing or lifting an arm. At this point Jane was a familiar extension of herself.

"Yes, I think so." Mon rubbed at the echo of an ache in her side. "I'd need time to work with each person to get them ready, but I'm sure I could handle two, maybe more."

It made sense. They'd want her controlling as many people as possible in a tough fight. The more dead they threw at the demons, the less live people needed to go into harm's way, but Mon would need something to block the pain, and weapons better than French nails and chiffon.

"This demon is dead," Mistress pointed her long boney finger at the lurker.

Yes, they'd established that.

"Bring it back." Eager breathiness made her instructor sound like she was about to have an orgasm.

"What?" Mon choked on the word as it exploded from her.

"Use your talent to animate this demon."

She crouched to examine the carcass that smelled of musk and urine. The revulsion she'd locked away broke free and rose with a vengeance. Mon slipped her magic from shredding tusks to wicked talons, then forced it to sink into the oily flesh. Bile rose in her throat as realization dawned. Her animations weren't going to need weapons after all. Mistress expected her to fight demons with demons.

6. Unlikely Visit

"T HEN I'LL HAVE the data correlated and select the hypothesis that fits best." I concluded my practice proposal with a shallow bow and awaited the applause.

And waited.

Gina and Bethany had turned the dean's guest chairs around to face me and had at least paid attention. Owen and Chad squabbled over a pile of tools they'd laid out on the workbench along the back wall of the office. Lars would probably be hurling soon because he and Mortimer played merry-go-round in the big leather chair behind Dean Gladstone's mahogany desk. The pencil gargoyle bounced up and down on Lars's knee, urging him to spin faster.

The gang kept showing up for our peer review sessions, but going last clearly had its disadvantages. Pulling the pitch together for my tinker project had taken longer than expected. Everyone else had finished their own briefs earlier in the week, incorporated the group's recommendations, and moved on.

"So if this football turns out to be some kind of magic generator, how do you determine what it powers?" Bethany asked with hand raised.

"Excellent question, Ms. Daniels." I liked fielding off the wall ideas because Mr. Girardi was sure to come up with some doozies. "That would require follow-on investigation. I'll provide an outline to guide further studies, the specifics of which would wholly depend on my project findings."

"And if it overloads?" Gina didn't bother raising her hand. "And you blow up Attwater during testing?"

Hopefully she was playing devil's advocate. I studied the tinker device sitting near the globe and mirror, then shifted my gaze to the dark paneling of Dean Gladstone's office. Given the amount of energy we'd felt coming off the football at its lowest setting, her question wasn't outrageous. But she couldn't think I'd be that careless.

"If the power output grows too large…" I chose my words carefully. "The best course of action would be to move my trials down into the vault. The magic dampening spell should be strong enough to stop any reaction from getting out of hand."

I'd already outlined the abundance of safeguards I planned to use in the study. Moving the equipment from my workshop down to the vault would be a royal pain and make access difficult, but wasn't impossible. Gina nodded, accepting my answer. After a few more questions and recommendations, I breathed a sigh of relief—just like I would after the real pitch to Mr. Girardi.

Of course, working in the vault would also rely heavily on Gina's schedule, unless Ms. Eisner was willing to grant me access too. I didn't think the latter was likely, but having someone who basically ranked second in Attwater's security department certainly had its advantages. Not only had Gina helped me inspect the vault for project candidates, she'd gotten us access to the Dean's office so everyone could practice their pitches.

We'd usually hash things out in the commons, but that was too open and noisy. Between signing up late for empty classrooms and working around Chad's travel schedule, there hadn't been a lot of options available. Plus we'd spent hundreds of hours in this room chasing down Mr. Gonzales and the dean last semester, which made the office feel kind of special to everyone.

The mirror, globe, and magic spectrometer still sat in the corner. Security had carefully removed the spider device from the lower left corner after their final trip to the volcanic tunnels. We still didn't know how the demons managed to plant the magical gadget that had hijacked the dean's security team.

Seeing the components of the system dark and abandoned made me sad. Since our people were lost in the past, attempts to home in on them had failed miserably.

I understood the precaution of removing the spider, but it felt like we'd locked away our only clue. Ms. Eisner had confiscated the pair of spiders I'd pulled from our training portal too. If getting to the dean was only a matter of the portal system being broken, I'd gladly take that on as my project, but the components worked fine. There just wasn't a target out there to find.

"Let's talk graduation." Bethany motioned everyone to gather around the desk.

"That's not until January." Lars slowed his spinning, but still occasionally kicked out a foot to send himself and the gargoyle around on another slow turn. "What's there to plan four months out?"

"It's called setting expectations, and it's hard to share at home without dancing around the topic of magic." Bethany turned to Gina. "You're the only one here who's been through the placement process. What can we expect?"

"Oh, well." Caught off-guard, Gina took a moment to consider while twirling a dark-red curl around her fingers. "The placement office is top notch, and you should get at least two offers—probably more."

"And they work with your desires too, right?" I remembered that from our first date—the one where I'd learned she was staying with Attwater for her first assignment.

"Sure do." She bounced an index finger at us. "Be up front with what you want. For me it was a coastal assignment so I can dive certify in my spare time. Don't be shy, and they'll do their best to find the perfect fit. No guarantees of course. Positions need to be strategic to counter demon activity. But Attwater won't push you out the door toward something you hate."

"What about reassignments?" Owen asked. "Like if your boss is a jerk, or the fit just isn't right?"

We settled into a comfortable back and forth as the group picked Gina's brain. Hopes, concerns, and desires trickled out along the way, including my own rising fear that industrial welding just wasn't for me.

"I'm doing well and all," I'd said. "But I need to build things that *do* something."

That was what made working with my robots so satisfying. Each little robot had a purpose, even if it was just to test out new components or improve my skill at integrating magic. There truly was no better feeling of accomplishment.

"There's a temporal forecaster over at Bashar School who might be able to help track down the dean," Chad said as career planning turned to gossip. "Heard the admin folks talking about it after my weather briefing. Interesting fact, hurricanes will be at a record high this year with widespread droughts on every continent except Antarctica—we don't track things like that here."

Chad got around even more than we'd suspected. Bashar seemed like the school of experts. I didn't really know what a temporal forecaster did, but it sounded like a step in the right direction toward finding our lost people. I glared at the silver portal system, the globe and tracker that should have led us to the dean, and the towering gateway mirror in its ornate silver frame. Gimbals halfway up the mirror let the surface swivel like a dressing mirror. Yellow light from the glow bulbs gleamed dully off scrollwork long overdue for a good polishing.

The mirror's position had it reflecting flashes of movement as our group shifted in our seats. It really picked up the spinning chair judging by the flash each time our comic relief came full circle. Distorted by the angle and dark corner, the reflection looked darker than the brown curve of leather.

"You've been awfully quiet, Lars." Bethany waved Mortimer down as the swivel chair launched on another orbit. "Where do you want to use your green-thumb talent?"

Mortimer jumped off as the OCD express came into the station, and Lars grabbed the desk to stop his momentum.

"Trees," he slurred wetly. "In the forest I'd be a goddamn god. They'll want me to—"

He cut off mid-sentence, swallowed hard, and tried again. A pitiful moan came out followed by more gulping. Our godlike companion looked paler than usual and distinctly green around the edges. A sheen of sweat popped out on his forehead as Lars grabbed his stomach, doubled over, and heaved into the trashcan at the end of the desk.

His chains jangled against the rim of the can, but didn't drown out the unpleasant sounds of our friend being sick. Everyone quickly found something else to focus on. I wandered toward the silver mirror, curious to see why shadows still flashed across its surface. Mortimer showed the most compassion. After a look to Bethany, he hopped off his creator's lap, shuffled over, and patted Lars on the back as the guy launched into another round.

It wasn't like we could do anything for the idiot. Lars just had to tough it out until his middle ear caught up. I turned back to the mirror and found the surface had gone wonky. My first thought was that the portal was activating, but the characteristic swirling vortex didn't materialize. The reflection morphed into one from a funhouse mirror made of old-time bubble glass. An opaque film covered the entire surface, and the scene in the frame stretched and shifted. My outline grew vague and shadowy, turning my red shirt to dingy brown.

The heaving behind me died down, replaced by shuffling and murmurs, but I didn't turn. *What's with this mirror?*

I lifted my left hand, waved, and jumped back when the blurry reflection jabbed out with the wrong hand and poked a stick at me. The stick came into focus better than anything, a narrow black rod with a silver grip shaped like a snake's head—Dean Gladstone's cane.

The silver handle rapped against an invisible membrane. The muffled thuds formed a soft rhythm that jumped past my ears and straight into my head. The silhouette holding the cane swelled and strained as if trying to break out of the mirror. White hair and trim buttons flashed into clarity for a moment before falling back into the shadowy outline, but it was enough to convince me I was looking at the dean. The cane tapped faster, its muffled almost-sound rising in pitch as though striking a taught drum.

"Uh, Jason?" Gina's voice sounded strained, and I couldn't blame her.

"Are you seeing this?" I spoke off to the side, unwilling to take my eyes off the image for fear of missing an important clue.

"Seriously, dude, stop preening in the mirror and help us out," Chad said. "Your high school buddy's possessed."

"What the—" I turned to find the other four in an arc around Lars.

Everyone crouched with arms wide as if they were ready to catch him if he fell. Which didn't make sense. Lars poked along the wall inspecting the dean's clock collection. He skirted a bookcase with jerky steps, probably still reeling from his spin-fest. But a turn of his head revealed his eyes. Both were clouded over, leaving only the outline of pupils, dark circles that twisted and stretched like the image in the mirror.

The rhythm of the cane throbbed faster as Lars stepped up onto a wooden chair and reached for a pendulum wall clock. The tempo from the mirror turned erratic, somehow communicating with Lars. His fingers ran down the glistening cherrywood, triggered a hidden catch, and the clock swung off to the side exposing a small door. The hidden safe lacked a tumbler but opened smoothly when Lars touched the gray metal.

The cane's drumming cut off, replaced by quiet, incessant ticking from the army of timepieces scattered around the room.

"They'll want me as a forest ranger on the front lines. Hey, who—" Lars balanced for a moment with a Wiley E. Coyote look and arms flailing before tumbling off the chair.

Owen and Chad caught him, but the clunk of heads connecting made the rest of us cringe. I shot a glance back to find the gateway was again just a mirror.

"Ow, geez! What the hell!" The white film faded from Lars's eyes as he rubbed his ear and glared at Owen, who was busy checking himself for a broken nose.

Chaos ensued as the guys yelled questions at Lars, who insisted he'd just been at the desk a second ago. Mortimer helpfully hopped from one man's shoulder to the next like an organ monkey on speed.

Bethany and Gina did the intelligent thing by staying out of the fight and investigating the compartment Lars discovered. Bethany pulled a slim leather book from the nook and jumped down from the chair Gina had been holding steady. Both tried to interrupt the argument before shooting angry glares at me, like it was *my* fault.

"Did anybody else see Dean Gladstone?" I bellowed, startling the others into silence. "Here, in the mirror. He had his cane."

Now that I had their attention, I described the image that had appeared. Amazingly, I'd been the only one to notice. Lars launched into bravado when I linked the tapping cane to his actions. He puffed out his chest and claimed a natural immunity to hypnosis thanks to his superior intellect.

"Dude, you were an absolute zombie." Owen smiled way too broadly, nearly touching off another shouting match.

"Okay, listen up." This time Bethany cut in before things boiled over. She held up the book. "Lars found something that I bet can help rescue the dean. So put away the testosterone, boys, and let's see what we've got."

She took her find over to the big desk, and we all gathered around. The book was small, maybe five by eight and less than an inch thick, with a supple brown cover. There was no title, but a raised bronze emblem shaped like an hourglass gave the leather some rigidity. The spine and back were similarly blank. With a shrug, Bethany opened the binding to the first page. A narrow border trimmed the off-white paper, but other than that the page was blank.

"Looks like they forgot the title," Chad said.

My stomach sank when she flipped the thin sheet over to a second blank page, and then a third. Bethany fanned through the book, skimming pages framed by a simple border—all of them blank.

"What's that mean?" I took the book, but changing hands didn't miraculously make writing appear.

"A blank journal isn't much help." Owen glared at Lars as if to imply he'd tried to trick us.

There was no denying the fact Dean Gladstone had directed Lars to the book. But why?

I strode over and double-checked the hidden safe, which of course was empty. The back of the swing-away clock didn't hold any clues either. But the pendulum was a bronze hourglass shape instead of round. That couldn't be a coincidence.

"The Dean's trying to tell us something about the Chrono-monks." I pointed from clock to book. "That bronze hourglass is the same design the order wore. Gladstone's got to be involved with them."

"Was involved," Gina corrected. "They disappeared a decade back. Why steer poor, clueless Lars to a blank journal?"

"Yeah, Sherlock, explain why the old man would—hey!" Lars turned puppy dog eyes on Gina after processing her insult.

"Maybe he was vulnerable to suggestion due to spinning himself silly. Or the dean wanted us to find more than just this one thing but lost control." I thought back to how the mirror's image had shifted and pulled, as if blocking his efforts. "He was pushing through a lot of interference to get at the gateway. Let's search for another compartment, anything marked with an hourglass."

We fanned out like kids on an Easter egg hunt, tugging at clocks, riffling through drawers, and checking behind the furniture. Chad even knocked on the thick paneling in search of hidden rooms. I wasn't sure that was a reliable method, but Lars joined him, which quickly drew Mortimer into the effort. Before long the office was a bit of a shambles, and the walls looked like a toddler with black finger-paint had run amuck thanks to bits of Mort's substance rubbing off during the search.

"So what *do* we know?" I felt the need to salvage the meeting and end on a positive note.

"The dean's alive?" Chad ventured.

"And he's trying to communicate." Owen jerked a thumb at the mirror portal.

"There's something we need to know about the monks of Skellig Island." Bethany bounced the slim book on her palm. "If he's stuck in time it stands to reason the Chrono-monks could help."

"Sure they could," I said. "Except for the pesky problem that they've disappeared.

"Or have they?" Owen was usually our resident cynic, but a strange enthusiasm lit his face.

"Explain." Bethany rolled her hand, wanting to hear more.

"Well, Cowboy says they're bringing in some time specialist. That guy's probably one of these monks in hiding."

"He just does forecasts like me, but for time." Chad looked like he wanted to say more, but Owen didn't give him the chance.

"I bet he's got more info about the order. He might even know where the others are hiding, the ones that can do the whole jump back in time thing. We find them, and we're golden."

"To bring Dean Gladstone and the others back, you mean, right?" I got a strange feeling Owen had something else in mind.

"Yeah, of course." Owen gave a kind of sideways head nod with eyes closed, and his face scrunched up like it always did before he added a qualifier. "But these guys could do a lot of good. It's time they stepped up and helped out again."

Yep, he has more in mind than simply finding the dean.

7. Life Goes On

DESPITE THE WEIRD encounter with our lost dean, school plodded on toward graduation. We'd of course reported the whole thing to Ms. Eisner. The acting dean had security give the office an even more thorough search. They found nothing. The Enchanted Items department—a group of in-house experts I'd never heard of—declared the blank journal was no more than an old book made a couple of centuries back.

On the upside, my certification moved along well, and Mr. Martin figured I'd graduate on time. I'd grown quite proud of my metallurgy knowledge and tidy welds, but the progress was soured by a seed of doubt. Did I really want to view the world through the dark little window of a welding visor? Was that how I wanted to spend my life?

I took to rebuilding my Amos series of robots as a kind of therapy. Heat-sculpted metal replaced the PVC body components, and extremities that had been predominantly plastic took on the appearance of medieval armor. The interior components of the Autonomous Magic Operating System were already as safe as I could manage. Compartmentalizing the tinker magic stabilized the system and provided the control link and life force beyond simple memory chips and processors. Servos, gyros, and other subsystems processed instructions solely through the CPU, avoiding any mismatch between tinker magic and technology—no more meltdowns. I'd even written a rudimentary machine language to prevent accidental complexity from endangering the robot.

With all the upgrades, I needed a new name, but "Amos Two" seemed like a cop out. After work was complete on both active robots—at home and at school—I dubbed the new series "Mel" and hoped neither robot developed a complex. I'd added armaments augmenting the bottle opener, which had been Amos's weapon of choice. Total weight jumped ten percent, but my shiny new Mels—Metallic Exoskeleton Landbots—looked like they'd be right at home in the robot wars Roxy used to enter.

It was funny and a bit sad how just over a year at school had changed my outlook. Now I thought in terms of weapons instead of tools when it came to my creations. But the therapy of getting my hands dirty worked wonders. Focusing on the new design helped me stay centered as things ramped up at Attwater.

Mr. Girardi gave me plenty of time to flesh out the proposal for my tinker project and seemed excited about my idea of investigating the football device. But he still hadn't given approval to start. After two non-committal weeks I pushed to formalize the plan. But he wanted to reassess several points and consult with a colleague to ensure he did my talent justice—seeing as so few tinkers came through the schools. No big deal, except time marched on. The mysterious nature of the football could easily demand way more hours than I'd estimated.

On a rainy Wednesday afternoon in early October, I headed for my tinker training in high spirits. Mel clomped along behind, having just assisted with welding repairs off campus. Students drifted through the inner ring heading to class. Someone scurried out of the doorway I was headed for, lustrous blond hair bobbing above a powder-blue sweater and short skirt.

"Roxy, wait up!" I hurried to catch her before she rounded the corner. "What brings you to this end of the school?"

"Not much." A brief scowl crinkled her forehead before morphing into a big smile that had me grinning along like an idiot. "Still trying to work out my talent. Ms. Schlaza has me interviewing with different teachers. Who knew Mr. Girardi covered so many specialties?"

"Yeah, the guy's a generalist, but don't worry. You could do a lot worse than land in his class next year."

"He's a dear, that's for sure." She patted her hair into place. "But that's quite the accent. Gotta run now."

"It's easy to get used to…" I trailed off because she'd spun on one high heel and clicked off down the hall. "Okay, see you later."

Mr. Girardi was ready for my lesson with the usual pile of broken items. Today's focus included musical gadgets, and I didn't recognized a couple of the stringed instruments leaning against the wall.

"You'll have to find a new tinker project. The device you found is not suitable." He delivered the proclamation in a flat monotone and blinked into the silence that followed before continuing. "Exploring the secrets of your football would certainly be fascinating, but there's nothing to indicate it needs repair. A tinker cannot fix what is not broken."

"But it belonged to a tinker, a powerful one judging by the shield he cast to protect it from demons. Isn't that enough?"

"I'm sorry." He spread his hands wide, sounding sincere.

I argued for several minutes, trying to wheedle the name of the colleague he'd discussed my proposal with. Maybe *they* could be reasoned with. But Mr. Girardi wasn't willing to part with that particular information, insisted the decision was his alone, and encouraged me to use the alternate project I'd passed up in the vault. In an attempt to make amends, he promised a quick turnaround on my new proposal.

The lesson was a blur that hardly registered. I mechanically went through the motions of repairing cracks, stuck valves, and insidious issues that ruined an instrument's pitch. I shuffled away from the session listless and exhausted, feeling like I'd been kicked in the stomach. Why had his tune changed so radically since my oral proposal?

Roxy caught me at the end of the day at our usual table in the commons, poring over a printout of my first proposal and drowning my sorrows in a carton of chocolate milk. I planned to replace the drink with a dark beer when I got home.

"Why the long face?" Roxy rubbed my back and plopped down next to me.

The rest of the gang usually drifted through after classes, but none had arrived yet. A corner of my brain wanted to skootch away from the warm thigh that pressed against mine. Roxy was just trying to console me, but my girlfriend wouldn't appreciate finding her so close and handsy. Still, I couldn't dredge up the energy to shrug her off. The thought of starting from scratch opened a gapping pit that sucked away my will.

"It can't be all that bad." Roxy caught my gaze with her emerald eyes and a slow smile that spread until she was all dimples and teeth.

My spirits bobbed a bit higher. With an economy of words born of fatigue, I explained my predicament. She nodded, asked a few technical questions, and drew me out of my malaise. As I warmed to the discussion, she reached over and took the thick sheaf of pages that were my original proposal.

"Let's see what we have." She flipped from the table of contents to the appendix. "See? You already have options listed."

"But I want to figure out that football before graduation," I said—okay, whined. Sue me. "I can kiss that chance goodbye once I'm out in the workforce."

"Oh, pooh." She waved away my words and turned the page. "Look here. This guidance device looks perfect. You've already formed a hypothesis." She read the description and jabbed a dainty finger at the diagram underneath. "Oh, this is the pretty hatbox we saw. You *have* to do this one."

Her enthusiasm tried to spread across the very short gap between us, but my stubborn streak was in the way. If Mr. Girardi didn't like my proposal, I wasn't going to give him the satisfaction of just dropping down to the next broken gadget on my list. I'd find a bigger and better project. Maybe Chad knew of something that had gone wonky at one of the other schools. A little voice in the back of my head said I was being stupid, that my spiteful inner child was going to keep me from graduating on time. That voice could shut it.

"I don't know." It was hard to tell the woman sitting so close that I didn't want her advice. Even harder when she patted my forearm, her emerald eyes troubled. I met her gaze and considered my options. "But I'll think about it."

"Think about what?" Gina's question cut between Roxy and me like a knife.

8. Football

"**I** HEAR YOUR girlfriend is pretty upset." Mr. Gonzales casually dropped the comment as he hooked power leads to a meter on his bench.

At five-eight, he wasn't a big man, and had to step on a stool to reach the retractable yellow power cord dangling overhead. He offered a smile beneath his bushy black moustache as he continued to set up his equipment. Anything that came out of the football would get recorded: magic, electricity, radiation, and more.

The Latino man finally looked like the brown-skinned dynamo he'd been before his ordeal. The moustache was once again trimmed to drooping perfection, as were the sharp lines of his buzz cut. The dark circles around his eyes had faded along with the fatigue. Those reminders of his demon possession were all but gone, and seeing him with tool bag in hand scurrying about the school always cheered me.

I shouldn't have been surprised that he knew about my problem. Plenty of people had been in the commons to witness a fiery side to Gina that matched her talent. We hadn't exactly fought. Hell, I'd barely gotten a dozen words out to explain why Roxy was consoling me. Everything I said just made things worse. By the time Owen, Bethany, and Mon arrived, I'd been ready to crawl into a corner to lick my wounds.

Gina didn't throw out explicit accusations, but the implication was there alongside the hurt look. I'd felt horrible—still did—and cursed the self-indulgent pity party that had started the whole mess.

"You've got that right, Mr. Gonzalez. I'm in the doghouse. But figuring this thing out might get me back in her good graces." I clipped the last lead to the gold end of the football device and backed away from the workbench.

"Please, I think we've been through enough together; call me Mike." He tugged at his moustache in thought. "Some people might say talking to the girl would help more than throwing yourself into another project."

I clamped down on a sullen reply because he was probably right. After our argument, Gina had marched me down to the vault, thrust the football device at me, and said to come back after I figured out what I wanted. Choosing the football was choosing Gina. There was no way I could take Roxy's suggestion and fix the guidance device. But I still needed Mr. Girardi's approval.

"The project is the problem, Mike, but these preliminary power readings might get me off the hook." My response sounded like a lame evasion. "The tinker ability pushes deeper when the football goes active. I just need a hint of a problem or alignment issue. If the football needs repair, I can re-pitch it for my tinker project."

"I'm happy to help, but re-submitted proposals are seldom accepted." He held both palms up when I looked his way. "Just letting you know. Do what you think is best."

Having graduated in facilities management himself, Mike Gonzalez knew his way around the school and its policies, but I just wasn't ready to concede. Wires trailed from the lonely device in the center of the heavy wood table to a set of instruments and meters we'd cobbled together on a rolling cart. The Frankenstein arrangement wasn't pretty, but would get the job done. Mike had efficiently pulled together what was needed as though he studied mystic objects every day.

"You know, I've had this gut feeling that figuring out your football there is important." He double checked the connections. "And I finally realized why. The Shadow Master didn't want this falling into the wrong hands."

"I don't suppose he left any specifics about why?"

"Sorry, afraid not." He sucked a breath in through his teeth. "I know my scattered memories haven't been terribly useful. Funny thing is…I got the impression he worried more about demons getting their hands on the device."

"That's a weird wrinkle. All clear?" I didn't want either of us getting zapped.

My partner in crime nodded and stepped behind the thick panel of leaded glass shielding his gear. Unfortunately, I had to put hands on the device to activate the football, so my personal protective equipment consisted mainly of a lead-lined vest. My back already ached, and even though neither of us thought radiation likely, I was determined to keep as many safety procedures in place as possible. I grasped a hemisphere in either hand, twisted clockwise a degree, and stepped back.

"No readings, but something's changed." Mike checked his meters and shrugged.

"I feel it too."

The room was charged with the kind of potential that preceded thunderstorms. I reached for the spectrum goggles perched on top of my head. Three types of glass on metal arms pivoted from the headband. Our training sensitized students to flows of magical energy, so we could often see power that would have otherwise been invisible. The goggles provided another level of insight. I'd gotten them from the dean for my independent study course. The gadget had been critical in gaining control of the tinker energy I accidentally sent into my robots.

I flipped through the colored lenses, settling on blue, which showed a glowing nimbus around the silver hemisphere. I stepped in and turned each half another degree, and the aura around that end intensified. Mike's meters still didn't register power flowing from the device. After a quick discussion, I tried again, turning both halves counter-clockwise.

This time the potential energy gathered around the gold half. Again, when I clicked the device up a degree, the glow intensified significantly—amazing and worrisome. Two degrees was only about half a percent of a full rotation. The thought of each increment doubling in intensity led to big numbers fast—really fast, exponentially fast.

"Still nothing on the meters," Mike confirmed after I relayed what I saw through the goggles and shut the football off.

"This thing is pretty simple," I said. "The only controls are twisting and pushing the ends closer. My tinker ability isn't helping at all. I ought to be able to see what's going on inside, but there's just nothing. Feel like pressing our luck on the lowest setting and bringing the ends in a notch?"

"Nothing ventured nothing gained."

We took up our respective positions to give it a go. I rotated the ends clockwise one degree, and the silver side again glowed in my goggles. The hemispheres pushed smoothly toward each other, pistons contracting maybe half an inch before there was a distinct click.

"Here we go." Mike's voice was muffled behind the glass. "Power readings coming through. No radiation."

The blue-white energy shot out in arcs that curved back to the gold hemisphere on the other end. Five crackling streams formed a cage around the three pistons. Similar energy mushroomed from the silver end, forming a side dome that bent into a full circle and returned to the metal surface. The effect looked like a textbook diagram of a magnetic field, except the small dome only appeared on one end.

"What do you have?" I asked.

"Stable readings." Mike flipped through a few different settings. "Still no radiation to worry about. Low voltage and current. Fourteen wheems for magical output, about equivalent to a low-level elemental spell. That drops off fast on the remote pickups, back to zero at a foot away. If I didn't know any better, I'd say the output is feeding back into the device."

"Take a look through the goggles." I stripped off the gadget and handed it over.

While Mike studied the football, I reached for the tingling core of tinker energy that sat below my sternum. This time, when I pushed out, my talent skimmed along just below the surface of the arcing power. A faint resonance had my senses buzzing. I couldn't exactly see into the device, but I'd cracked the surface. There were deeper layers there for sure. With a bit of work, the entry and exit points of that energy flashing between the nodes might provide a pathway to explore.

"Interesting, especially that asymmetrical node on the right." Mike handed the goggles over and headed back to his readouts. "Take it down to zero, then reverse the setting."

I did as instructed, twisting the ends counterclockwise one degree and again pushing the rods in to the first stop. Sure enough, the cage of energy sprang back, but this time the excess bulb radiated from the gold hemisphere.

"Predictable. I like it." Mike wore a self-satisfied grin as he tuned his gear. "I'll have to check the waveforms, but I'm fairly certain the magical polarity just reversed. Did that crown of energy shift to the other end over there?" He nodded at my thumbs up. "Can't wait to dig into the phase data and energy profiles. There's a lot to examine to characterize a magical signature. Just like the energy that makes up your talent, all magic uses the seven elemental forces as building blocks. At a glance, this thing is probably heavy on Fire and Air, but there's certainly more to it."

The man knew a metric ton more than I did about magical properties. My proposal largely relied on using tinker abilities to help me investigate the football, an approach I was certain would work if I could continue to plumb the depths of the device. But the maintenance manager's enthusiasm as he got lost in his instruments was something else altogether.

"What did you say your talent was again?"

"Mine?" Mike popped up from behind his panels like a prairie dog. "Officially it's called systology, which loosely means I have a knack for studying magic systems. But it's more than that. I absolutely love delving into all systems, seeing the interrelationships and possibilities. Unfortunately that isn't a skill well suited to hunting demons, and my command of elemental spells is practically non-existent. Attwater tried to plug me into academic circles, but I like getting my hands dirty. So basically I'm a misfit. That's how I landed back at the school."

"Looks like you've got no regrets." Something he said hadn't sounded quite right. "But you meant to say five, not seven elements, right?"

"I forgot how they teach now." He shook his head, but there was a bit of mischief in those brown eyes. "Earth, Air, Fire, Water, and Spirit do tend to be the base elements for most spellwork. But there are a couple of others out there that come into play on rare occasions."

"And those are?"

"Not important at this time."

And that was the end of the subject.

I left Mike elbow-deep in the displays full of data. Time had slipped away while we worked. Attwater's halls were pleasantly deserted, so I didn't have to worry about running into my friends. Strange thought, but they all seemed to be angry at me, not just Gina, the whole gang—except Owen. My girlfriend thinking I was cheating seemed to have made the cretin's day.

We'd known from the start that delving into the football wouldn't be a one-and-done effort. A few more sessions would put me on track to salvage my original proposal. In the meantime, I'd talk things out with Gina. Hopefully, she'd like hearing about our progress, because every other topic I considered leading with seemed sure to make her mad.

Mr. Girardi wanted another proposal in a week. That gave me plenty of time to figure out the project and how to get back in Gina's good graces.

9. Extracurricular

T IME TURNED OUT to be an elusive luxury. Ms. Eisner and Melissa Murdock grabbed me the very next morning before I'd managed a second cup of coffee. When the acting dean and head of security literally drag you off into an empty conference room, it's hard to think of anything good coming from it.

My mind immediately jumped to the football device locked away in Mr. Gonzales's workshop. Had word that we'd activated it outside the vault's protective field somehow gotten out? Gina had agreed to my use of the device, but given our current rocky relations, that support might have been revoked.

"How are your studies going?" Ms. Eisner led off what felt like an inquisition, doing nothing to ease my concern that I was in very hot water.

"Good? Um…really good." Now that wasn't the whole truth. "Still working my talent proposal for Mr. Girardi, but I've got a couple of viable alternatives lined up."

I cringed inside, glad Gina wasn't in the room to hear me include Roxy's recommended project.

"Not feeling over stressed or overworked?" At my head shake, Ms. Eisner stepped back, yielding to Ms. Murdock.

"I'd like you to head up student security for your class." The middle-aged woman with salt and pepper hair beamed, eyes full of feline intensity. "You've proven you can keep your head when facing shadows and lurkers. Mr. Gladstone spoke highly of you and so does Ms. Williams."

She apparently hadn't talked to Gina in the last twenty-four hours. The illusion of having time to study the football, revamp my proposal, and make up with my girlfriend evaporated. I thought back to Gina's last semester when she'd held a similar position. Student security pulled her into briefs and raids day and night. And like an idiot, I'd just told Ms. Eisner that all was well.

"I've got an awful lot to do already. There're plenty of people with better magic."

"It's a big responsibility," Ms. Murdock conceded. "Student missions are vitally important to prepare everyone for their duties after graduation. With my security team stretched thin, we're late standing up formal missions. Don't worry about your spell casting. We don't want the strongest mage. This is more about character, and you're good under pressure."

The conversation turned awkward as I attempted to dodge the unwanted responsibility. The women countered my excuses with reasonable arguments that made the extracurricular job into more of a civic duty. I'd be going out on missions either way, so why not take part in coordinating. Ms. Murdock insisted that demon activity had plunged to a record low and that this was the perfect opportunity to get the job on my resume with minimal effort. I had no idea who would read such a resume, but in the end I didn't really have a choice. They just needed to hear me accept.

"Okay, count me in." The writing on the wall was too bold to ignore.

"Excellent." Ms. Murdock pumped my hand, making me think she must lift weights in addition to the martial arts training underpinning her controlled grace. "We have a combined briefing at four today, just a status update and meetup between department reps and student leads. Bring a second if you'd like."

Bethany would have been my natural choice to take to the meeting, but she'd made herself scarce lately. At first I figured she'd been digging for more answers about the journal. She remained convinced the blank pages held answers. But Mon hadn't turned up lately either, so the two were probably spending time together. More power to them. Who knew where we'd all land come graduation.

So I brought Owen along as my second in command. We both struggled to see how our talents fit into the grand scheme. Even though I'd made a valiant effort to dodge the responsibility of being a student lead, getting involved could only help. The soon-to-be mechanic did his own fair share of evading, but in the end came along willingly.

Ms. Murdock welcomed the entire group in the commons, had her people check everyone in, and led us through the twisting halls of the inner rings to a command center buried deep in the bowels of the building. The secure location was where planning and strategy took place and also housed the portals that transported teams to their mission sites.

"I see you'll be in the driver's seat now." Gina came over to offer congratulations in her official capacity as Ms. Murdock's second in command. "With Owen at your side, no less."

"Hoping to do as well as you did. Nice digs."

"I'll be lucky to find my way back here again," Owen said. "There isn't even a room number."

"Don't worry." Gina eyed me as she spoke. "We'll key your badges for access, and the card itself can lead you in like a divining rod. Everyone's final projects in order?"

"All done with the Harley," Owen said. "Now, I've got an old BMW boxer to get ready for vintage motorcycle days and graduation."

"Working on mine too." The answer kind of exploded from my mouth. "Hoping to re-engage about studying the football."

Mike Gonzales was still working through the data, but we'd squeezed in a quick set of readings with the hemispheres dialed up two degrees. We figured collapsing the rods increased the power. If that hypothesis was correct, the device would be at max output when the ends were pushed fully together into a single sphere. For safety, we'd only brought them in one notch, the lowest power setting that produced measurable data.

"Good to have goals." She didn't sound as pleased as I'd hoped. "Listen up to the orientation briefs. Weird things are going on out there."

"Wasn't Murdock just touting the fact that sabotage and infrastructure attacks are down?" Owen asked.

"They are, and we're finding empty lurker nests more often than not." Gina shrugged. "It's kind of like the problem with those sites Mr. Gonzales identified. I have a hard time believing the enemy is simply giving up. More likely they're consolidating forces. We need to watch for something big."

"So much for easy leadership duties."

The joke fell flat, as did my attempts throughout the meeting to engage Gina on a more personal level. But we did get a thorough indoctrination describing how the combined student-staff security operation worked. Attwater's security took the brunt of calls from the field. Clear cut shadow or individual lurker problems would be delegated to a student team once it had cut its teeth in combined operations.

Three student teams consisting of twenty members each had been designated from among those graduating. We'd be contacting the general team members in the coming days, organizing training, and standing by for our first assignment with the main security force.

"Gotta admit, it's exciting," Owen said after the formal briefs concluded. "The poor noobs are in for a shock."

"Pot and kettle," I said.

"But you and I have already looked demons in the eye."

Point taken.

Over the next few days, Owen and I met with our peer leads and did a little player trading. Gina must have had a hand in the original team assignments because Bethany, Chad, and Mon were already on my roster. Still, it was good to find we were allowed to trade players to balance out strengths. Not every mission would require the full team's presence, so it was prudent to ensure each student leader had a couple of all-stars like Bethany on call.

Meanwhile, work on the football progressed. I managed to get a fingertip hold with my tinker magic, but had yet to find the thread of intuition that normally led me to the heart of a broken item. The only hint of a problem was that the football appeared unable to do anything on its own. The device was part of a larger system. That summed up my grasp of its function and wasn't enough to claim it needed repairs, but investigations continued.

10. Student Mission

"**O**UR TEAM WILL take the abandoned tunnels," I said as Gina concluded her briefing in the war room.

Having just come off the last in a series of field calls, she still wore her black tactical outfit. Bags under her eyes told me she'd been going full tilt. Although the last three nests had been mostly abandoned, security still had the responsibility of checking out calls from our network of operatives. Gina's people had mopped up a few low-level stragglers, but Ms. Murdock wanted the student teams to search for clues as to why demons continued to vanish.

"Are you sure?" Gina arched an eyebrow. "That site has the most ground to cover. It's more than the old highway tunnels. There's a warren of side passages and equipment rooms, and your team's down below half strength."

She had a point. We'd temporarily lost five members to an early flu season. Bethany and Mon were also out of play. Demands from their talent instructors continued to tie both women up late into the evening. But we had a secret weapon.

"Shouldn't be a problem." I looked to Owen, who nodded his agreement. "We've got an ace in the hole. Lori Warwick's talent is finding hidden things. And I've still got plenty of firepower to back her up and good schematics of the installation. We should be able to knock it out in under two hours."

"Okay, the tunnels go to Team Alpha." Gina marked the assignment on her whiteboard and turned back to the handful of people present. "Who wants the water treatment facility?"

I'd been lobbying hard for cool superhero team names. But when that left my people stuck with Team Tinker, I shut my mouth and let the traditional letter assignments stand.

Student Team Charlie took the water treatment plant, leaving Team Bravo with forest recon near a solar farm that had been plagued with shadow demons. The student leads and their seconds sat at the polished wood conference table going over details gathered by Gina's first responders.

After taking backseat for two training missions, this was like being all grown up and allowed to sit at the adults' table. At least, it felt that way if I ignored the security people standing along the back wall. Behind the occasional eye roll or grimace, you could almost see the wheels turning as each worked out how they would handle the searches.

A couple were more professional or simply harder to read. A tall thin woman wrapped from head to toe in dark pleats was the hardest by far. Long white fingers clutched the front of her black outfit—as if she were bitterly cold—and only the woman's piercing gray eyes showed from within the material shrouding her face. I assumed she was a woman by the slim figure, narrow waist, and quiet presence. She hadn't spoken during any of the security briefings—something none of the men managed—so perhaps was simply an observer from one of the other schools.

"Are you getting any sleep at all?" I asked Gina after the meeting.

"A few hours." She tucked a curl over her left ear and carefully collected the loose pages she'd used for notes. "I'm fine. You'd think fewer attacks would be good, but these deserted nests are disconcerting."

"When things settle down, I still owe you a night out."

I'd been slowly wriggling my way back into Gina's good graces, but things were definitely not yet cool between us. She really didn't want to hear about our work with the football, so I'd tabled that topic until my final project got formally accepted. Lately, it seemed the only safe subjects were security matters, but at least we were talking.

"Wouldn't that be nice." Her tentative smile was an olive branch. "They will eventually."

The problem with "eventually" was that I only had a few months until graduation, which left our relationship back on the shores of Lake Whereisthisgoing.

That evening I gathered our small team for the tunnel mission. Several more dropped out with the flu. Lori's talent would still set the pace, but with only half a dozen people, including Chad, Owen and me, getting through the warren of tunnels might take two nights.

"Everyone keep hold of your maps, lights, and buddy." I signaled the end of the pre-mission briefing by pulling on my leather tinker hat and running two fingers along the brim in my signature salute. "No wandering off alone. We want a good showing for our first solo mission. Radios will be unreliable in the tunnels, so stay close. This nest has been cleared, but keep your eyes and ears open. You've had basic combat training; lurkers could look like anything. Standard room clearing protocols are in effect, after which Lori has point until the next zone. Everyone ready?"

Nods and nervous excitement flowed around the circle of students. Our dark street clothes and sneakers were better suited for a party than a raiding a demon lair. We'd been issued tactical outfits, but a follow-up search mission didn't warrant the fancy gear. We carried a few shadow demon traps and tasers, but our weapons of choice were phone cameras and magic. The traps looked like big batteries that could suck up shadow demons. Tasers would slow down most lurkers, but folks like Owen could fire off a fireball just as fast.

I gave the guard manning our portal a thumbs up, and she activated the control panel—another example of machine-magic interface. Security maintained its own portal system. The oval doorways looked similar to the metal ship hatches used in Practical Exploration classes, with a cross bar controlling six latches.

"We'll watch the door. Stay safe." A black-clad man lifted the handle, swung the door open, and stepped into the swirling portal.

I followed him through. Magic tingled over my skin and the familiar lurch hit my stomach with a moment of freefall. My team assembled on the far side under a dim sky approaching twilight. We gathered on a cracked street that was more grass and saplings than blacktop. The dark maw of a long-abandoned freeway tunnel gaped from the base of the mountain looming over us.

"Three hours max," I told our portal guard before leading the others into the tunnel.

The stench of lurkers grew stronger as we merged into the gloom, flashlights cutting brilliant swaths across a floor littered with broken glass and walls decorated with stylish graffiti. There wasn't likely to be much in the dark reaches of the main passage, but we gave the mile-long cavern a quick once over just to be sure.

Lori walked in the middle of the group, leading us left and right as she swept the area with her talent. Judging by the pockets of bedding and debris, the place had been home to plenty of vagrants and parties over the years.

Demon activity became much more evident in the service tunnels that led off from about mid-span. Shadow demons didn't disturb their surroundings except for the machinery they sabotaged. Lurkers, on the other hand, tended to "decorate" their nests with odds and ends they found interesting. Lurkers were packrats, constantly on the lookout for enchanted items but seeming to not have much ability to distinguish between true artifacts and discarded junk. We passed several gruesome splashes where walls and floor had been painted by lurker innards. Funny, I'd thought Gina's people had only encountered straggler demons at the water treatment plant.

"Stay close until Owen finds the emergency lighting," I said after we'd gone about twenty yards.

Fortunately, the breaker panel was right where the map said. The clunk of relays brought glass domes along the ceiling to life throughout the complex. The lighting was by no means bright, but at least we could navigate without flashlights. We worked our way through narrow corridors and the first two larger rooms.

"The original call was about lurkers, right?" Owen asked.

"Yep, a mixed nest of mid-level demons that security had been watching," I said. "At least one of them had magic, but they cleared out suddenly."

Security wasn't always able to sweep in and eradicate problems. This threat had been minimal and placed under observation until a raid could be mounted. Our night man at the adjacent power station was the first to notice when the lurker scouts stopped casing his facility. Changes in demon behavior could mean bad news. Attwater took patterns seriously, so the drop off in activity led to more missions and was running Gina and her people ragged.

Lori bobbed along amidst the team, her short, straight hair glinting with subtle blue under the emergency lights. She'd be certified as a private investigator upon graduation, a career that matched her talent of finding lost items perfectly—unlike some of us. The compact thirty-five-year-old was easy to imagine as a pleasant but hardboiled detective hunting up missing heirlooms or spouses who'd skipped town.

"Bag!" Lori called out the moment we entered a four-way hub in the tunnel system.

We'd been following piping and cables that joined up in a knotted array of manifolds, relief valves, and junction panels. I nearly burst out laughing when Lori whipped out an honest-to-goodness magnifying glass to inspect a workbench near the electrical panels. The lens in its metal hoop matched the blue in her hair, making me wonder if the glass had properties like my spectrum goggles. Bradley, a nervous little guy with curly red hair and big guns when it came to common spells hurried over with a pair of magic-dampening bags.

Lori carefully lifted a small wood case from the top drawer, inspected its contents, and slid the whole thing into one of the soft black bags.

"Dangerous?" I figured knowing was important.

"Don't think so." Lori had a clipped New England accent that drew out vowels before chopping them off. "An enchanted sextant or surveying instrument."

Yep, demons would collect just about anything.

Sweeping around the adjacent corridors took another hour and landed us back at the hub without turning up anything else.

"We've been everywhere right?" I asked Owen while consulting my laminated map.

"Far as I can tell, but—" He double checked his own map. "Where's she off to? Hey, we've already been that way!"

He called after Lori as she headed down the left-hand passageway. Everyone hurried to follow. I did too, feeling thoroughly out of control.

"Lori, we're done," I said when she slowed at a blank section of wall.

"I can't help feeling that I've missed something." Lori ran her hands over the wall and stepped back to pull out her magnifying glass. "There's a tingle right here, but just a general glow."

She held the glass in front of her face for a solid minute. I slipped the spectrum goggles out and flipped down the blue lens. A subtle glow came off the cement walls—very subtle. If I hadn't been looking for it, I would never have noticed.

"I see what you mean. Let me try something." I flipped down the yellow lens, then the red. A vertical seam high up on the wall throbbed dull amber. I ran a hand over the area and found a small hole. "There's a slot here with a socket at the top, like maybe the lever is missing."

"Oh, I can do missing." Lori put away the magnifying glass and rubbed her hands.

The hairs on the back of my neck came to attention. I jerked my hand off the slot and backed away. But the sensation came from behind. Through the rose lenses, Lori shone bright with golden light pouring off her. My intuition told me she'd opened herself up to the universe, asking for guidance. And the universe answered, coalescing and caressing the woman's aura, feeding her information. I pulled the goggles off against the glare, but also to keep from intruding on the intimate moment.

Lori turned in a slow circle with eyes closed, walked back the way we'd come, and knelt against the wall. The presence faded, and she opened her eyes.

"Here." She tapped a section of wall that rang metallic.

Owen helped pry open a small door painted to match the concrete. Lori reached inside and withdrew a metal bar with a flattened handle. The two-foot length ended in a six-sided nub that would fit into the socket back at the glowing wall. By its weight, I guessed the bar was aluminum under its matte-black powder coating. Close inspection showed wear along the edges of the hexagonal socket fitting. The lever had been used recently and often.

"Nice work, Lori." I looked the bar over with my goggles, but found no trace of magic. "Is everyone up for an experiment?"

The team fanned out in a ring, magic held ready along with a couple shadow demon traps. Owen fit the lever in its socket and pulled. A thump was followed by a grating screech, but the wall stayed put. Heads swiveled as we scanned the hall trying to spot what had shifted.

"It's open," Lori whispered with a nod at the section of wall by Owen. "Illusion."

11. Hidden Room

A PEEK THROUGH the goggles showed Lori was right. Magic flared in a ghostly illusion concealing the open doorway. I poked the surface with a shadow trap, then eased halfway through the wall. The tunnel beyond opened into a small room after a short distance. I waved the others to follow.

There was no sensation of vertigo, so we'd crossed through a hidden door rather than a portal. My team formed up on the other side, flashlight beams playing in a wild display across block walls. Glints of metal showed a table and chairs sat in the dark room beyond.

"Slow and easy." I kept my voice low, motioning Owen to lead half the team down the left wall while I took the right.

We'd taken maybe five steps when two shimmering creatures rushed from the doorway at the end of the passage. Owen launched a fireball, while I threw a whirlwind. Both spells winked out on contact, one demon absorbing the flames and the other swallowing my strongest air spell like it was nothing. *Hell.*

"Flashbangs!" I got out the call for defensive grenades just before an electric jolt slammed my jaw shut.

Chad was quick on the draw. A small cylinder flew over my head, landed in the corridor beyond, and split the air with a concussive blast. The demons rushed us, getting in too close for us to toss more disruptive devices without bringing everyone to their knees.

The burly demon nearest was just a glowing outline that slashed with talons of lightning. Pain exploded, blue arcs of electricity scorching my shirt and locking my muscles in convulsions as the phantom claw passed through me. The sparking outline caught on the shadow demon trap, nearly tearing it from my left hand. Thanks to the electric jolt I couldn't have let go if I tried. My clenched hand jerked as the trap tried to draw in something it was never meant to handle.

The cylinder was basically a battery that absorbed shadow energy, but it could only hold so much. The trap grew hot, then shorted out with a puff of smoke. I dropped the trap, clenched my burnt hand, and looked straight through the ghostly creature as it turned on Chad. Our attackers were made of electricity—form without substance.

"Energy trap, not lurkers," I managed between clenched teeth as another spasm dropped me to the floor.

Demons or not, the defenders ripped through Owen, me, and the second wave of our team. It was like swimming with electric eels; just as you started to regain control, you'd get zapped. But our attackers seemed to be tethered to the far doorway, not quite able to reach Lori and Bradley by the illusionary wall.

"Find the off switch!" I yelled over the confusion.

Lori didn't waste any time, pivoted, and pointed to the right-hand side of the room ahead. "Silver control panel."

Of course it was beyond the leashed attackers. I fumbled for my other shadow trap. Owen had been staggering my way, saw what I was up to, and pulled out his own trap.

I meant to say, *"Owen and I will hold them off for a few seconds. Bradley, get in there and take out that panel."* What came out as another jolt took hold was more along the lines of "Owen and I...I...I off ... Bradle...e...e...y ... pa...pa...panel."

Hoping he'd understood, I rolled onto my stomach and jabbed the cylinder in my aching hand at the butt end of the apparition attacking the woman behind me.

This is gonna hurt like a son of a bit—

My arm convulsed where it contacted the energy. White pain exploded across my palm. Owen crouched against the opposite wall, his own trap stabbed through the back of the other guardian and jittering like he gripped a live wire. I knew the feeling. Someone swept past, stepping on my good hand. I would have spat out a curse if my jaw wasn't locked shut.

Smoke curled up from the trap and my hand. That palm went cold and tingly, which was a relief but couldn't be good. The trap whined high and clear, then blew out with a pop and puff of smoke. The energy I'd held captive swung around, its shaggy, crackling outline looking like a great lion's head as it lunged and...vanished.

The roar of static that had accompanied the attack cut off, leaving behind the sound of shifting bodies, moans, and coughing. It took several tries to unglue my tongue from the roof of my mouth, and I had to pry the half-melted trap out of my burnt hand.

"Who needs help?" I croaked.

"I need a beer." Owen clutched his fingers as lights clicked on in the room beyond.

"Everyone's alive." Lori took stock as she scurried between team members.

She scooped a smoking hat off the floor and handed it to Chad as he pushed to his feet. After slapping out the smoldering brim, the cowboy smashed it on his head and started helping others up.

"You guys have got to come see this." Bradley called from the room ahead, then seemed to catch on that we weren't exactly in stellar shape. "No more traps, so no hurry. I'll grab some pics."

He moved around, presumably documenting his find. The attack had turned most of our electronic devices into scrap. Even the tasers were fried. And my damn phone contract wasn't up until next year.

"Thank god no one has a heart condition," Lori said as we shook off the lingering effects.

The burns were our worst injuries. A quick wrap would hold Owen and me until we got the nurse to look at our hands.

"There could be more surprises," I declared when everyone was on their feet. "Stay alert."

The room beyond turned out to be more orderly than the rest of the lair, with chairs neatly tucked under a small conference table, message boards lining the walls, and even a single-serve coffee maker on the corner bookshelf. Judging by the dark screens above two control stations with fixed swivel chairs, the room's original purpose had been to monitor the facility. But it was the contents of those wall boards that spoke volumes.

"This was a war room." I was certain of it.

Drawings and diagrams were pinned on the walls, and stacks of maps were sorted into cubby holes along the edge of the table. I let out a low whistle at the damaged panel by the entrance—or more precisely at the ragged hole filled with smoking, twisted metal that used to control the defenses. Great chunks of the surrounding wall were missing too, having been blasted away by a combination of elements. Moisture dripped down the wall underneath, so even Water had been involved.

"Nice work, Brad." I blinked at the carnage and took a mental note to ask him about the spell later.

"Jackpot!" Owen ran a hand over one of the wall maps. "Unless I miss my guess, this is the power grid with targets circled. There's another for water distribution. And cell towers." His enthusiasm mounted as he worked his way around the room. "This has to be the work of mimics. Lurkers don't sit in cushy chairs drinking lattes and drawing up battle plans."

No they didn't, which made our find a big deal. We did our best to catalogue the scene. Lori used her dowsing abilities again, but didn't find any more magic items. Those with working cameras snapped pics and video, and we grabbed a handful of samples to take back. Attwater would have to send in experts to figure out what it all meant and how the information could be leveraged.

I pulled one final paper roll from the files. No sense trying to take it all back, but I wanted to add a building schematic to round out the equipment drawings and maps. A peek at the first few inches of the giant sheet showed rooms marked off along corridors. Standard drafting notation showed dimensions, but the notes were in an unfamiliar language. I was just rolling the drawing back up when the fountain in the open atrium caught my eye. That winding path looked really familiar.

"Guys, we have a problem." I unrolled the drawing fully. Sure enough, beyond the atrium and office areas, the rooms were arrayed in concentric rings. Many of the side corridors were incomplete, breaking off into blank areas that would presumably be filled in later. "This is Attwater."

"Crap, you're right, there's the commons!" Bradley let out a blistering curse that surprised everyone.

"Everyone, lend a hand and look through these stacks," The command came out harsher than I'd meant. "We're taking back anything that might relate to the school."

I waved Owen closer and showed him several areas of the school drawing that had been outlined in red.

"That's the admin wing for sure." He pointed to a narrow corridor along the left side.

"And this has got to be the vault." I jabbed a finger down on a big room with a round doorway nestled deep in the labyrinth, then slid it over to a section floating off the main building. "But where's this?"

"I'm guessing a lower floor." Owen scratched the stubble that passed for his beard. "Maybe near the heartstone chamber, but there's really no way to tell. These others seem to be scattered at random. It would help if Attwater had told us they have their own language."

A fifteen minute search pushed us well past the two-hour mark and pulled up two more items. One was a drawing of the back of the school, complete with rolling hills, circular drive, and the three massive doors to the auto shop. The other was less easy to recognize.

"It's the Bashar School," Bradley insisted. "This central arena in the auditorium is a dead giveaway. That's where they hold grudge matches."

The interior of the massive round building with spires and tiers was only about twenty percent completed. Instead of concentric rings, side rooms tended to hug the exterior walls in a haphazard arrangement and had been penciled in with only light outlines. More detail went into the cavernous central room with its tiered seating and open center stage. According to rumors, Bashar held magic duels to resolve student disputes. If so, our sister school must be rougher around the edges than Attwater.

For now, the important thing was to get back and warn Attwater. "I'll take your word for it." I pointed to the mound of items we'd set aside. "Bring all this along."

We headed back at a brisk jog, spells at the ready—just in case. Bradley and Lori hustled along in the center of the group, bristling with tightly rolled maps and drawings.

"Made it with twenty minutes to spare." Our portal security man called out as we emerged from the main tunnel. "Looks like quite the haul too."

"I have to get this stuff to Ms. Murdock ASAP." I jerked a thumb at our find. "We found a hidden room that's a planning cell. The school may be a potential target, so this stuff is time sensitive."

"Let's get you all back then." He motioned us to the swirling portal. "I'll call it in for an emergency debrief."

We swept through the portal one at a time. I brought up the rear with our guard right on my tail. We stepped into total chaos. The other guard yelled into her phone as she flipped switches to shut down our portal. Her words were lost in the wail of sirens and stringent blares from white boxes near the ceiling. Strobes on the front of each unit flashed at steady, one-second intervals.

"What's going on?" bellowed the man behind me as he dogged the door down over the deactivated portal.

"I'm trying to find out!" The woman with the phone yelled back. "The watch office should shut off audible alarms any—" The alarms stopped mid wail, and silence crashed in. "Gods, that's better."

"Do we need to evacuate?" The only other time I'd heard building alarms had been during fire drills.

"It's the general emergency tone, not a fire code." The woman at the console shook her head.

"Where's Murdock?" our man asked. "If it's an attack, the team has intel."

"She's off station. We don't even know who tripped the alarm. Perimeter sensors are all quiet." The woman held up a finger, listening to a tinny voice from her phone. "Gina Williams is the duty officer and gathering everyone in damage control central. Get going. I'll join you after securing my panel."

We headed into the hall under the flashing strobes. My heart thudded against my ribs, hoping the emergency didn't have anything to do with what we'd found.

"I don't think anyone set off this alarm." Chad crowded in close enough that I smelled the charred felt of his hat. Satisfaction settled in a stupid corner of my brain at the thought that my leather hat had fared far better.

"Someone had to," I pointed out.

We piled through a set of double doors into a room lined with desks, monitors, and consoles. Two of the four seats had security personnel in street clothes manning them and flipping through video feeds from various locations in the school and the surrounding grounds.

Gina stood behind the woman to our right, quietly asking her to pan the camera and bring up proximity sensor reading. The big desk dominating the center of the room stood empty, nestled in a half-ring of heads-up displays and a communications bank. My team stood off to the side, waiting for our chance to report.

Lori broke away to talk with a guard, returned with a first aid kit, and treated Owen's burnt hand. At least some of us were thinking.

"I think Attwater herself set off the alarm." The big cowboy leaned against the wall with both hands on the familiar stonework. "It's something bad."

"Demon attack?" I looked to Bradley and Lori to make sure those maps had made it through.

"Don't think so." Chad had a funny look on his face like he was sampling unfamiliar food and trying to work out the flavors. "Attwater's pretty sensitive to those. She's worried about there being too much power gathered within the walls." Again with the grimace of biting into a sour thought. "She's worried about an explosion!"

12. Football

"THERE'S A BOMB." My statement got Gina's attention fast. Hell, no competent leader would ever ignore those words.

"I've got no indications of that." Gina looked to her people for confirmation and got head shakes in return.

I hurried over, towing Lori along as the woman tied off the bandage she'd applied to my abused palm. Chad kept pace, his grim expression urging me to explain in as few words as possible.

"You know Chad has a link with the building, right?" I continued at her nod. "He's getting a read on a big power build up. Attwater says it's about to blow."

"Where?"

"She can't tell me." Chad got that perplexed look again. "But she'll guide us!"

"Track my position and find somebody who knows how to disarm a bomb," Gina told the woman at the displays before going to the shelves and jamming several items into a carry bag.

"I don't know if it's related, but we've got something else to worry about." I grabbed the Attwater schematic from the demon lair, rolled it out on the desk, and pointed to the highlighted areas. "We found a stash of maps in the tunnel raid. The demons are planning something for Attwater."

Gina cursed and turned back to the woman who was handing a binder to the other guard. "Bring the on-call staff in too and make sure Ms. Murdock gets an update. I'm authorizing full perimeter sweeps and portal lockdown protocols."

We left Bradley and Lori to help and darted into the hall. Chad led the way, dragging one hand along the wall. Halfway down the inner ring we took the stairs, spilled out onto to the second floor, and headed down a spur. Wiring and plumbing from side passages converged overhead, and I had a sinking feeling that I knew where we were headed.

"Not far now." Chad's face glistened with the exertion of keeping up running communications with the semi-sentient building. "Just a few doors down on the left. She's never seen anything like it."

We could all feel it now, a blistering hum of magical energy that registered more in your gut that ears. The power had a familiar rhythm to it, and my heart sank further when I figured out where I'd felt it.

"That's Mr. Gonzales's work room." I tried to dart ahead, but Gina pulled me up short.

"We go in as a team in case the demons laid a trap."

My ears burned, partly because she was right. My people had been ambushed by a demon trap just an hour ago because we'd gone in blind. But another realization fed the guilt clawing its way up my gullet.

"I don't think this is demons," I said. "The energy signature is from that device we found with the dead tinker. Mike Gonzales was helping test it. Something must have gone wrong."

"Clock's ticking." Chad stopped a dozen paces short of the workshop door.

"You're the strongest spellslinger." Gina jabbed a finger at Owen. "Go first and roll right. I'll go next and take left. Jason, you're last. We secure the room first. You see hostiles, you take them out. If you're unsure of a target drop it anyway. Chad, I'll wave you in with the all-clear. I can't afford to lose your link with Attwater in case there's more to this. Everyone ready?"

We surrounded the door in a loose arc. Owen took point with a whirlwind spell primed and ready. Even an opponent resistant to magic would be knocked back by the air element. Gina held one of our standard issue tasers in her right hand and an Earth spell in her left. I followed Owen's example, not wanting to unleash anything more damaging in the close confines.

Owen reached for the handle, but the door flew open. A fuzzy pink blur topped with wild blond hair rushed from the room and slammed into him with a startled yelp. Quick-draw Owen fired off his whirlwind as he and Roxy collided. The funnel cloud roared down the hall, tearing an occasional bulletin board from the wall.

"What the hell?" Owen's glare shifted between his retreating spell and the woman as they got untangled.

Roxy looked like a deer caught in the headlights, her eyes round and wild. No surprise since she faced four grim people with spells ready. She narrowed her eyes when a growl rumbled in Gina's throat.

"What's going on in there?" Gina demanded.

Roxy shrank back and hissed like a cornered cat. She looked ready to claw her way past, but took a deep breath instead.

"I don't know." Roxy shot a look over her shoulder, and turned back with frightened eyes focused on me. "We have to get out of here! It's some kind of bomb."

"And how would *you* know that?" Gina raised her taser.

"It's kind of obvious." When that didn't work, Roxy threw up her hands, gaze still on me. "I was working late on exercises from Dean Eisner. A weird sensation hit me, magic so strong I couldn't ignore it. I came to investigate, found the janitor passed out, and that thing in there going nuts. I was just running out to find help when I crashed into this idiot."

She sidestepped Owen, but with Gina in her face had nowhere to go. Our monitoring station with its radiation shield was visible through the door. A man in tan overalls was slumped over the controls.

"Mike!" I rushed inside.

He was breathing steadily, but out cold. I pulled him back into the padded chair, but couldn't rouse him.

"Something knocked him out." Roxy stood behind me, and the others crowded the doorway.

The energy coursing through the room throbbed against my skin and drummed in my ears. The football sat where we'd left it, nestled among the various sensors that fed the still-active equipment. But instead of being set on the first or second notch, the device formed a perfect sphere, gold half pulsing opposite the silver side in an alternating double-beat that built toward a crescendo. Why on Earth had he set the football to maximum?

"Whatever we're doing, we need to do it fast." Chad had both hands pressed to the doorframe as though he were trying to keep it from bending inward. "Attwater's pretty sure your toy there is about to take out half the building."

"Just leave it." Panic rose in Roxy's voice when Gina took a step toward the workbench. "The people are what matter, right? Evacuate, get everyone out. We can carry your friend."

Even at this late hour there would be students and staff scattered around Attwater, not to mention the extra security Gina had called in. I looked to Chad with eyebrows raised and mouthed "time?" He shook his head, an emphatic no.

"Jason, options?" Gina squinted at the pulsing sphere, dug around in her bag, and held up a magic suppression pouch like we used on missions, except this one was big enough for a bowling ball. "Without true bomb disposal gear, this is the strongest suppression carrier we've got. If we could get the sphere to the vault, the dampening spell might deactivate it. But this thing's giving off incredible power. I doubt the pouch would contain the blast if we didn't make it to the vault in time."

"Five minutes tops," Chad called out.

Definitely not enough time.

"The controls are pretty straight forward. I should be able to switch it off." I dashed over to the workbench.

"I tried prying it apart," Roxy wailed. "Let's just go!"

"Owen, watch the power readings." I squinted into the blinding aura, looking for the seam between halves. "I need to know if anything spikes. Watch the waveform too. It was looking pretty erratic. I need it to settle back down to a square wave."

"I'm on it." Owen rolled Mr. Gonzales back and manned the monitoring station. "Uh…there's like five displays."

"Center monitor's your close up view. It's set up like an oscilloscope. The barrel switch along the bottom hops between magical spectrums and frequency graphs. Read the labels."

That was all the instruction time I could spare as I blinked back tears and reached out a tentative hand. Damn, I needed sunglasses. The spectrum goggles would help me see if the magic was going unstable, but the intensity would blind me. My left hand went cold and numb when my bandaged palm hit the silver half. A moment later, painful tingles zapped through my right from the gold side.

"Here goes nothing." I tried pulling the halves apart, but just like Roxy had said, they were locked together. So I gave a little counterclockwise twist, backing off the amplitude five degrees.

"Levels are dropping," Owen called out.

In our testing we'd always set the degree of rotation before adjusting the distance between hemispheres. Thinking of it like a sound system, this was like adjusting the equalizer settings before clicking on and ramping up the volume. I gave an experimental tug, and the seam along the joint between metals widened.

"Backing off the power now," I pulled the ends apart a half inch until I hit a natural stop.

Separating the ends was like pulling magnets apart, except in this instance the attracting force was magic. I slid the ends out to the second then third stops. It was moving easier now.

"Hold up!" Owen squinted at the screen. "Readings are going wonky. Everything dropped fine at first, but now I've got funny spikes shooting up all over the place."

"How about now?" I pulled the ends out to about a third of the fully extended distance.

"It's a damned light show."

"Is amplitude or frequency going haywire, or is it both?"

"Time's short, really short." Chad pulled his cowboy hat low as though that might deflect the blast.

Even without the goggles, I felt the power rage and had to blink back tears. If we got out of this alive, I'd need a seeing-eye dog—or a seeing-eye bot. I could equip Mel for the task, maybe get a cameo in Scientific America. But I wouldn't get a congratulatory write-up if I didn't stay in one piece.

"Okay, bringing it back up. Let me know when it's stable again." My fingers were like swollen sausages that barely obeyed my brain, but I managed to click the hemispheres closer.

"There! No—" Owen slicked back his hair with both hands and leaned in close. "Maybe. Yeah, I think—"

"Oh for crying out loud. Move over." Roxy bulled Owen out of the way, pulled up the second chair, and started flipping switches. "Amplitude's still off the scales, above a hundred thousand wheems. Frequency is erratic between spectrums." More clicking. "It's like you're out of phase. Bring it in farther."

Another click brought the halves within an inch. "How about now?"

"Better. Frequencies have all dropped back to within five degrees of phase."

I backed off the rotation setting a few degrees just to see what happened.

"There you go! Wait, too far." Roxy nodded when I added a bit of clockwise twist. "Try bringing down the power again."

This time when I slid the ends apart a click, the readings remained stable, and the prickling in my fingers eased a fraction. But going further threw things out of whack again.

Unraveling the settings took a lot of back and forth, like opening those stupid padlocks on gym lockers—three turns left to your number, then two full rotations right, miss the number by a hair, and start again. It felt like we worked at it forever, but it couldn't have been all that long. By the time the device was halfway open, Chad stopped his countdown to Armageddon.

"Several channels are flattening out. You're closing in on square waveforms again." Roxy said after another round of adjustments. "I assume you want to bring them all down to standing waves?"

"Ideally." I squinted at the inner collar, estimating we were currently at about a quarter rotation.

Given how erratic the football could be, we weren't out of the woods yet, but we were close. The readings seemed to be less finicky with the device tuned down this low, so adjustments came fast and furious—a degree or two here, pulling the ends apart a fraction there. Sometimes I had to reverse course and increase the power output, but the overall movement was in the right direction.

"Drift's slowing," Roxy called out as I eased the hemispheres down below five degrees of offset. "Slowing…stop! You're all lined up. Go for it."

With a deep breath, I pulled the halves apart until they clicked out to full extension. When no one yelled, I twisted the ends to the neutral position and stepped back. I whipped out the goggles, not bothering to strap them on to look. The football was off.

"I think that's it," I said. "We good there, Roxy?"

"The patient is flat lined. Dead as a forgotten pharaoh's doornail."

"Chad?" I wanted every angle covered.

"Yep," He patted the door frame. "Old girl's happy."

The room let out a collective sigh of relief. I crossed over to check on Mr. Gonzales, who still hadn't budged. Being near the blazing football had certainly been uncomfortable, but its power hadn't affected the rest of us the way it had the maintenance manager. After fighting through the demon trap in the tunnels, I had to wonder if he'd accidently triggered a latent protective spell by turning the device settings up so high.

"Can you call the infirmary?" I knew Gina's phone would work. In fact, it was already in her hand.

"Hey!" Chad squawked as a heavily armored team shoved him aside and rushed into the room.

Their burly suits and thick face shields made the five people look like dark astronauts. Two of them carried a heavy chest supported between long poles. The bomb squad had arrived.

The exchange got pretty heated as we tried to tell the new arrivals that everything was under control. At Gina's insistence, the bomb squad finally departed amid reluctant mutters.

"Do you know how long it took me to gear up?" one squat team member—a woman by her voice—asked her companion as the pair stomped off.

The duty nurse arrived panting and out of breath to give Mr. Gonzales the once over. Her findings were inconclusive, so Chad helped get him on a gurney and they rolled him away for further tests and evaluation. The nurse didn't seem to think he was in danger, but something certainly kept him from waking.

"Pretty fancy driving there on the equipment," I told Roxy as things settled down.

"Not much different from running robot diagnostics in the pits at competitions." She looked at her feet and slid a mass of hair behind her ear with one hand.

"Except these readouts track magic." Gina strode over, hands on hips.

"True, but there's only so many ways to measure and display power," Roxy said. "All ends up looking pretty much the same."

Gina's lips pursed as if she'd just tasted something sour. My stomach twisted in a knot of tension as my girlfriend eyed the other woman. The tension grew to a breaking point.

"Thanks for the help." Gina thrust her hand out, and I think my jaw dropped open.

"Sure thing." Roxy lifted an eyebrow, and her cautious look morphed into a satisfied smile as she shook Gina's hand. "Glad I was here."

I didn't delude myself into thinking the two would be the best of friends. There was a certain gleam in Roxy's eye that told me that particular ship had sailed. But at least the gloves seemed to be back on. Hopefully, we could all just focus on graduating and the other problems at hand.

13. Bethany & Mon

"**Y**OUR TEACHER'S MONDO creepy." Bethany shivered, remembering the woman in black gliding soundlessly across the floor and how she never showed her face.

"Oh, and your battle-axe Hilda is such a delight," Mon said with little enthusiasm. "I thought she was going to take her riding crop to your butt when she found out your giant beetle wasn't poisonous."

"Ms. Baxter's all about the weapons."

"We're screwed, aren't we?" Mon asked.

Rather than answer, Bethany slid her hand into Mon's, reveling in the warmth as their fingers intertwined. It had been a long day and even longer night. The simulators with their battle programs and magic holograms were bad enough. Bethany had grown to hate training in the special talents wing, even as she reveled in honing her talent. But to find that Attwater kept demons prisoner and turned lurkers loose on students was simply barbaric. All just to gauge the effectiveness of a few special talents.

Practical Exploration with its tightly controlled encounters and the real life missions by student security were clean and wholesome compared to what she, Mon, and the handful of others were subjected to in Attwater's forgotten basements. Ms. Baxter said they should feel honored, that few students had the potential to achieve greatness in the fight against demonkind. *Aren't we the lucky ones?*

"Do you think Dean Gladstone knows they're building an army?" Bethany tossed a pebble into the atrium fountain.

In her mind's eye the ripples spread out like waves of lurkers under the control of the alliance, the group responsible for her and Mon's special study sessions. Her own drawings would march right alongside the monsters destined to wipe out the demon hordes that Attwater and the monks fought. But when you fought fire with fire, something was always left burning. If the alliance didn't destroy their own minions…well, then the demons wouldn't truly be gone. Would they?

"Not exactly an army," Mon said. "But any demons within Attwater's walls is too many."

Mon shivered, and Bethany wrapped an arm around her shoulders. Making drawings that could quietly take out shadow demon guards was bad enough. But her heart went out for what her girlfriend had been forced to do, to endure. The thought of sweet Mon pushing her talent into a demon, even a dead one, and then having to animate the soulless being was unthinkable.

Bethany didn't bother lying to herself. Accepting Mon's necromancy had put a strain on their relationship. She wasn't staunchly religious, but raising the dead seemed a fundamental violation. Those doubts were bad enough, but Mon struggled with the nature of her own talent. Bethany knew the toll of internal conflict. Coming to grips with her drawings being so similar to shadows had taken all her strength and the support of her friends. Mon deserved that same kind of support, and Bethany was determined to stick by the girl's side. Mon wasn't going to sink into the darkness and despair that pulled down so many necromancers, not if Bethany could help it.

The Atrium was their sanctuary, a refuge after training sessions defiled their magic. The babbling brook, grass, and trees lent peace and serenity to their roiling thoughts. But it was only a bandage. They always had to go back out and face the situation that had ensnared them.

"Ms. Baxter talks more than your mistress." She didn't dare share too much soul-crushing information, but Mon needed to know the scope of what they were dealing with. "The alliance is capturing demons all over the world. Baxter says they're stockpiling hundreds—maybe thousands—of shadows and lurkers. They can't control mimics, so those have to be destroyed. The group keeps hunting for innovative ways to control the rest, to weaponize demon against demon. There's a big battle coming."

"Doesn't seem like Gladstone would condone poaching students if he were here," Mon said.

"Chad's visiting the Bashar School tomorrow. He'll poke around a little to see if the same thing's going on." At Mon's horrified look, Bethany hurried on. "Don't worry, I didn't give him details and certainly didn't talk about your talent. He's just going to find out if they have a 'special' training wing like ours. Oh, and he's bringing that time forecaster back to double check the findings on the dean's disappearance. I plan to pick that guy's brain the first chance I get."

14. Bedside

I STOPPED BY the infirmary at lunchtime to see if Mr. Gonzales was any better. Attwater darn near had a field hospital tucked behind the administration offices in the east wing, a necessity given security's frequent run-ins with demons. The in-house staff handled emergencies and hard-to-explain problems we needed to keep out of civilian hospitals—like, say, magically induced comas.

"He has stirred occasionally, which is encouraging," the duty nurse said when I checked in at the front desk. "No signs of trauma or physical injuries. We're hopeful that he'll wake soon."

They'd swapped out his work clothes for a hospital gown, the kind with little blue flowers and inappropriate openings designed to cure lollygagging patients through embarrassment. Only truly ill people would endure a gown for long.

The man was liberally covered in little white pads with trailing wires connected to monitors on a stainless steel cart. He looked like the device we'd been studying, the thing that had landed him here.

What were you doing, Mike? I didn't voice the question. He didn't answer.

A comfy chair had been set up for visitors, and the welding specification manual that Mr. Martin wanted us to memorize sat heavy in my bag. I toyed with the idea of reading out loud, but aside from feeling silly, things like that were reserved for people dying in intensive care. Mike was going to be fine. He just needed to wake up. So I settled back to study the joys of tensile strength and dissimilar materials.

"If you say 'as you wish' to him, I swear I'll hurl." Gina startled me out of my search through the appendix as she slipped into the room. "You know, like from *The Princess Bride* movie?"

"Yes you're very funny. Shut up." Now I was really glad I'd decided against reading out loud. "Thought you had security stuff to do all day."

"I did, and it's done." She pointed at the clock on the wall behind me. "It's quittin' time."

"No way." I spun around. "Crap, I missed afternoon classes."

"You'll live. How's he doing?"

"Mumbles in his sleep and tries to roll over every once in a while." Those pregnant moments of expectation were likely what had me losing track of time. "Nurse checks in every thirty minutes, but says it's just a waiting game. His condition's still a mystery."

"Well, your football device is safely back in the vault so it shouldn't be hurting anyone else. I don't think you'll be using it for a tinker project anytime soon."

"No, you're right." That sort of limited my options, but I didn't want to get into a sensitive topic.

"There's more." Gina pulled up a chair and lowered her voice. "Our teams scoured that secret room you found off the tunnels. We recovered a boatload of information, mostly just maps you could buy online. Even the ones that weren't annotated should definitely help the experts better understand the demons' objectives."

"I sense a 'but' coming."

"But a bunch of it focuses on the schools, mostly Attwater, but Bashar and Chingyow were definitely being cased too. You saw some of it. They had the vault and a few other key locations targeted as treasure stores."

"They're obsessed with magical objects," I said.

"True, and they also had pinpointed three-quarters of our portals. Plus, we found topological maps of the surrounding area. They know exactly where we're located."

"Southern New Mexico right?" That was our group's best collective guess.

"Doesn't matter." Gina gave a noncommittal shrug. *Damn.* "What does matter is there has to be a mole in the organization to get that kind of information. They could have infiltrated any of the schools. But since more details about Attwater were found, my money is on a spy right here. We've got to ratchet up internal security again."

They'd just recently relaxed the in-person checks at each entrance, and a bunch of security's top people were still missing.

"Bet you'll end up here longer than just one semester." Oddly, the crisis eased the strain in our relationship, and my mind immediately turned toward the future.

"Maybe." She waved away the idea. "But I'm not interested in a permanent position. My salamanders are going to revolt if I don't get somewhere where they can frolic in molten metal."

"Is there enough info to stop the demons cold and keep the schools safe?"

"Still working through the data," she said. "The idea that we're being targeted is mostly conjecture based on the marked-up maps and drawing. It's a logical conclusion, but without real substance. All we can do is keep tightening up any holes in our normal security measures. Portals continue to be a major weakness, but they're also essential to daily business."

"Maybe the abandoned nests mean the lurkers are giving up or focusing effort elsewhere." I didn't have a clue where that elsewhere might be, but it was a happy thought—that Gina immediately squashed.

"That's the thing." She leaned in closer. "I don't think some of those sites were simply abandoned. Your team must have seen signs of a fight at the tunnel."

"Just some unsightly splashes from your mop-up mission." We hadn't been focused on those things because a cleanup crew would take care of the janitorial end of things.

"That's just it, Jason. By the time we were called in, there weren't any lurkers left. All we dealt with were a couple of shadow guards, and those seemed terrified. Something drove out the demons occupying that nest."

"That's a first." I didn't like the implications. "Is there a new monster on the loose?"

"It's actually happened twice before. The demons seem to have simply walked away from most of the recently abandoned sites, but this is the third that shows signs they were driven out. Forensics is working overtime on the samples we collected."

"Sounds like there could be different factions." Not a huge surprise given we already knew the Shadow Master had been stealing from the mimics.

"Maybe so," she admitted. "Life was simpler when we knew exactly what we were dealing with."

"Why am I wearing a dress?" The bed creaked as Mr. Gonzales shifted, blinked down at his clothes, then noticed us. "Jason? Please tell me I wasn't possessed again."

His voice was cracked and dry, but he took in the room with clear eyes. We hurried to his side as he fell into a coughing fit.

"You passed out working on the football." I handed him a cup of water from the nightstand, and Gina hit the nurse's call button.

"Yes, I was in the workshop checking readings." He coughed again, took another sip, and scrunched up his face in thought. "The room lurched sideways. I remember thinking earthquake as something thudded on the floor behind me. Then...nothing, I wake up here in a dress. Where are we?"

"School infirmary," Gina said. "You've been unconscious, a bad reaction to the magic from the sphere."

"You should have waited to up the power until I was there to help." Although that might have just put both of us in a hospital bed.

"Up the power?" He shook his head and winced. "What are you talking about? I was just reviewing the logs. I don't even remember turning it on. If I did, it would have just been to verify the settings we'd already tried."

"So nice to have you back with us, Mr. Gonzales." The nurse swept into the room, efficiently shooed Gina and I back from the bed, and launched into an examination. "Can you tell me your first name?"

"Mike."

"And the year?"

Questions rolled from her mouth like a well-rehearsed monologue, presumably designed to ensure he didn't suffer lingering brain damage. Gina and I faded into the background when it became clear we wouldn't get another word in until the nurse was satisfied.

In the end we never really got to talk more. Despite being asleep for a day and a half, the interview exhausted him. Mike was sawing logs again before long. There really wasn't much more to discuss. He was back with us and none the worse for wear, except for not remembering what had gone wrong.

15. Time Forecaster

T HE DAY FINISHED uneventfully, but my dreams that night were full of demons that overran the school and made me late for my final welding exam, which I showed up to without pants.

Lunch in the commons the next day had us discussing classes and how Mr. Gonzales would soon be released. The whole gang crowded around the table while we waited for Chad. The pillar seat awaited him, but the benches were getting crowded as our small circle of friends grew to include Mon, Lars, Gina, and now Roxy. The latter two weren't exactly best of friends, but had been passingly cordial after Roxy helped defuse the football. Still, they sat on opposite ends of the table, Gina by my side and Roxy next to Owen.

"You two have been awfully quiet today." I'd been wondering if Mon and Bethany had a fight, but probably not, given how they huddled together.

"Talent training's getting hard," Bethany said after exchanging a look with her girlfriend.

"I hear that." Owen's statement drew a groan from everyone because he'd taken to crowing about the motorcycle he'd have running any day now. "Can't hardly step away from the shop without getting called back in to try my hand at another engine. You'd think they'd figure out by now that I can't be fooled."

"Yeah, you'd think they would." Bethany nodded, clearly relieved he hadn't launched into motorcycle nostalgia, but also with a resigned look that said he didn't understand what she was going through at all.

"Howdy, gang!" Chad swaggered into the commons with his Montana accent in full gear and towing along a red-haired guy wearing slacks and a sweater. "Meet Herman Krauss, a newly minted graduate from the Bashar School of Vocational Interests. Herman, this is our Attwater posse."

Chad walked his smiling but dazed guest around the table and introduced everyone by name. Herman had startlingly pale skin and an infectious boyish grin. His sweater had big buttons, and his slacks laced up the side. The outfit seemed to be a cross between traditional lederhosen and current fashion.

"It is certainly nice to finally meet you all." Herman sat with Chad by the pillar. "And refreshing to be out of those volcanic caves."

"Speaking of which, how did it go in Hawaii?" I asked.

The dean and his security team had disappeared from the volcanic caves under Mt. Kilauea. Everyone at the table had either been in on the chase to find them or heard most of the details already. At the occasional assembly, Ms. Eisner provided terse updates on the search that mostly consisted of platitudes and assurances that everything possible was being done.

We knew better, knew that the situation wasn't likely to improve unless a specialist like Herman could shed more light on the situation.

"Not altogether badly." The easy-going smile slipped off Herman's face as he wrestled with an answer. "That is, no massive surprises—good or bad."

"Ms. Murdock doesn't want him talking about it where prying eyes might hear," Chad clarified. "He confirmed what we already suspected, but now we have a firm date."

"Sorry, I blinked. Can you repeat that?" Owen grinned at his own wit, then doubled over when Roxy elbowed him in the ribs.

Those two were getting quite chummy. I didn't mind Roxy's attention turning elsewhere. That made life with Gina easier. But I gaped at the playful way he counterattacked. Owen had better be careful or people would see through his carefully crafted lone-wolf persona.

Chad started to repeat himself before catching on. "I'll deal with you later, gearhead. But having a narrow timeframe can only help the search."

"So, without divulging details about the current job, how the heck does time forecasting work?" I asked.

"It's really kind of fascinating." Herman planted his elbows on the table and used both hands as he spoke. His choppy German accent softened into something vaguely British. "My talent extends in a bubble or envelope over the area under consideration, much like my friend Chad here reads weather. The smaller the area, the more focused this bubble and accurate the results."

"Actually, my magic opens me to the environment." Chad threw his big hands wide to illustrate. "Like astral projection, except my consciousness drifts out onto the wind. That lets me feel the different pressure fronts and temperature gradients that the talent interprets."

"Now that *is* interesting." Our guest turned his back to Owen and Roxy so he could face Chad. "Time isn't the homogeneous fabric of progression that most believe. It has definite whorls and vortexes that sound very similar."

The two chatted on, hands flying and comparing forecast techniques, ignoring the rest of the table. When Chad reached into his book-bag, intent on drawing out the elements of his daily forecast, the rest of us knew something had to be done.

"You two either need to get a room or speak in English so the rest of us can follow along." Gina's statement put an end to their private confab.

"Sorry." Despite Herman's fair skin turning bright red, he recovered quickly. "I don't get a lot of opportunity to talk shop. We in the time business have a rather tight community." He scratched his chin. "It's just Dean Gladstone, me, and a hundred-year-old woman in Scotland. She doesn't really count anymore. Poor thing has dementia. Certain talents are thought to exacerbate that sort of condition." Gina's scowl jerked him away from the rabbit hole before he darted in. "Anyway, my bubble lets me…observe, for lack of a better term, events and disturbances across the timeline. Present, past, and future converge, and sometimes I can untangle them enough to make sense of things. It's all passive. I can't manipulate the time stream the way the dean and others used to. But sometimes my skill comes in handy."

To be honest, envisioning how his talent worked was difficult. We discussed it for a few more minutes, Chad trying to compare it to his own abilities and Owen insisting that if the magic let Herman see pockets in time he ought to be able to influence it too. The conversation devolved into general discussion about everyone's talent and the biggest challenges associated with each.

Mon didn't participate and excused herself saying she was late for training.

"Will you be okay on your own?" Bethany caught the girl's chin and lifted her face until their eyes met.

At Mon's solemn nod, Bethany wrapped her in a hug, promising to check on her later. Something odd was definitely going on there.

Herman and Chad got ready to depart as enthusiasm waned, but there was something else we needed to show our guest.

"So, fun fact." I pointed at Bethany. "We've got an item you might be interested in."

"Oh, yeah." She rummaged in her bag and brought out the blank journal.

Bethany was a bulldog for details. Forgetting about the journal was out of character.

"Ah, the Chrono-monk symbol." Herman brushed his fingertips over the metal-embossed hourglass on the cover. "Contemporary design rather than an ancient relic."

"Dean Gladstone wanted us to find it, but the pages are blank," Bethany said. "We were hoping you might have some insights."

He flipped through book from cover to cover, nodded, and placed his hands to either side with palms down. Herman didn't exactly go into a trance, but his eyes went out of focus as though he looked through instead of at the tabletop. I stretched my magical senses, trying to catch a whiff of magic.

"Tricky devil." Herman cupped his hands as though patting snow into a ball, never actually touching the book.

"This isn't blank. The writing's just off our temporal axis, out of phase if you like."

"Can you read it?" I asked.

"Let's see." He flipped open the cover to the first bordered page, the interior of which remained blank. "Unusual topic." He skimmed through a few more pages. "Not a lot of detail."

"Care to enlighten us?" I had hoped the temporal bubble would let us all see the contents.

"Oh, sorry. It's just that talking about the monastery and Skellig Michael—the real activities there, not the touristy stuff—isn't something that usually gets shared with outsiders." He grimaced an apology. "You're certain that Dean Gladstone wanted you to have this?"

"He walked me to it like a puppet!" Lars still hadn't gotten over the ordeal.

"It was like this." I explained how we'd come to find the book.

"Makes sense." Herman nodded, drawing his conclusion. "He's trying to give you information that can help the school in his absence."

"And?" Bethany prompted impatiently.

"He's used a tricky temporal shift that puts the journal entries a fraction of a second out of sync with the current timeline. I think I can do one better than just read this to you."

Herman closed the book and went back into concentration mode. His brow furrowed, then eased, then furrowed again. Nothing happened for a good two minutes. Between one second and the next, a title appeared in gold script under the hourglass. It read simply, "Skellig Michael."

"All yours." Herman nodded and slid the book back, his distant gaze looking right through Bethany. He cringed and dropped his voice to a whisper meant just for her. "I'm so sorry. You and your friend have a terrible decision coming." Herman shook off whatever he'd seen and continued on more briskly. "The journal entries were shifted out of phase by a tricky little temporal lock. I managed to deactivate it. Everything should be there now."

Bethany opened the cover, revealing blocky handwriting. She flipped through more pages, some light with text, others heavy, and still others containing various sketches.

"Hey, that's the hatbox from the vault. Go back." Roxy leaned across the table, nearly knocking Herman off the bench.

Bethany scowled, but complied. Sure enough, the prior page was taken up by a pencil drawing of the funky guidance device with its three ornate legs and jeweled inserts. The facing page held a drawing of the silver portal mirror and globe. Bethany flipped pages on the thin journal, muttering to herself. She jumped around so fast that it was doubtful anyone else caught more than a word or two from the text.

"At a glance, these are instructions for reaching the monks at their monastery island off Ireland." She rifled back to a picture of the portal assembly. Rough coastline showed through the mirror, and the ornate cabinet was stacked on the globe's rolling framework. "It's the how-to manual for setting up a portal using these three components."

"The monks would be the only ones with a chance of following the dean's trail through time," Herman said. "But they've been gone for years."

"Could a portal reach across time?" Owen asked.

"I doubt it." Herman shook his head. "At least I've never heard of anything like that. Too many different mechanisms and principles involved."

"Wouldn't work anyway." I thought back to my brief examination of the old tracker in the vault. "That guidance cabinet is busted."

"Is it now?" Roxy's lips spread into a seductive smile. "If we only knew someone skilled at repairs."

"I'll give this a thorough read before we jump to any more conclusions." Bethany cradled the journal like one of her beloved sketchpads. "We really appreciate your help, Herman. I'd like to bend your ear on another issue before you head home."

16. Project Peril

I HAD DONE a good job of avoiding Roxy and any impression of impropriety for the better part of a week, right up until Tuesday's general assembly. Bethany and Owen spotted her heading for the seats I was saving and hurried to crowd in on either side, leaving Roxy to sit two rows back.

"So I got all the way through the dean's journal and it's about what we thought." Bethany leaned in close. "The whole book describes the monastery on Skellig Michael. Part of it reads like tourist information, describing how the initial monks settled there to wage their battle against the forces of darkness. It even goes on to modern times and how to hire boats to ferry out from the mainland."

"But the portal's the exciting part," Owen added.

"Yep, it seems like the globe and mirror combo was originally built solely to provide easy access to the Chrono-monks. The language for that part gets a little vague, but I think the mirror was able to follow them. Sometimes the winters out on the island got to be too much, so the order would move over into Ireland for a few months. That broken component down in the vault is the key to tracking them."

"So you want me to fix it?" Dread coiled in my belly at the thought of how mad that would make Gina.

"You do need a tinker project," Bethany said. "And Dean Gladstone must have wanted us to try, otherwise why give the book to us?"

"The world needs the Chrono-monks back." Owen punched me in the arm for emphasis.

He'd taken quite an interest in Mr. Grawpin's lessons about the ancient order that set up the world barriers, but I hadn't realized the depth of his enthusiasm. Owen's eyes damn near glowed with intensity as he willed me to go fix the stupid tracker. Luckily, I was saved from answering as the lights dimmed and people walked onto the stage.

Since the Dean's disappearance, Ms. Eisner's focus for the weekly gathering turned increasingly toward security. Today's lecture was no exception, and she was joined onstage by Gina and Ms. Schlaza.

Ms. Eisner assured the students that the experts were making progress in returning Dean Gladstone and expressed her eagerness to give the man back his executive level hokum so that she could return to teaching. Everyone liked Ms. Eisner, and laughter echoed through the auditorium at the face she made when speaking of her current leadership role.

Annette Schlaza made her own face, which was less than pleasant. Her expression hovered between hungry wolverine and pissed-off feline as she added her two cents.

"All foolishness aside" —Schlaza shot a pointed glare at Ms. Eisner— "immediately report any, and I do mean *any,* suspicious activity to a teacher or security, especially if a portal is involved. We want to be absolutely certain that the rest of the semester runs smoothly. Out of an abundance of caution, your home portals will be deactivated for first year students between the hours of eight p.m. and six a.m. Do I make myself clear?" A subdued chorus of "yes, ma'am" rose from the students unfortunate enough to have class under the Ice Queen. She accepted the response with a royal nod and clapped her hands once. "Very good. Now, are there any questions?"

"Phhht, as if!" Owen's reaction sent a moist spray across my arm, but I couldn't disagree with his sentiment.

Since no one was brave enough to step up with a question, Ms. Schlaza yielded the stage. The program moved into familiar and relaxed territory. Student officers recapped several fundraising events, including a winter talent show promising to be the highlight of the year. The student council was determined to resurrect the traditional event that had fallen by the wayside a few years back.

To get people's creative juices and excitement flowing about showcasing talents, a group of volunteers launched into an exhibition demonstrating possibilities.

"Don't let the title of the show fool you." A tall man with black hair and an outrageous waxed moustache stepped up as ring master for the demonstration. "Entering with your unique magical talent is not required. Have a special elemental spell you're dying to show off? Enter it. Do friends back home rave about that graceful ballet routine? Bring it on. Everything magical and mundane is fair game."

As he spoke three people stepped on stage. A thin woman with arrow-straight black hair carried a cello, took a seat, and began to play. The melody was smooth and beautiful, filling the room with dulcet tones from a slow classical piece. The opening strains melded into a faster contemporary march, then classic metal as her montage progressed. She was a gifted musician, mesmerizing the crowd with the music pouring forth.

A blue flash glinted off her bow as the tempo raced on, then a spark of gold. Soon the air around her shimmered with explosions of pastels and richer tones. The light show matched the music so well, so naturally, that it took me a moment to catch on. I clapped my hands over my ears and the lightest brighter colors winked out, while the darker bursts grew faint. I dropped my hands and the full display burst back to life.

"We're actually seeing the notes," I said to Bethany. "Like projected synesthesia."

The woman finished with a flourish to thundering applause as a small dark-haired man wearing green spandex stepped to center-stage. He looked to be in his fifties and with deliberate care held both arms out as if to stabilize himself. A drumroll sounded from backstage as he slowly drew up his right leg. The drum cut off with the crash of a symbol when his foot reached his knee. He held the pose for five seconds. Murmurs drifted across the uncomfortable silence. A sharp beat of the snare started another drumroll, and the foot descended. The cymbal crashed when the guy was back on two feet. He took a deep bow.

A smattering of uncertain applause turned to a collective gasp as the guy pitched too far forward. He should have smashed into the floor face down, but tucked and rolled, executing three somersaults before pulling up into another one-legged stand—but this time on tiptoe with the raised leg hugged to his cheek as it extended straight over his head. He flowed smoothly though complex tumbles and gravity defying flips, never missing a beat as the crowd roared their approval at being duped. Best of all, there was no undercurrent of magic. The man was an incredible athlete.

A portly woman dressed as a baker took the stage last. She pushed a silver serving cart laden with an elegant cake. Five massive tiers decorated with a complex string of roses, petals, and other intricate designs would have done any bride proud. Not much of a show after Mr. Gymnast, but she carted her creation in a wide circle, receiving well-deserved applause.

Then her cake exploded—or at least the decorations did.

Flowers, pearly strings, and all the random design elements blew out into the audience, leaving the impressively iced creation bare. A yellow tulip hovered in front of my face on two slowly flapping green leaves as if daring me. I plucked the living bit of icing from the air, and nibbled a petal—sugary lemon!

I don't think anybody heard the closing announcements. We funneled out through the double doors laughing and munching on cake decorations. Bethany started to ask a question, but spotted Mon in the crowd and dropped me like a hot potato. I hadn't wanted to get into my tinker project anyway. *Bullet dodged.*

Then Roxy struck.

She hit me from behind with a playful bump. At first I thought it was Owen, but he'd already drifted off.

"Have you been dodging me?" She slipped her hand into mine before I could answer.

Sparks exploded when our fingers touched, an electric burst like the first day we'd met—only stronger. My thoughts grew fuzzy. There was something wrong about her holding my hand, but I couldn't quite figure out what.

"Um…no." I focused on her question.

I hadn't been. Had I? What the heck was in that frosting?

"So when do we start working on that hatbox?" As she spoke her fingers massaged mine with a surprisingly strong grip, crushing really, that ground my knuckles together as more electricity zapped up to my elbow.

Despite the grip growing painful, I didn't let go, didn't want to. What I wanted to do was to give this lovely creature whatever she needed. But the damned sugar rush and baker's magic had my head spinning. We'd had emoji pudding shots at last year's Spring Fling, and I had a sneaking suspicion I knew the mage responsible. But those blasts of emotions wore off in seconds, while this one seemed to be growing stronger. Roxy's need rolled over me, not sexual, but similar and just as intense.

"Hatbox?" I couldn't quite track what she wanted from me. "Oh, the tracker to get to the monks."

"That's the one, genius. Let's go fix it."

"Can't." I smiled like a fool, a drunk fool—stoned on magic mushrooms.

"Focus for me." She sounded sweet when she was mad. "Why not?"

"Hatbox is in the vault." Her grip eased up, as did the effects of the cake decorations, and I found it easier to string thoughts together. "Vault's locked."

She pouted pretty too—with a little too much teeth.

"And my girlfriend wouldn't like it," I added, thinking myself very clever for remembering that bit.

More teeth showed and a cute little growl escaped her throat.

17. Intervention

"EVERYONE WANTS ME to fix that old guidance system in the vault." My hand still tingled pleasantly from yesterday's talk with Roxy. The woman had put forth a good argument about repairing the 'hatbox.' Very compelling, even if I couldn't recall all the details. "But Gina's going to hate me if I take Roxy's suggestion."

The disappointment on Gina's face when she'd first found Roxy helping me pick a project sent a sobering chill down my spine. As much as Roxy deserved my help, I couldn't stand the thought of doing that to my girlfriend, not again. Even so, I had to pick another project or risk not graduating this winter.

Something deep in my gut told me that working on the guidance system right now was a very bad idea, which didn't make sense. The feeling wasn't easily put into words, just a bone-deep dread that bad things could happen. And I didn't think it had anything to do with disappointing Gina.

Having such a good listener helped me work through the conflicting internal monologue, even if sitting on the floor in Bethany's tiny studio had my butt going numb. Mortimer lounged on the miniature sofa in his leafy apartment, which was actually a large bird cage that Lars had grown from thorny vines.

Even Bethany didn't understand how her gargoyle had acquired furniture. Every time I visited her storage-closet-turned-art-studio, the cage sitting in the corner held some new luxury. Today's improvement seemed to be working electricity. Mortimer had been reading under a tiny table lamp when I showed up and let myself in for my meeting with Bethany. She must have gotten hung up, which gave me the chance to vent.

It was difficult to gauge how much the gargoyle understood, but Mortimer leaned forward as I walked through my options. When I'd circled back around to using the guidance system for my final project, he nodded in sympathy, shuffled to the doorway, and patted my hand.

"It's the only reasonable alternative at this point." I blew out a big breath, and Mortimer nodded in agreement. "I'm just going to have to bite the bullet and let Gina know it has nothing to do with Roxy."

Mortimer straightened and gave a curt nod at my decision, tusks gaping in approval. Sometimes it was your quiet friends that said the most.

"Thanks for having my back, little man." I held out my fist, and Mort bumped charcoal knuckles to mine, both our hands pulling back with exploding fingers. "Awesome."

My numb hand and a tightness in my chest eased at having made the decision. Mr. Girardi had hinted pretty strongly that he'd accept my alternate proposal, so my biggest hurdle would be breaking the news to Gina. Mission complete, Mortimer drifted back to his couch and the thumb-sized book full of colorful comics—a vibrant contrast to the gargoyle's grayscale.

A few of Bethany's other drawings had wandered off their page during our chat and now sat or hovered over their respective sketchpads that were on display along one wall. I was contemplating the massive blue tentacles slithering among the ceiling pipes when the door burst open.

"Sorry I'm late." Bethany bustled in carrying her book bag. "Getting everyone together was like herding cats."

Mon followed in Bethany's wake. Then came Chad and Owen. When Lars squeezed into the small room and shut the door, I got the feeling something big was up.

"No problem," I said carefully. "I thought you wanted to talk about the journal."

"In a way. It's time for 'the talk.'" Bethany put air quotes around the last two words and looked way too serious.

"Which talk would that be?"

"The get-your-head-out-of-your-ass talk," Owen said.

"Not helping." Bethany glared at Owen's grin and then at me as I eased my way toward the door. "Tina!"

I found myself facing a pebbly blue wall as the massive octopus drawing slipped off the pipes and blocked the exit. *Wonderful.* I turned back to the group with my hands raised in surrender and took a seat by the cage and my new best friend.

"This Roxy thing has to stop," Bethany said.

Not again.

"Can you believe this?" I looked to Mortimer and did a double-take. "Et tu?"

My tiny confidant perched on a wooden chair just inside the doorway. He peered at me over wire-rimmed spectacles that had appeared out of thin air. A pencil clutched in his right claw hovered over his book.

"Look." I tried to keep my voice reasonable. "I'm going to have to work on that old guidance system if I want to graduate."

"Yeah you do," Owen said. "It's the only way we'll find those monks."

Nice to have backup, but it was so weird that Owen had a thing for the monks all of the sudden. I waited for Bethany to contradict him, but she just nodded.

"We get that," Bethany said. "But you don't have to make googly eyes at Roxy all the time."

"I don't—"

"You do. We all see it." She was getting up a head of steam, and the others nodded like bobble-heads. "You held hands with her right there in the hall yesterday where everyone could see, where Gina saw."

Crap! Did she?

The exit from our assembly was a confused blur. Everyone had been jostling and laughing. Sure, I'd talked to Roxy. And she *had* grabbed my hand—briefly. What the heck had I been thinking?

The gang asked the same questions several times over, in a not-so-subtle attempt to get me to admit I had the hots for Roxy or that I was ready to dump Gina. Neither could be further from the truth, yet I found it increasingly difficult to defend my recent actions.

As far as interventions went, the interrogation was a thoroughly miserable experience. My adamant denial of any sexual interest in Roxy and having to wipe my eyes when admitting Gina deserved better finally won them over—if grudgingly labeling me a clueless idiot instead of a selfish jackass could be considered winning.

"We *will* be watching you, mister." Bethany included the entire group and her drawings with a swirling finger to drive home the fact they believed but didn't trust me. "You need to talk to your girlfriend, stay focused on your work, and keep the hell away from that blond bimbo."

Chastened as I was, a small part of me lunged to the surface to defend Roxy. But I managed to keep my mouth shut and nod in agreement.

"Good." Bethany pulled the dean's journal from her pack. "Now let's talk shop."

18. Repairs Begin

G INA TURNED OUT to be pretty elusive. Between my classes and her work schedule, I couldn't catch up to her for the rest of the day. The talk we needed to have wasn't something that could be done by text—even *I* wasn't that clueless. But once I was home and out of the school's no-signal zone, I managed to pin her down for a meet up after school the next day.

Unfortunately, I had talent training in the afternoon. With little choice, I pitched my new proposal to Mr. Girardi, explaining the guidance cabinet's basic function and sad state of repair. When I finished summarizing my research and repair plan, he practically bounced in his seat and congratulated me on finding a worthy project. That was the easy part.

"Hey, how's it going?" I asked as Gina joined me in my workshop.

I'd cleared my bench of miscellaneous parts and tossed the scrap that tended to accumulate into the corner. Mel had helped deep clean away my anxiety as I waited. He now stood gleaming in the corner. His new metal framework had gotten a thorough polishing too. Not that a clean room was likely to make the discussion any easier.

"Busy, busy." Gina looked around my small workspace and whistled low. "Someone's been a busy beaver. You're lookin' good too, Sir Mel."

She hadn't seen my robot since I'd fabricated his new body, back before the welds had been ground down and buffed. I almost launched into a description of how well his auxiliary functions were coming along, not the least of which was a higher reasoning module that gave him increased decision making capabilities without risking a magical meltdown. But I bit my tongue and focused on what needed saying.

"Listen, Gina. I've been acting stupid lately, and I'm sorry." Instead of commenting, she crossed her arms and let me keep digging. "I know you must hate me, but I've got zero interest in Roxy, honest. She just keeps running into me."

"And your hand seems to keep falling into hers."

Ouch.

"Like I said, stupid. There's no good excuse, but I promise it'll stop." I put as much sincerity as I could behind the words, willing her to believe.

We talked for a good twenty minutes. She expressed cogent, intelligent thoughts on the nature of relationships and the inherent trust needed to help them flourish. I just seemed to keep repeating my apology and promising to do better. Deeper sentiments were right there on the tip of my tongue, but I couldn't quite frame them properly.

"I think it's time we moved on," Gina finally said.

"Oh." Not what I wanted to hear at all, but I didn't have a leg to stand on. "If that's what you want."

"Now, none of that." She actually smiled at my slumped posture. "Move on together, as in put this behind us." I must have brightened up too much as understanding dawned. "We'll take it slow, a kind of reboot. Deal?"

"Deal." I couldn't ask for more than that. "But I've got to let you know about my project too."

"No, you don't." Her smile stretched to the thing of beauty I remembered. "You're going to fix that guidance system, and that's fine. My issue has never been with your final project. You'll be needing the entire mirror portal system for your work. Access requires approval from security, especially in our heightened state of readiness."

"Oh, I hadn't thought of that." I felt stupid on several levels now.

"Luckily you have an in with the department. I'll handle coordinating with your instructor. You can have the guidance cabinet for the duration, but the globe and mirror need to be locked back in the vault each night. We'll have to sync our schedules because my boss and Ms. Eisner aren't giving out additional access privileges until we're sure that Attwater's no longer a target."

"It's still weeks away, but what about field trials? I'll have to activate the portal at some point to test the repairs." At least the mirror wouldn't try to blow up on me like the damned football.

"Again, we'll work out the details." She waved at the room. "As a precaution, we may want the portal in a more secure location. At a minimum, I or another officer will need to be present for any operational tests."

"You," I blurted out and was happy to see that made her smile.

* * *

Rebuilding our relationship was slowed by our misaligned schedules more than any reluctance on Gina's part. After some lively debate, Ms. Murdock allowed me to operate out of my workshop, but insisted on installing a high-security lock. The system would stop all but the most determined thief, while giving Gina access to the room in case of emergency.

Gina took me down to the vault to retrieve the guidance component. The mirror and globe stood ready in their little nook, and the fact that they were on wheels would make it easy to roll them out and back in on the days I needed them.

Before we left, I did linger in front of the football device that had caused such problems. Gazing at the gold and silver hemispheres sitting placidly on their connecting rods, it was hard to shake the feeling that I'd let the long-dead tinker down. He'd been protecting the football for a reason.

On the bright side, Mike Gonzales made a full recovery and was back to work. He still couldn't shed any light on why the device had overloaded, but our equipment had recorded a ton of data that he intended to go through with a fine-toothed comb. On the rare occasions I found time to pop in on him after hours, he was always elbow deep in waveform mathematics that made my head hurt.

"Track me down when you're ready for the mirror," Gina said as she closed the massive vault door.

"Will do." I leaned over the rolling cart carrying the broken component, intent on a quick kiss. But she moved away and managed to turn the motion into an awkward half-hug.

Back at my shop, I gave the tracker a thorough inspection, letting my tinker magic slide over, around, and though the device. I was again struck by the age of the unit and the spells woven throughout. There weren't many moving parts aside from the four rings of inset gems that encircled the upper half and could be rotated to different settings. Deciphering those settings would take a deep dive into the dean's journal, which Bethany had reluctantly turned over.

Magic was the main mechanism, its flow and interconnections making up the machinery that was the guidance system. But many of those spells had been truncated so that they stopped just shy of a key nexus or interface. The problem cropped up in so many places that I started a log to keep track. Bethany's drawing skill would have come in handy since my sketches looked more like those of a crazed ten-year-old da Vinci. No one else would be able to decipher my chicken scratch schematics and cross sections, but I could—usually.

Days blurred together as I plodded between classes and my workshop. More often than not Mel was my sole companion, and I think even my upgraded robot was growing weary of the running dialogue. Roxy hadn't tried to intercept me for days, seeming content to ply her wiles on Owen when he emerged from the basement garages on a break from his own project.

"It's like someone deliberately cut all the critical connections in the stupid thing," I told Bethany when she found me sulking into a much needed cup of coffee in the commons.

My interim review with Mr. Girardi had left me feeling down. I'd always imagined my tinker skill as a panacea that could breathe life back into anything. It did work that way on simple problems. Intellectually, I'd known my final project would be more involved, but the massive task ahead had me reeling. Magic was supposed to be easy, wasn't it?

"Is the dean's book helping?" She took a seat and bit into the cheese Danish she'd paired with her own morning cup.

"A little, but it's like relying on the owner's manual to rebuild your car or doing brain surgery based on a textbook. There are just so many spells to rebuild. Think layered wards that have been added over the years, hundreds of tiny spells interconnecting to act as a whole. That's what I'm dealing with. The journal gives a feel for the general functions. That rocket component in the front office replaced the locator function, but the original tracker could follow people on the move and more. There's a whole journal section about tuning the portal system to different locations on Skellig Michael. I'm not sure what that's all about yet."

"Will hooking it up to the globe and mirror help?" she asked.

"I've got a lot more to do before I'm ready for that." I took a deep breath and tried to focus on the positive. "Even though I don't know what most of the spells do, intuition is built into the tinker magic. It's slow going, but the talent guides me. I've managed to get the first handful of severed spells reconnected. Funny, using my talent to fix broken spells is kind of like welding with magic instead of flux and rods."

"Keep plugging away. You'll get there." She jabbed a finger glistening with sugary glaze at me. "You *are* taking time off for the talent show, right? A night off might help you see things from a fresh perspective."

"You won't catch me on stage." Between her pointed question and frown, I conceded the need for a break. "But sure, I'll be there to watch others make fools of themselves. Have any interesting acts signed up?"

"I'm going to let the comment about fools slide—this time." She noticed the sticky residue and licked the finger she'd been waving at me. "Mon and I will be doing a special juggling routine. I expect you to heartily applaud when the time comes. There are also whispers about a wild animal exhibit by one of the vet techs. It sounds like she'll be pushing her talent to the max. And believe it or not, Chad's signed up with a musical act."

"Really?" I could just picture the cowboy lounging against a log by the fire with his trusty guitar, but Bethany shook her head at the idea.

"No guitar, and obviously nothing to do with his weather forecasting talent. Chad's being tight-lipped. Says we all just have to wait and see. He's been sneaking off to the lower levels to rehearse, but no one's caught him yet so we don't even know what instrument. Maybe he'll just be singing."

"A crooning cowboy. Damn, now I *have* to go to the show."

19. Portal Testing

M Y GOAL WAS to the conduct an initial test of the
entire portal system before the talent competition.
Between security briefings and welding classes, reattaching
the web of spells by then would be a challenge.

There was a state of flow involved in selecting an
enchantment's severed end, finding the matching strand, and
fusing the two into a whole with tinker magic. I fell into a
rhythm that melted away the hours as I picked my way
through the intricate web. Green spread across my map of
the guidance system's inner workings as I marked off
completed areas and gained a head of steam.

One saving grace was the fact that student security
missions had been suspended due to the intel we'd
recovered. But my team still got called in occasionally to
patrol the halls and fortify accesses I'd never even known
existed.

The Friday before the talent show, I ran out of things to
fix. I triple-checked my notes and spent a solid thirty minutes
immersed in the tracker as my tinker talent did its thing.
There were no loose ends, and the magic felt solid. An odd
gap still sat at the center of the spell-work, like the opening
in the middle of a web where a spider would wait. There

wasn't anything I could do about that. It was time to hook this baby up to the rest of the system.

I cornered Gina in one of the Practical Exploration classrooms, where she was spot-checking portals. "Can you get me into the vault?"

The set of metal doors in each room looked like they belonged on a ship. Most of us had met our first demon on the other side of the hatchways that ported student teams into tightly controlled situations—except the time our portal had sent us into demon-infested ruins. That event had been a wake-up call. Portals were vulnerabilities, thus the current schedule of inspections to ensure no one tampered with them.

"I'm a little busy at the moment." Gina ran her hands around the metal lip of the next doorway, checking for hidden devices. "This isn't another visit to your precious football is it?"

"Nooo." I stretched out the vowel for emphasis. Geez, ask to visit a cool gadget a couple of times and all of the sudden it's a crime. "I need to check out the silver mirror and globe."

That got her attention.

"Oh really?" She checked the clock, waved over a helper, and told him to continue the inspection. "It's already three o'clock. You remember the rules?"

"Roll 'em back into the vault every night, no exceptions." I nodded and crossed my heart. "A couple of hours will give me a chance to tune all three components and see if my repairs hold up. I've got a lot of checks to do before even activating the portal. How late can you stay?"

"Honestly, it's been a long week, and I'm working tomorrow. I'd really like to be out of here by seven."

"Great." I nodded, eager to get going. "Perfect Friday night."

It wasn't until we were rolling the mirror and globe up to my workroom door that I realized the room wasn't arranged to accommodate the entire system. In fact, I'd been in such a rush to go find Gina that I hadn't even picked up the wrappers and empty drink cans that had piled up during the long nights.

The access panel tingled with warmth under my hand as the magic lock recognized me. I shouldered the door open and made a production of lining the mirror up to fit through sideways—stalling and firing off a flurry of mental commands that had Mel zipping around inside to pick up trash. Some fit in the overflowing trash can, a few empty chip bags landed in Mel's auxiliary tool pouch, and the rest got stuffed into my late-night snack locker above the workbench.

"That's got it," I said when the coast looked clear.

"Steer much?" Gina huffed in exasperation when I finally moved out of the way and let her push the globe through. "Where do you want it?"

With a little rearranging we set the mirror to the left of the workbench and the globe on the back wall to the right. The three curled feet of the guidance cabinet fit cleanly into the clamps set in a triangle on the globe's cradle. That was the one physical connection between the devices and only necessary due to the tight confines.

"That's different." I flipped open the journal to double check a couple of items.

"Problem?" Gina pulled a stool over and sat by Mel while I worked.

"Whoever constructed the spectrum analyzer—that rocket-looking piece that replaced this guidance cabinet—

added subroutines to automate the system set up. Just leaves a little more for me to do."

Linking up the three components was much like setting up any wireless system, but instead of radio waves, a linking spell discovered and connected each piece. Without the spectrum analyzer to do the work, I had to tease out the right spells and manually initiate what, on a computer, would be scanning for other devices. Luckily the journal specified the physical settings made by positioning the gem rings around the top of the cabinet. Those decorations had been the things that originally led Roxy to dub the guidance cabinet as a hatbox.

Even being careful to triple check everything, the entire process only took half an hour. Clicking a blue sapphire down to accept the final link with the mirror rewarded us with a low hum that tingled along my magical senses. Gina felt it too, judging by the brilliant smile she shot me.

"All good?" she asked and hopped to her feet when I nodded. "Then I've got to get back to the shop for evening reports. I'll stop back at six-thirty."

"Perfect. That gives me time to take baseline readings."

In addition to documenting the natural ebb and flow of magic with the system at rest and quietly communicating among the components, I realigned a few strands that drifted out of tune. A more mundane task involved listing out what I'd need to safely test the portal. There'd been one too many instances lately of people ending up in the wrong place, so my trusty robot would go through first to scope things out.

"Mel, you're going to need a GPS upgrade."

No need to build anything fancy. The guts from my old cell phone would work just fine once he got beyond Attwater's cell signal jamming. The video feed had worked before through the portal, so I'd also need a laptop on this end. The main thing was to know where in the world the portal led before stepping through myself—or ourselves.

Bethany would want to come along. Repairing the guidance component of the system might be *my* talent project, but more than a good grade was at stake. The dean had led us to the journal, had wanted us to discover the secret to finding the long lost Chrono-monks. We were betting that the monks could bring Dean Gladstone and the others back.

I needed basic supplies too. The monks preferred desolate coastal sites like Skellig Michael off Ireland, places where the order could live a life of devout sacrifice without modern amenities. Such places weren't likely to have pleasant weather. Outerwear, flashlights, and more would be needed along with the journal and a decent map. The school had access to a worldwide geographic database. Once Mel came back with the coordinates, I could print whatever was needed. In the unlikely event that the monks had gone tropical, we'd just have to shed layers.

Ideally, the silver portal would drop us right on the monastery's doorstep, but my gut said that was unlikely. The guidance system's delicately balanced spellwork didn't feel as though it was attuned to a particular person or group of people. The newer tracking unit resonated with the magic in an item to find the mage that had made it. There was no such feel with the old guidance system. It either used a different mechanism to track down the monks in their nomadic phase, or I'd missed some key element—another good reason to quietly use Mel for a test.

Once I had a portal to the monks, we'd bring along all the data on Dean Gladstone's last location, and—if Gina agreed—Herman's conclusions about the dean's time-jump spell. All necessary, but way out of scope of my master repair project. Just getting the portal stable and operational would let me write up my findings and claim success.

Maybe going above and beyond simple repairs would give me more leverage with placement. I expected to get some job offers closer to graduation, but the welding jobs I'd been sent out on hadn't exactly wowed me. Chances were good that finding a decent fit would be a challenge.

20. Robot Recon

T HERE WASN'T MUCH more to do the next day without firing up the actual portal. Being a Saturday, the halls were quiet. Security remained on high alert, so there were extra black-clad people prowling past my shop every so often. First thing in the morning, a pair of new recruits had challenged us as we pushed the mirror and globe out of the vault. But the guards had gone pale and apologized profusely after recognizing Gina, despite her reassurance that they were doing a great job. After getting me set up, Gina used the morning to attack the mountain of paperwork that had accumulated during the week.

I got to hear all about the administrative nonsense during lunch in the commons. In return I assured her that my final adjustments had held and that the portal was ready for the operational test. She must have been as curious as I was to see where it led, because talking her into an afternoon rendezvous was a breeze. Of course that was needed anyway to stow the gear for the night, but I still took it as a win.

"See you at three, and you can show me what you've got." She leaned in and kissed my cheek before we went our separate ways.

That was the moment I knew that I had been fully forgiven. Gina didn't hold the stupidness with Roxy against me. We'd been building up to this point in fits and starts, hampered by the simple fact we saw each other infrequently. Our discussions had flowed more easily with each passing conversation, fewer awkward silences cropped up, and we'd even held hands a few times. And with one simple kiss, she'd brought "us" back. The glint in her eye told me she knew it too.

The next few hours would have dragged if not for my frantic rechecking of every detail. I'd pulled together Mel's GPS tracker overnight and tested it on his brother unit back at my place. One wildcard was that GPS satellites didn't cover one hundred percent of the globe, but the risk of hitting a dead zone was low.

I was busily trying to wear out my notes by reading them over yet again when the quiet hum-click of the lock told me the waiting was over.

"Knock, knock." With one hand on the access reader, Gina pushed the door open and slid into the room.

"We're all set." I waved Mel to my side and pointed out the gear. "Cameras, directional mic, GPS tracker, video feed to laptop."

"Okay, tiger." She laughed at my eagerness, which only increased my enthusiasm. "Fire it up easy. No explosions."

"Not a chance." I kept my voice light, but the casual reference to the football going critical landed like an icy blanket.

That was probably the point. This first test needed a rational, metered approach more than schoolboy enthusiasm. The latter could lead to mistakes. I carefully initiated the system and coaxed the magic to flow. Hard as I tried, I couldn't keep the grin off my face as ripples flowed across the mirror and the surface swirled into the characteristic green energy of an active portal.

"Checking power and flux." Mostly this entailed opening my sight to the magic coursing between the components, but the journal had also recommended ensuring a pair of gemstones on the guidance cabinet glowed blue and that they each sat at the top of their adjustment slot. "Check the video feed?"

Gina moved to the bench and gave me a thumbs up. "I see your butt. And if you ask, 'but what,' I'll smack it."

"Hmmm." Definitely back on full speaking terms. "I think we're clear for launch." I turned and crouched low to look my robot in his glowing red eyes—really just a reflection from the camera lenses embedded behind his polarizing face shield. "Take it slow and easy, Mel. This is just a quick recon. We need about three minutes to grab that satellite link and get coordinates. Come right back if anything is confusing."

The words were more for my own benefit, helping ease the nervous knot in my stomach. I felt like a dad that couldn't let their kids drive off without giving the OCD mantras to drive safe, keep each other awake, and the ever popular "call when you get there."

"You gonna let him go or not?" Gina raised an eyebrow.

I studied my feet and shuffled out of the way. Mel strode to the portal with confident steps. His metal frame clinked more than the old PVC design as servos drove arms and legs, and he disappeared through the swirling green surface.

I rushed to Gina's side, catching the barest flash of the mirror frame on the screen before the video feed changed to swirling static. Pouring green paint over a TV screen between stations and stirring would roughly approximate the video that came through, and that was normal. The Picasso image lasted only a second or two, then the screen went black.

"What the—" I fiddled with the gain and checked the link, which indicated we were still connected. "Where'd he go?"

"And what's that sound?"

Static came through in rolling bursts, ending with a roar. The sound repeated two, three times.

I instinctively reached out with the tinker magic that forged my bond with Mel, but of course that didn't work. Portal magic interfered with most spells. My creations could continue to do their job on the other side, but I couldn't communicate with them, except through technology. Radio waves didn't bounce off the portal surface the way magic did.

"Are you there, Mel?" I asked into the mic.

These were the times you took note of necessary design enhancements. In this instance, my robot needed a way to answer. We hadn't done much reconnaissance and telling Mel to turn toward the sound didn't work with blank video. I took a mental note to give him a basic vocabulary. I'd even take Morse code at this point.

"That static is oddly rhythmic." Gina tilted her head and turned up the volume as the sound ended with another thunderous crash. "Those are waves! He's at the beach."

Two things confirmed her conclusion almost immediately. A high-pitched call in staccato bursts faded off into the distance—a seagull. And the dim outline of a rocky shore slowly resolved in gray tones against the black screen. White lettering flashed in the lower right corner, "Low LUX Mode."

"Clever boy." Even more so because he was saving his batteries by not jumping straight to floodlights. "Mel, pan around in a slow circle, but watch your footing."

The image clarified as low-light compensation kicked in, giving the gloomy outlines that distinctive night-vision-green cast. Jagged rocks rose in front of Mel, sweeping into dark promontories rising from roiling water. Another crash of surf sprayed fine mist high as wave hit stone. The scene panned out over open water, a speck of land rising in the distance. More rocky shoreline could be anywhere from Maine to California, as could the massive rock wall that came next. But nowhere in the United States would be that dark at this time of day.

"Are those steps?" Gina squinted at the rock face.

There did seem to be a lighter ribbon cutting its way against the black. I had Mel move forward for a closer look. The rollercoaster of a camera ride over the next few seconds meant he'd climbed and scurried over rocks.

"It's definitely some kind of fissure." But the image was still too dark and grainy to tell for sure. "Mel, shift to floodlights."

The screen went black for a moment as he disengaged low-light mode, then dazzling light played across the rock wall. Vibrant green moss and mottled patches of lichen clung to the rock face to either side of a narrow fissure. Sure enough, a rough stairway curved up—and up. Mel's lights were bright, cutting a swath into the misty night, but the stairs went farther.

"Can he climb those?" Gina asked.

"I'd rather find another path."

Another sweep of the area revealed a rudimentary boat dock consisting of a big squared off rock that jutted out into a relatively calm pool. We wouldn't have even recognized it except for the iron rails driven into the stone and the connecting safety chains. That was about it. Without swimming to another landing spot, those steps were the only way to go. Mel wasn't designed for swimming. Hell, I was already worried about corrosion from salt spray. It was possible he was on the shore of a massive lake, but the angry water certainly had the look of an ocean.

"Stairs it is," I said as Mel returned to the foot of the path.

He climbed slowly, documenting as much as possible and shining his spotlight up the incline ahead in search of the top, or even a landing. The stone looked slick, and despite Mel's gyrostabilizers the image lurched a few times as he slipped. And still the steps went on.

Occasional breaks in the right-hand wall were edged with rails and chain similar to the dock, the metal old and pitted. Beyond the safety chains were vast drops that looked down onto rocks and more rocks and swallowed Mel's stark beam in roiling mist.

Mel had climbed the equivalent of five stories when the video bounced again. This time we got a close up of the chiseled stone, a fibrous patch of moss, and Mel's left foot before the image righted itself. And still there was no end in sight.

"Mel, hold up." I muted the mic and turned to Gina. "I don't want to push him any farther. With bad footing and the drain on his batteries it isn't worth the risk."

"Think he got a GPS lock?"

"He's been there plenty long," I said. "Making it to the top would have been better. It'll just come down to whether the cliffs block the signal." I keyed the mic again. "Mel, that's enough. Come on home."

Coming down took longer than climbing. The stairs were sized for humans, not pint-sized robots. But Mel worked out an effective sit-twist-step maneuver and made it down safely. Watching his rollercoaster video feed had Gina and me ready to hurl.

He came through the portal with a wash of briny air that left little doubt he'd been near the sea. I dropped the portal into standby, and the green surface faded back to being just a mirror.

"Let's see what we've got." I walked Mel over to my laptop, downloaded his GPS info, and typed the coordinates into a map application. "Fifty-one point seventy-seven degrees north by ten point fifty-four degrees west, and we search." A digital globe appeared on the screen, spinning on its axis before the image zoomed down to a jagged island outline in the northern hemisphere's Celtic Sea. Zooming out showed the speck of land sat off the southern tip of a much larger island, Ireland.

"I guess that shouldn't be a surprise." Gina shook her head. "I mean, we knew the monks were originally based there."

"Except Skellig Michael is a tourist trap now and deserted. It doesn't make sense."

"Everyone says the Chrono-monks vanished over a decade ago, but I'm certain that people were visiting the Skellig ruins before that." She tugged on a curl of hair while talking through her logic. "If that's the case, the monks must have some way of concealing themselves. They probably worked right alongside visitors that had to stick to the marked paths."

"Except Gladstone and the experts insist they're gone now." The dean's wistful look whenever I'd asked about the monks told me he believed they'd vanished for good.

"Apparently they've come back."

21. Talent Show

"**M**URDOCK GAVE PERMISSION for hops with the silver portal as long as I monitor from Attwater's end," Gina said on our way to meet the others.

"I'm ready anytime. There isn't much more I can do with the system." But that hadn't kept me from going over the guidance device with a fine tooth comb.

I still couldn't pinpoint where its spells linked to the monks, but by definition magic wasn't a precise science. Sometimes you just had to go with the flow. Getting official approval from security and the acting dean had eaten up half the week. Bethany and Owen insisted on going with me, and we'd agreed to a weekend excursion, which was the first opening where everyone's schedules aligned. That put the dreaded talent show between me and finding the monks.

"Over here, but no peeking." Bethany waved us away from our normal table in the commons.

She and Mon had set out a makeup stand in the far corner. They'd dressed to complement in yin-yang style, a white square-neck dress against Bethany's dark skin and Mon's black clothing contrasting with her alabaster completion. Both outfits were damned sexy. They wore matching eye and lip liner too.

"Nice work." I nodded to Mon as she applied blush to a middle-aged woman in a sparkly green suit.

"She's doing up anyone who needs help before the show." Bethany beamed at Mon before giving us her full attention. "It's been like party central today. The show's going to be a blast. Performers have to queue up backstage, so we won't be able to join you. And Owen's moping around here somewhere. Something's gotten under his skin, but he insists he's ready for tomorrow's outing."

"That mound of gear in my workroom would agree," I said. "You'd think we were planning a month-long expedition."

A quick internet search confirmed that the island was less than a mile long, but the terrain was beyond hilly, treacherous, and dotted with ruins of the old monastery. We'd gathered an impressive array of equipment to handle steep slopes, rain, and whatever else might hit us.

All indications were that the portal had been aligned properly. If you believed the dean's book, we'd find the Chrono-monks on the other end. The journal spelled out the purpose of each stone building on the island and even discussed their contents. The matter-of-fact tone of the little text rekindled the thought of magic allowing the monks to coexist alongside a steady stream of summer tourists. All very unlikely, which made my head hurt.

Early November was safe from commercial visitors and virtually guaranteed miserable weather. The temperature rarely dropped to freezing, but windy, wet, and cold wouldn't be much better.

* * *

"Are these seats taken?" Gina laughed and dropped into the spot next to a grouchy looking Owen.

I scooted in next to her as the auditorium filled. The room buzzed with excitement, and I waved to several familiar faces. Mike Gonzales was on the job at the far back near a big panel that controlled stage lighting.

"Cheer up," I told Owen. "We've got to represent for this thing."

Our group was down by half, so we'd have to be extra loud to make up the difference and cheer them on. It was a little lonely sitting there as a trio, but Lars showed up and took the seat behind Gina, fleshing out the group. There was no sign of Roxy, which was a relief. Maybe that was what had Owen bent out of shape. Those two had gotten tight, even as the woman distanced herself from the core group and me in particular.

"What's the scoop on tomorrow?" Owen didn't exactly smile, but at least he was talking.

"Early start. Island time is five hours ahead of us. With those insane stairs, we'll want to be back before nightfall."

The lights dimmed, and the roar of the crowd settled into background murmurs as Ms. Eisner and her staff took the stage. Announcements were blessedly short, consisting of reminders to resist heckling, be polite, and pick up your trash.

The gymnast who'd performed at the general assembly was the first act out to warm up the crowd. He danced to classical music—not my usual taste, but the piece fit his extraordinary movements perfectly.

The acts were broken into categories like athletic, musical, and a variety of other classifications. An asterisk alongside listings in the program denoted the entrants using magic.

The cake lady came on right before Mon and Bethany, but instead of being limited to confections, her act filled the room with everything from flying hotdogs to popcorn clusters. Every snack got scooped from the air and a chorus of crunching accompanied our friends as they danced onto the stage. The two women flowed and twirled from one step to the next and finished at center stage in a curvy hug that melded them into the yin-yang symbol their outfits represented.

Magic flared as they separated, and Bethany tossed a bright blue ball to Mon. She followed with a yellow one and then a green. Mon juggled the balls in an ever expanding circle as Bethany fired them out of thin air. I counted a dozen by the time Bethany produced a black one the size of a bowling ball. Its surface was far from smooth, almost jagged.

I glanced down at the program. The act was annotated as magic. The dark ball launched, arms, legs, and a tail unfurling as it flew towards Mon. The room let out a collective gasp.

"That's Mortimer," Gina whispered.

The little gargoyle made a valiant attempt to bite Mon's hand off, but she deftly plucked a green ball from her circle, shoved it in his gapping maw, and swept the little guy into her routine. The crowd roared as the startled creature spit out the ball and clawed the air cartoon-style. The flying balls became a treadmill as he hopped from one to then next to avoid getting tossed back into the circle by the blurred mechanism that was Mon's hands.

Mort made headway around the circle, but a deft air spell reversed the balls and forced him to scrabble for his life. Bethany faced Mon, and balls flew between the two women. The pattern shifted. One stream of balls arced high and another crossed it midway down.

Mortimer spent half his time running in place as he skipped across the projectiles trying to get at either of the women. Then the pattern would shift and he'd be fighting to avoid being sucked into the juggling.

"Clever. They're making letters," Owen said.

I saw it now. That double-bounce formed a W followed by an A. Others noticed and started to voice what they saw out loud. Bethany shot the room a dazzling smile and nodded encouragement as she and Mon circled each other, giving the shifting letters three dimensions.

"A…T…T," the crowd chanted. "W…A…T…E…R"

That R must have taken some pretty complex air flows to pull off, especially with Mortimer running inside the upper loop like a hamster.

"Attwater!" we all cried.

The balls exploded into miniature fireworks that shot out smoky streamers. Mortimer tumbled into a forward roll and came up like a gymnast sticking the landing. He bowed to audience with the women bracketing him.

"I bet the balls were more of Bethany's drawings," I said as we stood and clapped until our hands stung.

After a few more acts, the lights grew dim, and a blue spot fell on Chad, who sat on a stool up against the stone wall off to our left. A U-shaped table laden with thirteen water goblets surrounded him. The glass to his far left was nearly empty, and each successive glass held more water so that the one on his far right was just shy of full.

Chad reached out and ran the tips of two fingers around the rim of the middle glass that was half full of water. A clear tone resonated through the room, louder that I would have thought possible. He worked his way down the line making three or four circles around each rim until it issued a pure note and occasionally dumping a splash of liquid into a jug by his feet.

"I've seen this before," Bethany said. "The different water levels give each goblet a distinct sound."

Everyone pivoted in their seats for a better view when they realized he wouldn't be taking the stage.

"It's the water boy," someone called out from the back of the room, followed by, "let's hear 'Free Bird!'"

So much for not heckling.

Chad took it in stride, nodded out across the audience, and began to play. Those beefy arms and ham hands danced across the goblets, flowing with gentle grace and dispensing delicate caresses to the glasses. What issued forth from his makeshift instrument was no ancient rock ballad. In fact it barely had an identifiable beat. Notes drifted over top one another, sometimes left to linger hauntingly, other times stopped short with a gentle palm.

"Whoa!" Lars, king of hip-hop and rap, looked like he might start drooling.

I couldn't blame the guy. Chad's music mesmerized us all, filling the massive space with impossible resonance. Each note echoed back louder than it went out. Those echoes grew deeper, more pronounced, an ultra-bass woofer several octaves lower than the crystal-pure goblet notes.

A subtle shift had the echoes coming faster until they played in syncopated harmony. Those deep notes took lead, with Chad following. The refrain shifted to a stately song of welcome as walls, floor, and ceiling reverberated, an ancient presence accepting the audience into its embrace. Attwater spoke to us through the music.

Pride shone in the cowboy's eyes as he played. The rhythm built, taking on a note of urgency, of warning.

Jim Stein

Attwater was glad to have us, but called for caution and vigilance. Finally, the beat slowed to a soothing throb, somehow projecting a promise that all would be well, that we would get through the trying times ahead, that we were family. The final note hung in the air and in my chest like a mother's hug until all grew silent.

No applause. No whispers. Stillness settled over the room as the ancient presence faded.

After a time, I wiped my eyes. I wasn't the only one. Chad looked dazed and uncertain. I clapped quietly, not wanting to disturb the reverent atmosphere. Others joined in, the subdued applause thanking the spirit of our school as much as Chad.

Had we just experienced how Chad felt every day when running his hands over the building's stonework? The thought brought a wave of admiration for our friend's natural ability.

The two acts that followed relied on physical comedy and glitzy magic, bringing energy and enthusiasm back to the crowd. As unbelievably awesome as Chad's performance was, I breathed easier as the somber mood lifted.

Then came Roxy. The reason she hadn't been down in the audience became obvious as she slunk onto stage accompanied by sultry jazz. Her jaw-dropping iridescent outfit consisted of a skin-tight red dress that disappeared into lacey silk trailing behind in a split-tail. She moved to the music, slow and sensuous.

"Oh, please," Gina said under her breath. "Why is this acceptable?"

The spotlight followed Roxy as she stepped down off the stage and worked her way around the room. She sang in a smoky, sultry voice, urging her listeners to "do right" by her.

Or maybe she just lip-synched to the soundtrack—hard to tell. She'd done something to her hair too. It draped in front of her left shoulder, hanging low and still blond but also shimmering red occasionally to match the dress.

My talent instructor, Mr. Girardi, sat in a folding chair by the fire exit. Roxy sashayed past, trailing a hand down his arm. A tiny flash lit the space between their fingers as they separated. I only saw it because he sat near us. Maybe my eyes were playing tricks. My instructor certainly didn't seem to mind as he swayed to the music, eyes half closed.

I checked the program, but the act was billed as a non-magical recreation of Jessica Rabbit singing "Why Don't You Do Right" from the cult movie *Who Framed Roger Rabbit*.

"Slut." Gina didn't bother pulling any punches, but there was an odd vibe as the woman sang, more compelling than blatantly sexual.

"At least she's an equal opportunity slut." Lars stuck his head between us, nearly giving me a heart attack.

His meaning was clear though. Roxy worked her way through the song and audience, reaching out occasionally to slide a hand over a shoulder here, down an arm there. The crowd hooted in appreciation when she included Ms. Eisner at one point and later Gina's boss, Ms. Murdock. Both women played along and grooved to the clarinet and tickling piano coming over the sound system.

As the song wound down, she sauntered toward our row and reached out a hand. Gina growled. Roxy changed course, bestowing her final flourish and a pouty air-kiss on Owen. He certainly didn't mind.

I ran the last few seconds back in my mind and concluded I was safe. Sure, I'd watched the show, but I hadn't been leering or done anything else to encourage Roxy. For once, I was free and clear. So I joined in the applause.

"You are in such hot water, mister." Gina elbowed me as she clapped, a metered cadence full of sarcasm.

22. To Skellig

T HE STEPS WENT on, and my legs burned. There hadn't been fog down at the landing, but mist now clung to the stone, making the hike cold, miserable, and slippery.

"Are we almost to the top?" Owen asked from a few steps back.

Through Mel's camera, I'd imagined the stairway was neatly carved into solid rock. In reality the steps mostly consisted of stacked stones. Some were level single slabs, but many had irregularities to catch a toe or put the unaware off balance. On top of that, once away from the boat landing there were no safety rails, just the occasional chain hammered into the wall to our left. When one of these glinted ahead you could be sure there was a huge drop off the open side of the stairs.

Then there were the switchbacks. The trail zig-zagged up the cliff face, regularly taking sharp turns. There might be a little white sign with its red arrow pointing the way, but no appreciable landings. It would be easy to take one step too many and plunge off the edge. To stay safe we had to take it slow, painfully slow.

"I think we're about halfway." I looked to Bethany, who was a few steps further along.

Luckily, I'd come across a safety video online while trying to find a more contemporary map of the island. The journal had a lot of details, and I wanted to see how they jived with the tourist info. I'd made everyone watch the short film because none of us had been to a desolate rock off the Irish coast. The simple documentary was an eye-opener. We'd hastily adjusted our supplies, trading sneakers for sturdy hiking shoes, paring down the equipment, and adding a small backpack for each of us to keep our hands free.

Bethany had gone one better and brought Mortimer along to scout ahead. The little gargoyle scurried over the rocks like he'd been born here. I'd lost count at two hundred steps, so the half-way estimate was only a guess.

We hadn't seen anyone, and the only sounds—aside from the thundering of my heart as it tried to rip through my ribs—came from pounding surf and screaming seabirds.

"Mort says there's a little valley at the top," Bethany called over her shoulder. "Not far."

"That little dude is severely distance-challenged," Owen grumbled. I wholeheartedly agreed, but saved my breath for the climb.

Even though it was socked in with fog, reaching that little haven felt wonderful. I could have slept for an hour on the cushy boulders after stripping off my pack.

"This is Christ's Saddle," Bethany read from her copy of the commercial map we each carried. "We came up on the west side instead of the normal tourist route. The main monastery should be off to the left. Visitors only get to view a couple other observation points and old sites, but the dean's journal reads as if both the lower and upper slopes are chock full of buildings, fields, and more."

"Upper!" Owen choked and sprayed out a mouthful of water. "No more climbing. We need to stay down here and focus on the monastery. That's got to be where the monks are."

"We aren't even up *to* the monastery level yet," I said. "Didn't you read the map?"

Instead of answering, Owen hunkered down and tore into his snacks, which wasn't a bad idea. We'd just climbed a forty-story building and had farther to go. I dug around in my pack for a chocolate-covered granola bar and leaned back on the cold, damp stone.

"Quite the show last night." Bethany decided I'd had enough rest.

"Can you believe the cowboy actually got the building to communicate?"

Chad had been absolutely euphoric after the show, going on and on about how he hadn't expected Attwater to take the lead on his act. The sentient school had apparently been harboring a desire to speak to the students that roamed its halls for centuries. Chad unwittingly gave her the mechanism to communicate.

"I'm happy for him." Bethany grew serious. "There was definitely a warning there."

"Not surprising given all the crap going on recently."

She shrugged, her tone carefully neutral. "Then there was Roxy's shtick. What was up with that?"

Oh, so that's how it is.

I'd gotten an earful last night from Gina about that damned number. I don't think she truly expected me to do anything, but by association I became the subject of her ire.

I'd listened and agreed. What else could I do, revoke my sponsorship of the woman into Attwater? That wouldn't make any difference. Despite never getting labeled with a particular talent, she was already under contract with the school.

"Don't bother pumping me for more info." I shrugged. "I'm clueless too. You can report that back to Gina."

My ill-worded response made her smile, but I got my point across.

"Okay." She held up both hands in surrender. "But something's off about that woman. I couldn't pick out any elemental magic during her song, but I'd bet my best sketchpad that she enhanced her performance with some kind of spell."

"Maybe her elusive talent was coming though," I offered. "A natural charisma of some sort."

We'd seen odder things. The more I thought about it, the more sense it made. The idea would also explain why common sense tended to fail around Roxy. Some magical pheromone she couldn't even control made people like her.

Break time ended and we climbed on. Given how tiny the island was, you'd think we'd be able to see if anyone was in the monastery area. But between the sheltering cliffs and misty afternoon, only stacked stone was visible as we approached. *Oh wait, there—nope, just more rocks.*

We stopped just shy of a low rectangular doorway that led to the main area and sent Mortimer ahead. The gargoyle returned in less than a minute, made straight for Bethany, and damned near climbed up under her shirt. It took her longer than he'd been gone to get the drawing settled down, but still he wouldn't leave her side. She ended up hoisting him onto her left shoulder and feeding him bits of charcoal, which darkened his outline and made him look more substantial through the mist.

"What's the verdict?" I finally asked.

"Something has Mort really agitated." She handed Mortimer her last pencil nub and dusted off her hands. "He won't say what, just that there's magic ahead."

"Wonderful." Owen squinted through the doorway and readied a fire spell.

I did the same with my whirlwind spell. When you were up against the unknown it was good to have diverse defenses. Bethany must have been thinking along the same lines because she drew on the earth element, although I didn't recognize the exact spell.

"This could be a good thing," she said. "The order would need magic to obscure them from prying eyes. So don't get trigger happy unless there's a clear threat."

"Let's go find some monks." I ducked through the opening onto a grassy path.

The monastery was a simple collection of stone huts, beehive structures made a thousand years ago of stacked rock. Dark rectangular doorways faced the central trail. I pulled my flashlight off its loop and peered inside the first structure, finding only an empty square room. We worked our way through the dwellings. The smallest were ten feet across, others about twice that size. All were deserted except for an occasional dedication plaque.

Mortimer stopped clinging to Bethany and took to exploring with a vengeance. He ended up singling out a bare patch of ground where one of the beehive structures had failed to weather the years. Nothing was left of it except a couple of foundation stones, which the little gargoyle kept sniffing around.

"He's mad because whatever spooked him has left," Bethany said when I asked what her creation was doing.

"This is a bust," Owen dropped the spell he held at the ready. "We snuck halfway around the globe to get a free tour of a deserted rock."

"There's more to check out, right?" I threw the question to Bethany, who already had the dean's journal open.

"Plenty more. A couple of overlooks to the south with dedication mounds and an oratory near the northernmost point. More steps, but not far."

Paths led where we needed to go, and it was unlikely we missed much considering the cliff edge a stone's throw to our left. A break in the fog gave me a dramatic view of the coastline far below where another seaside road looped around the island. A couple more modern huts studded the deserted area down there and would house seasonal workers.

Negotiating the trail was no picnic. Skellig Michael was literally a giant craggy rock sticking out of the sea. The occasional face with sufficient topsoil to support wispy grasses and tangled weeds would have accommodated the order's gardens. But even those small fields slanted off at a twenty-degree angle toward sheer drops.

"What a way to live," Owen said as we left the third and last area on the southern island.

"It's all uphill from here." I didn't like the sound of that any more than he did.

So far we'd struck out big time, finding nothing of interest. Mortimer had regained his composure and resumed his scouting to no avail. If the guidance cabinet had steered us correctly, our last chance of finding the monks would be on the highest promontory at the northern overlook.

"Tours aren't allowed up here." Bethany hopped over the chain blocking the narrow stairs. "The climb won't be as long as coming up from the water."

Cold seeped into my bones as we climbed in shadow between steep walls. There wasn't a deadly drop to deal with, but pushing on through the mist with stiffening joints became a chore. A trip down after sunset was definitely off the table. In fact, I was considering calling it a day when the fog broke and we emerged onto a grassy field under dazzling sunlight.

Upslope from the head of the staircase, perched on the bitter edge of the rock that was Skellig Michael, sat a stone dais with a slab roof supported by four stone pillars. The open-air structure was made of carved blocks instead of the stacked stone used everywhere else.

"Still no one." I tramped along a hard rock path the grass couldn't reclaim and climbed three steps into the structure. "I'm guessing an oratory is for praying?"

A massive stone wheel took up a good portion of the floor. The raised altar was darker than the surrounding rock and had a shallow bowl hewn into the center. Chiseled lines radiated out from the depression like the ordinal points of a compass. Arrow-straight seams in the floor extended the pattern in all four directions.

"It's like looking over the edge of the world." Awe crept into Bethany's voice as she pivoted from east to west.

Three sides of the oratory opened onto empty space, overlooking the vastness of the sea below. The main coast of Ireland lay on the horizon off to our far right. The mist we'd been fighting all day clung mainly to the island itself, leaving a clear view of the angry waters just offshore. Halfway to the horizon a gray curtain extended from a flat expanse of dark clouds to the waterline.

"That's pretty heavy rain off to the northwest." I sighted between the compass lines. "Something to keep an eye on. No way do I want to be on those stairs in a storm."

"Check out Mortimer." Owen pointed to where the gargoyle perched on an outcropping at the edge of the field.

The little guy shifted from one foot to the other as if trying to work up his nerve, then scampered over the rocks and disappeared.

"What's he got?" I followed Bethany over with Owen close on my heels.

The rocky ridge was too high to climb, but stopped short of the cliff. As we scrambled uphill around the jutting formation, an arc of stacked stone came into view. The lone hut was set back from the cliff and built right into the jagged natural rock so that only the entrance and half of its dome was exposed. Mortimer crouched in front of the doorway, tossing stones into the darkness.

My tinker magic flared. "There's magic here."

Bethany and Owen went still. They were stretching their magical senses, trying to catch what I felt.

"Not getting anything." Owen shrugged.

"My talent certainly is." Moving closer felt like walking toward a speaker stack blasting at full volume, except there was no sound, only a throbbing pressure against the tingling core of my magic.

"That means it's not an elemental spell." Bethany knelt by her drawing and scratched behind his ears. "Mort feels it too, same as before. He still doesn't know what to make of it, but it's got him more curious than scared."

"Not much time." I looked back to gauge how much daylight we had left and noticed the squall was closer and wider than before. "Go big or go home, right?"

I gritted my teeth, pushed through the invisible force, and entered the hut. Once inside, the pressure of the ancient magic eased, and I could breathe again. There was no way they couldn't feel that. But Owen sauntered through the door, flashlight whipping around the chamber as he let out a low whistle. No, he definitely hadn't felt the power.

Just like the other huts we'd investigated, the square interior was at odds with the domed construction—durable design. Unlike those other huts, there was a writing desk piled with books, shelves, and a rear door made of heavy planks set in a metal frame. It opened without a sound, and a red-robed man bustled into the room.

He sat at the desk, lifted a quill pen from the ink pot, and began to write in the margins of a book that lay open, so intent on his work that he didn't even notice us. His hood covered half his weathered face. The flickering candle revealed heavy brows above a flat nose that looked to have been broken a few times. Stringy brown hair dangled down either side of haggard-looking eyes.

"Uh…excuse me." I cleared my throat, but he just kept writing. "Sir?"

I looked to my friends. Owen shrugged and shook his head. Bethany urged me forward with a wave. This was definitely what we'd come for. I hadn't missed the brass hourglass dangling from the man's belt.

I stepped farther into the small room. The monk's head jerked up and his eyes went wide, but the angle of his gaze was off—as if he looked past me. I turned to see if Owen or

Bethany had caught his attention, but neither was quite in the man's line of sight.

"We're looking for—" I bit off my words when he shook an angry fist and spoke.

His mouth formed words, but no sound. He grew visibly angry, eyes tracking something off to my left. The monk surged to his feet, yelling at the empty spot and jabbing a gnarled finger at the entrance. His wooden chair toppled over backwards onto the stone floor.

The scene played out in absolute silence. The falling chair hadn't even made a sound. It was as if a dampening spell separated us from the man, but that didn't explain why he argued with thin air.

I inched forward, intending to tap the guy on the shoulder. Before I reached him, the monk spun around, robes flaring and arms flailing. He rushed to the wooden door that now stood open behind his desk and hurried through, hourglass swinging wildly on the end of his rope belt. He slammed the door shut behind him—all without a sound.

"No!" Owen surged forward, darted around the desk, and yanked the door open.

The doorway opened onto a stacked stone wall. Owen floundered to check his momentum. He threw both hands up, managed to stop short of the wall, and stepped back to lean on the desk.

"What the hell was—" Owen fell to the floor, his butt sinking right through the weathered desktop like it wasn't there.

The wood surface turned pale and translucent. All the furniture from the overturned chair to the squat bookshelves with their thin leather volumes and scrolls grew insubstantial, their outlines fading. A moment later we stood in an empty room. Well, Bethany, Mortimer, and I stood. Owen was still sprawled on the floor looking stunned.

"Door's still here." Bethany was first to recover, and strode over to examine the rear exit and the solid wall it opened on. "But the knob's gone."

"What the hell was that?" Owen scrambled to his feet and retrieved his light. "Ghosts?"

"No idea if the island is supposed to be haunted," Bethany said. "I don't even know if ghosts exist. None of our classes talk about them."

"Magic is definitely involved." I thought back to that pulsing sensation. "It resonates with my tinker ability. Which you'd think would mean that something's broken."

"Except there's literally nothing here," Owen said. "Unless the whole thousand-year-old monastery needs a touch up."

A few minutes of searching didn't offer any further clues, and that storm front had drawn uncomfortably close. Bethany sent Mortimer on another round of the upper plateau. He shot off so fast that I was certain he'd found something useful, especially when we caught up and found him hopping out onto the rocks beyond the oratory.

My knees felt like water as I edged way too close to that thousand-foot drop. Visions of a secret cave on the cliff face kept me going. Mortimer sat with his legs dangling over the void. He gripped a hardy purple wildflower in one clawed hand and sent its fluffy seeds off into the rising wind with the other.

When I yelled at him to get back to searching, he looked over, seemed to calculate the probability of my clumsy human feet carrying me the last ten feet, and returned to his careful dissection of the plant. Sometimes the gargoyle acted very cat-like.

We spent the last few minutes taking a boatload of pics and videos. I doubted there was much I could do from Attwater to solve the mystery of our ghost-monk, but documenting everything possible could only help. The setting sun and rising wind soon had me calling the others in for the hike down.

"Any chance of getting your portal to land up here next time to avoid the death-march up those stairs?" Owen asked when I promised we'd be back.

"Not sure." I pulled out my GPS and set a waypoint. "Remind me to grab position and elevation info at a few spots on the way down, and I'll try to figure something out."

Mr. Gonzales had cracked the code on the spider devices that redirected portals. They were demonic bad juju, but maybe the principles involved could help me dial in a better landing spot for our next trip.

23. Recalibrating

"WE FOUND A GHOST!" Owen crowed as he emerged from the mirror.

"Sure, and Dracula stopped by while you guys were out playing tourist." Gina rolled her eyes and gave me a sharp look. "By the way, thanks so much for the booby trap. Very funny."

I had no idea what she was talking about, and still didn't get it when she thrust the trashcan into my hands. Even though I'd emptied it yesterday, the can was full to the brim with empty wrappers and crushed cans.

"Hey, I said no parties while we were out." I frowned at her scowl, then noticed her shirt held several chocolate smudges and drying dribbles of liquid down the front. The locker over her seat at the workbench was open and crumbs were strewn across the bench. An image of Mel frantically hiding trash the other day flashed through my head followed by me stupidly telling Gina to help herself to my stash if she got hungry. "Oh crap. That wasn't on purpose."

"Not important." She cut off my floundering explanation. "Tell me about the ghost."

We described our island hike, how Mortimer had discovered the hidden stone hut, and the surreal encounter with the red-robed monk.

"I'm going to try to get the portal to put us in a better spot next time." I jerked a thumb at the mirror. "We didn't get to most of the lower island either. Do you think Ms. Murdock would let our student security team check it out for a few hours? They'd be able to cover a lot of ground fast."

"We've still got a bunch of folks out sick, but you can always ask." Gina shrugged. "So far we've been able to cover watch rotations without pulling people out of class. I agree with checking every angle. To be honest though, your mystery monk should be where you put the most effort, especially since he had your talent flaring."

"At least that ties back to my project a little." I eyed the globe and the guidance element I was supposed to be fixing. "It's ninety-percent operational, but something's not quite right. The journal says it should lead to the monks themselves, not just their island—any portal could be set up to do that."

"Maybe they're all dead." Owen threw up his hands at our aghast expressions and seemed oddly angry at his own line of reasoning. "What? Makes perfect sense. That's why the box steered us to a monkly spirit."

"I seriously doubt you're dealing with a ghost," Gina said. "If anything, what you describe was more likely an echo from the past. Remember, we're dealing with *Chrono*-monks who manipulate *time*. Go have your geek-fest with Mr. Gonzales. I need to talk with Ms. Murdock anyway and can see about getting her approval. But first, let's get your gear back to the vault. I was only half kidding about the Dracula visit. The door handle jiggled a couple of times while you were gone, but I couldn't catch whoever was testing the lock."

I found Mike Gonzales working overtime on a Saturday night rebuilding a steam regulator—no surprise.

"Do you ever go home?" I asked as he waved me through the door to his shop.

"It's more fun here." He set the valve body down and kicked off the workbench. His rolling chair glided across the room and stopped just short of the bank of monitors we'd used to test the football. "Damn, almost made it that time." He pulled himself the rest of the way with his feet and flipped open a laptop under the meters. "I've been going through the readings I recorded while passed out. Take a look."

Not what I'd come for, but it was hard to resist the allure of good data and the man's enthusiasm as he pulled up graphs and charts.

"Just a quick look," I said, to offset the guilty pleasure. "Then I need to ask you for tips on recalibrating my portal."

"Of course, school comes first." He meant a distant second and hours later, in this case. "Overloading our football unit was the best thing that could have happened as far as characterizing its performance." He pointed to a pair of colorful graphs containing thousands of data points. Statistical curves went asymptotic as they shot off the top of the graph near the right edge.

"Discounting the fact it almost blew up your shop." I felt compelled to remind him that he'd nearly died, but the fact didn't seem to faze him one bit.

"Water under the bridge." He waved away my statement. "We've got hard evidence now. The football is most definitely a storage device, a rechargeable magic battery. Our early work at low power showed that the polarity could be reversed, but even as it went critical, the opposing pole absorbed a massive amount of energy." He flipped through his findings at a dizzying rate, finally settling on a simplified set of two-dimensional graphs that were easier to grasp.

"Interesting comparison." I studied the screen. "There's an order of magnitude difference, but otherwise those match." The scales were the giveaway on the power differences.

"Yes!" He stepped through the graphs, starting at the top. "This is from your basic lithium battery. The next one down benchmarks the typical method used to tie off a ley line to power irrigation pumps or plumbing in remote villages we support. Then there's a standard magical ward. Notice the power in and out show very little transference loss, as do the final curves from data reduction of the football's operation."

"Nice work." It was the kind of evaluation that I'd hoped to present as part of my thesis.

That ship had sailed, but I took a mental note to compare my repaired guidance device with the newer spectrum tracker.

"I'm still digging for information on an artifact this powerful. This thing could power a small city, if cities ran on a complex mixture of elemental magic." He tugged on his moustache. "And before you even ask, no, it's not a weapon. It just acted like a bomb because the magical stops were fully open and the football couldn't reabsorb its own output fast enough. You'd need a very special spell or device to consume that much energy."

We talked a little about unintended consequences and how inventions with the best of intentions could often be repurposed for warfare. No matter how you sliced it, the football had the potential to blow things up. The best course of action was to leave it safely locked in the vault.

"I need your take on the spider devices. Is there a way to build their relative offset function into a standard portal? Let me draw out what I'm thinking."

I laid out what I knew of the silver mirror, its portal system, and my need to control the landing point on Skellig Michael. We built reference vectors from the coordinates and elevation data in my GPS app. Mike drew out the basic principle behind how the spider devices hijacked portals. By the end of a two-hour discussion, we had a working theory on how to tweak the guidance system to avoid those ridiculous stairs.

I spent the better part of Sunday noodling through how best to adjust the guidance system. One perk of being a team lead was that I could come and go through my local portal despite the current restrictions. The personnel checking access credentials were running on fumes and had the vacant expression of people just this side of total exhaustion.

I also put my own team on standby for a visit to the Celtic Sea—only to discover we were back down to six active members. Now that I thought about it, the halls had grown sparse between classes lately. I vaguely recalled a couple of announcements urging students to swing by the infirmary for flu shots. The epidemic must have spread wider than I'd realized.

I caught Gina early Monday morning, checked my equipment out of the vault, and tested the new modifications. A few trials with my robotic guinea pig confirmed they worked. The far end of the portal could be set to the boat dock, mid-island at Christ's Saddle, or up by the oratory. To find a flat spot on that uppermost level, I had to back the gate off to the top of the stairs.

Repositioning the portal's exit just took a mental nudge to engage the proper position translation before activating the mirror. Similar to the demon-made spider devices, my spells added horizontal and elevation vectors to the coordinates and relied on the portal's built-in safety mechanisms to open the gate at ground-level. Planting my magic subroutines in the ancient artifact felt intrusive, but the nodes and switching mechanism could be easily removed.

Returning to the island was a fun afternoon excursion, but my pared-down team turned up little more than puffins and terns. They discovered the path around the lower island connected the caretakers' quarters and lighthouse, but found no clues to the missing monastic order.

A passing fishing boat noticed our team and kept station close offshore. We couldn't hear what they were yelling, and the rough seas prevented the craft from docking. The captain would no doubt report us to the authorities. The incident was a good reminder that we were trespassing and needed to conclude our business quickly.

After the team turned in their findings, I hopped the portal up to the oratory level. Gina was dying to inspect the hidden beehive hut, and Bethany enthusiastically volunteered to stay behind.

"I'll watch the shop." Bethany sent me through the portal with an unexpected wink. "Go show her the sunset."

24. Ghostly Allure

GINA SUCKED IN a deep breath as we stepped through the portal onto the coarse grass of Skellig Michael's highest plateau. A light breeze ruffled my jacket. The temperature was still in the fifties and pleasantly cool. That would change rapidly once the sun set.

"Smell that salt air." Gina exhaled, pulled in another lungful, and looked to the open-air structure on the point up ahead. "That's the oratory?"

"Yep. Killer views from up there. The hut Mortimer found is out around those rocks." I pointed off to our left.

"Business first, I guess." She bumped my shoulder in that old familiar way and nodded at the ridge. "Lead on."

Gina followed me up the slope, scrambling on hands and feet across the steepest section and around the rocky outcropping. Our last visit had been so surreal that I half expected the beehive structure to be gone.

I needn't have worried. The opening to the hut beckoned just like before. The sensation that had overwhelmed my senses on the last visit was gone, but as I followed her inside, an uncomfortable tingle rose beneath my ribcage.

"The residue of what we experienced yesterday is still setting off my tinker magic, but it's nowhere near as intense."

"The only thing different about this building is the back door?" Gina crossed the room and ran her hand over the weathered planks.

"Just that and the fact it's hidden up here and half buried. When the monk appeared, there was an old wooden desk and chair here." I panned my light across the floor to outline where the furniture had been. "Low bookcases took up this space and ran along the far wall there."

"Wild. And you still feel it." She turned in a full circle with eyes half-closed, trying to sense the lingering magic. "Nothing at all for me. I wonder why your particular talent reacts with this place."

"That prickling sensation usually kicks in when I examine something that's broken, but I've never felt anything like the flare of power that hit me last time. It was strongest at the entrance, but didn't fully dissipate until the monk vanished."

"Let me try something." She sat her flashlight down and called up elemental power. "Tell me if you get a reaction."

Gina sent out a mild waft of air, followed by a spray of water. I sensed each element as she wandered around the room working through all five. After her spirit spell faded, she turned with a raised eyebrow.

"Nothing new, just the tingling. I sensed your magic, but only in the normal way."

"It was worth a shot." She shrugged and grabbed her light. "I wanted to see if maybe the room itself was amplifying magic and making you oversensitive."

"Like hitting the right frequency that resonates with my talent." Except for lots of experimenting, I wasn't sure how to go about ruling that out. But another idea occurred to me.

"This might be a long shot, but there's a chance Lori could pinpoint what's getting under my skin. I could bring her in to try."

"So, you bring all the girls up here."

"What? No!" I sputtered. "Just you…and Bethany. But Lori's talent could—"

"You are simply too easy." Her tinkling laugh set me back as she linked her arm through mine. "Let's go check out that altar and beautiful sunset."

Walking together had my blood pumping, but we eventually separated to skirt around the rocks. The breeze cooled the warmth where Gina had pressed against my side. A pang of loss replaced the tingling as we moved away from the hut.

"About ten minutes left." I figured the sun would drop those last few degrees fast.

It had already squashed into an oval by the time we stepped into the oratory. Gina ran a hand over the stone table and the inside of the depression at its center.

"I hope this wasn't for a blood sacrifice." She traced the grooves radiating out from the bowl. "Times were tough back in the day, but that practice never gets associated with European monks."

"Owen and I think it's a compass. Maybe the bowl gets filled with liquid to support a magnetic needle. Those thick outgoing grooves align exactly with the four major cardinal directions. There are more on the floor set at regular intervals."

"I like that idea better." Gina circled the altar, joining me to look out over the water. "Have you ever seen such a magnificent view?"

"Ireland's over there." I pointed to the far right. "And that rock sticking out of the water to the left is Little Skellig. It's even smaller and rockier. Almost impossible to land a boat, but they've found one structure up high that's similar to this one."

Too much online research had seeped into my brain. I couldn't seem to stop spewing random facts that popped into my head as the distant fiery ball touched the water.

"Shhh." Gina put a finger on my lips. "Let's just watch."

We watched in silence as the sun slowly sank, its outline deforming until just a small sliver sat above the horizon. She huddled close, and I put an arm around her shoulders, reveling in the warmth as her head settled on my shoulder.

Gina slipped her hand into mine as that last bit of gold dropped beneath the water. But instead of winking out, the light spread across the surface like an explosion, picking up color from the sea and lighting the horizon with a brilliant green flash. Our hands gripped tight, and we both gasped at the wondrous display.

The last vestiges of light drained from the horizon over the next few minutes. Gloom crowded our little bluff, and the wind grew cold.

"Guess we should head back." I spoke quietly, not wanting to disturb the moment.

Instead of agreeing, Gina snuggled closer and laid her free hand on my chest. The heat of her touch burned through my leather jacket and shirt, grew hotter when her fingers slipped inside my collar and she pulled my head to hers.

Our lips met, soft and wonderful and urgent. The need for air ended the kiss. I gulped down a quick breath and headed back for more, only to find her finger on my lips.

"We *could* head back." She rubbed her fingertip in little circles, squishing my lips around and tapping the index finger of her other hand against her own lips in thought. *Too many fingers in the way.* "Or we could head over to that nice soft patch of grass by the rocks and watch the stars rise. Unless you're in a big hurry?"

"Nope, no hurry!" The words tumbled out too enthusiastically, and I ended up with the tip of her finger between my lips.

I led Gina by the hand, zigzagging across the field searching for a spot that wasn't rocky. The roaring ocean, the twilight call of seabirds returning to nest, the ocean tang—all perfect.

Damn! The slope might look flat, but it was absolutely strewn with jagged chucks. There just wasn't a good place to…sit. My search through the grass grew frantic.

"Here." Gina guided me around the outcropping to a level ledge we'd cross on the way to the hut.

I eyed the patch of wild grass dubiously because it sat right at the edge of the drop-off. She laughed and pulled me down to the surprisingly springy surface. A depression in the ground eased my anxiety about being near the cliff and also hid us from sight of the gently-glowing portal.

"So which constellations can we spot from here?" Her hand was back on my chest, brown eyes sparkling in the failing light. "Maybe Leo or Orion the Hunter." She wasn't looking at the sky as her hand traced lower. "We might find the little dipper, the big dipper, or the really big—"

I cut her off with a fierce kiss. She laughed as our mouths pressed together, a throaty rich sound that soothed something deep inside—even as it drew my hunger to the surface. Her mirth melted into the heat of our embrace, and I wanted…more.

Discounting the sparking explosions behind my eyelids, very few stars got counted.

Time became a resilient, fungible thing, stretching to glorious hours, compressing down to urgent minutes, and finally leaving us breathless in the darkness. Even then, I resisted looking to the blazing canopy of lights overhead, preferring to take in Gina's dim outline. But two people could only gaze at each other for so long.

"You were wonderful." I brushed my thumb across her cheek, in no hurry to rush conversation yet longing to hear the happy, fuzzy satisfaction I sensed put into words.

"What the hell was that?" She shot bolt upright and gaped at me.

The stringent reply wasn't what I'd hoped for. Who would? I blinked into the dark, uncertain how to respond. "Uh… I really like you, and thought we—"

"Oh, not you, stud." She patted my chest and planted a quick kiss on my lips—awkward, since they were still stammering out confused thoughts. "You were awesome and then some. We'll talk about it later, but right now—" she straightened her clothes, pulled on her coat, and spun me around by the shoulders. "There's a light in your hut."

Yellow flickered from the rectangle of blackness that was the entrance below the beehive dome. If the structure had been hidden before, the shadows under a moonless sky made it damned near invisible.

We crept to the structure with flashlights held low. The wall of energy I'd felt before hit me full in the gut. I forced my feet to follow Gina as sweat popped out and turned to ice on my forehead. She paused at the entrance to look me over and mouthed her words. "Are you okay?"

I sucked in a ragged breath, nodded, and waved her forward. Which—as everyone familiar with international sign language knew—meant, "I'm fine, but keep moving or I'm going to hurl."

As it had before, the pressure and roiling in my stomach eased after we crossed the threshold. The monk again sat scribbling by candlelight at his desk.

"Sir, we'd like a word!" Gina kept her light pointed off to the side to avoid blinding the man, but moved it closer when he ignored her.

The bright spotlight landed on the page under his pen, walked up his front, and settled on the hooded face—still no reaction. Oddly, Gina's light did nothing to further illuminate his clothes or features. The lower half of his face remained hidden in shadows cast by the candle.

The monk looked up, then leapt to his feet and launched into a silent argument with thin air.

"This is exactly what we saw before." I didn't bother keeping my voice down. "In a minute he's going to chase someone out through the back door."

Sure enough, that's what happened, exactly like last time, even down to the furniture fading from sight. Gina played Owen's role and ran over to open the door covering the blank wall.

"You felt it again too, didn't you?" She pressed on the stones as if to ensure they were real.

"Big time, but it's back down to a tingle now."

"I should have had a camera out," she said. "I'd love to know if he'd show up."

"Probably not. Did you notice how our lights never touched his face? Aside from being incorporeal, that whole scene doesn't seem to interact with the physical world."

It took an effort to resist the urge to search for more clues. Nothing had changed, so there was no point. We headed out into the night, skirted the rocks near "our" spot, and took the portal home.

25. Missing Piece

"**H**OW OFTEN DO you think that scene repeats?" Bethany asked, then conveniently answered. "I bet it's at regular intervals, or maybe keyed to an astrological event. Or the monk might only show up when Jason's close enough to set him off."

We'd returned to my workshop to find Bethany playing tic-tac-toe with Mortimer and gave her the rundown of our Chrono-monk sighting. As long as she kept talking about Skellig Michael's apparition, she wouldn't be asking uncomfortable personal questions.

"Could be that anyone with magic brings the monk out." Gina was checking her phone for updates from security.

"That's true," Bethany said. "How close were you two when you saw the candlelight?"

"Doesn't matter." I jumped in to head off that particular line of questioning. "We'd already investigated the hut for a good twenty minutes and nothing appeared that time."

"So why'd you go back after dark?" Bethany was just *not* letting go.

"Routine double-check." I didn't like the speculative look in her eye. "Listen, I think we ought to get Lori up there to see what she can uncover. That boat that tried to run us off earlier would have reported seeing trespassers, so we need to put a ribbon on this thing fast."

"Yeah, I don't know how easy that'll be." Gina flashed her phone's screen at us, but the text was too small to read from a distance. "Lori's still out sick and isn't expected to be back for at least two days."

Two days turned into three, and still no Lori. Gina gave her a call, but unless we wanted crackers and Gatorade spewed all over my workshop we'd have to give her more time to recover.

Everyone went about their classes as if we hadn't been popping in and out of one of the most beautiful and terrifying places on Earth. The delay gave me time to finish drafting the report documenting my troubleshooting and repairs. After a few days of pulling out my hair over structure and style, I was certain Mr. Girardi would pass me even if I never got any further with the guidance unit.

Gina and I even managed to grab a quick dinner one night between shifts. Nothing wild like our time on the island, but I think it said a lot about our relationship that we were still relaxed and enjoyed each other's company. Things hadn't strayed into the dreaded awkward zone.

All good, except I still needed to push the guidance system that extra mile if we were to find the Chrono-monks and help Dean Gladstone. The only lead was the ghostly monk and the strange power calling to me from our little island at the top of the world. Which brought us full circle to needing Lori.

"When's the return trip to rock island?" Owen caught me sneaking into my shop between classes.

"Still waiting on Lori." The security lock vibrated under my palm, and I pushed the door open. "She's keeping food down, so I guess that's progress."

Mel was busy sweeping and dusting. A curious aspect of my budding relationship with Gina was that keeping my shop and apartment clean had suddenly become a priority. A few days ago, it hadn't really mattered, but now...well, let's just say that both Mels were on track to get the good-housekeeping robotic achievement medal.

"Damn it! I'll drag her butt in here myself if she doesn't come back soon. Lori's our tickets to finding those monks."

"*Might* be." But my instincts screamed that the stone hut held the key to making the guidance system fully operational. "The real flu's not like a cold. Some people are down for weeks."

"Well, her time's eating into our time," he grumbled, and took to shadow boxing with poor Mel while I collected books for my afternoon classes. "So Roxy's been asking about you."

"What?" I squawked and ridiculously looked around to make sure no one heard. "Why?"

"She's just got her geek on." He answered too smoothly, so was trying to get under my skin. "Wants to be sure you finish your tinker project. Sure mentions you a lot though. I think she's still sweet on you."

"Like that wouldn't be a time bomb waiting to blow. Why are you even hanging around with her?"

"Well..." He scratched his chin in thought. "She stops by the auto shop occasionally. You gotta admit she's cute, likable too."

"Too likeable," I said recalling some of our ill-conceived moments. "It's kind of hard to think straight around that woman."

"Roxy does make it hard to tell which way is up. Don't sweat it though. I know you and Gina are getting pretty tight. I'll tell our blond bombshell that you've just got a couple more portal tests before wrapping up your project."

"Owen, seriously?" How could I phrase this? "Don't tell her anything."

"You got it, boss." His sly grin seemed to contradict his words. "But at least tell *me* how skinny-dipping with fiery Gina went."

"Oh come on! We were like a thousand feet above the water."

"So it was skinny only?" He leered in triumph.

But there was no way I was biting on that particular bait.

* * *

Bethany glared at Mon's instructor as the woman drifted deeper into the restricted wing, back towards the alliance planning area. She rarely interacted with the strange woman, but hated her more with each passing day.

Mistress had left her classroom door unlocked, and Bethany pushed her way inside. At first glance, the sterile room looked deserted. A steel gurney sat in front of the bank of square refrigerator doors that housed the morgue's long-term guests.

Quiet sobbing came from the end of the counter along the far wall, from a dark shape huddled in the corner. Bethany rushed over, knelt, and hugged Mon tight. *Damn Mistress and all the other sadistic bastards that teach down here.* Mon leaned in, nuzzling under her chin. Bethany rubbed her back, offering quiet support.

"I don't want to do it anymore," Mon whispered. "Not like this."

"Shhh, it's okay. We'll get through this." Bethany rocked and hummed a wordless tune the way her grandmother had when thunderstorms threatened.

After a time, Mon sat up and wiped her eyes with the back of one hand. "Sorry."

"Don't be." Bethany fussed with the dark strands plastered to the girl's wet cheeks, preening and tucking them back out of the way. "Do you want to talk?"

"Animating demons feels wrong." Mon shrugged, spittle flying on a bitter laugh. "Sounds funny saying it out loud, acting like bringing back regular people is okay. My whole talent is a disaster."

"Don't say that." Bethany had survived a similar crisis of doubt, the crippling thought that her own drawings might be demons. "Our gifts are special."

"Is it wrong that working on Jane Doe feels wholesome by comparison?" Mon bit her lip as she worked through her thoughts. "I struggled with that until something dawned on me. Bringing someone back is a kind of tribute, the shadow of a second chance. You know? I get impressions from them sometimes, little glimpses into who they were, their hopes and dreams. Bringing them back gives the person that tiny bit of time to work toward closure if they aren't misused. It must be a condition of the human psyche. They all have something to prove; they all want time to do more." A crooked smile raised one corner of her mouth as she nodded to herself. "I give them the chance."

"That's my goth-girl; dark and creepy can be a good thing. We've just got crappy teachers trying to exploit us."

"It's only going to get worse." Mon's tentative smile vanished. "They're planning something big, organizing the students, and Mistress will want me to…perform. A raid will bring in more bodies."

And more live lurkers too. Bethany shivered, stealing another hug, this time for her own comfort. She was pretty certain she knew what the alliance wanted from her scriptomancy. At first it had been the obvious, fighting shadow demons, a task for which her creations were uniquely suited. That was why Ms. Baxter had pressed her to draw ever fiercer creatures.

But when her instructor got wind of the Shadow Master controlling lurker demons, the lessons had changed. Instead of toxic venom and claws, Ms. Baxter pushed for digging foreclaws, barbed appendages, and slim bodies modeled after burrowing insects and plants.

Mon would be their secret weapon to control dead lurkers. Bethany would control live ones. She was certain that was Ms. Baxter's end game, to have Bethany send drawings into live lurkers and to control them the way the Shadow Master had. The thought of sending her creations, those extensions of herself, into demons was revolting.

The fact that something big was in the works didn't bode well. The wing was abuzz with speculation but few facts. Several of her fellow students were on tap for whatever was coming, but were being closed mouthed about details. Bethany hadn't been recruited. Like Mon's, her skills weren't useful in clearing out lurker nests—yet.

"We'll get help." Bethany lifted the girl's chin, forcing Mon to look her in the eye.

"Help? We can't even tell our friends what's happening down here."

That certainly did make the situation more difficult. At first Bethany had been embarrassed by her special training and how dirty perverting her drawings made her feel. She'd shied away from giving Jason and Owen details even when they pressed.

But when the manipulation became clear, she'd gone to them for advice and found herself unable to talk about problems in their special wing—not just unwilling, physically incapable. Trial and error proved it was impossible to speak, write, text, or communicate in any way if her intent was to undermine their much-vaunted "special" training. Students in the wing could talk among themselves to an extent, but not to anyone else.

"Listen, we're going to find Dean Gladstone. He'll know what to do." She had to believe it. "There's still hope."

26. A Rocky Trip

F OUR DAYS LATER Lori made it back to school, and we gathered in my workroom. Owen and Bethany rounded out our party of four. I had the portal system set up and ready to go. We were just waiting on Gina, who was off finishing prep for a security matter. She'd be back on guard duty watching over the mirror while we attempted to solve the mystery of the ghostly monk.

I'd tried to get Herman to come along. His ability to look through time might tell us if the monk writing at his desk was an event from the past. Unfortunately, the guy was tied up in his duties at the Bashar School. Chad managed to have a quick discussion and relay an outline of what we'd been seeing. Herman promised to do a little research, but remained skeptical. Apparently people without temporal talent rarely—if ever—observed echoes from the past that fell in line with the type of encounter we'd described.

"Do you need the bag?" Owen thrust a plastic shopping bag at Lori.

"Put that thing in my face one more time, and my talent's going to find a pointy boot to fit your anatomy in the most uncomfortable way possible." Lori clung to the edge of my workbench, staring daggers.

Owen was being…Owen. But I didn't totally discount his sentiment. Lori looked like she'd dragged herself from death's doorstep to join us. A fine sheen covered her face, and she broke into shallow panting every few minutes. We hadn't even hit the island yet. Even her shiny blue highlights had fled, leaving dull turquoise streaks in hair that looked as tired as its owner.

"Sorry that took so long," Gina said as she unlocked the door and entered. "I had something special to attend to."

"No problem." I did a double-take when someone followed her in—two someones. "Oh, Ms. Murdock…and Dean Eisner. What brings you ladies to my humble lab?"

I elbowed Owen back a step to make room for our unexpected visitors, which put seven of us in the tiny room. I wanted to jump through the portal just to get some fresh air. Lori looked even greener around the gills, if that was possible.

"Ms. Murdock's kept me up to date on your activities." Ms. Eisner nodded at the mirror. "But the school has received complaints of trespassing from Ireland's Heritage Ministry."

Those fishermen must have had a hotline straight to the top. Not hard to imagine considering the prominence of the tourist attraction. Even if only a hundred or so people a day could visit the island, it probably enticed ten times that many to visit the mainland.

"How did they even know about us?" Bethany asked.

"It seems that someone" —the acting dean fixed Owen with a glare that could melt stone— "posted a number of outlandish selfies with unmistakable landmarks in the background. The authorities had already received reports of an unauthorized group on Skellig Michael. When those pictures grew legs, they put two and two together."

"I do have quite the following." Owen actually seemed proud of himself until Ms. Eisner turned up the wattage on her frown. "But it won't happen again. Promise." He crossed his heart and gave her that scoundrel grin, the one reserved for fictional Casanovas and eccentric pirates.

"Well, no harm done, or at least not much." Her lips curved into a reluctant smile. *Dang.* "We convinced them it was just photo manipulation for a school project—not hard considering we're five thousand miles away with records that you've been in school every day. It helps that high seas are keeping investigators from landing, but at some point you're going to run out of time. I suggest you finish your project quickly."

After warning us all to keep a low profile and double-checking that Lori wasn't going to faint, Dean Eisner left us to get on with the task at hand. Owen took lead before Ms. Murdock decided to give him her two cents' worth, which seemed a smart move given his charm hadn't impressed the security chief. The women went through next, and I brought up the rear.

Gina and her boss launched into discussing a tactical pincer movement to surround and overcome, no doubt an aspect of Attwater's new defensives. But I missed the details as my stomach did a portal-induced somersault and seabirds shrieked their animated conversation overhead.

The time difference worked against us again. The sun had already started to sink toward the horizon by the time we stepped onto the upper bluff of Skellig Michael. Most newcomers to the island wanted to take in the magnificent views for a few minutes, but Lori seemed intent on avoiding looking out to sea—no mean feat given the locale. As we worked our way around the rocks, she kept her eyes glued to the ground. She was afraid of heights, trying to keep from being sick, or both.

"Just don't look down as we round the point." I offered a hand so she needn't get closer to the edge than necessary. "The hut's just around the bend."

Lori survived the final bit of gymnastics it took to clear the outcropping, but it left her pale and gulping down air like a winded runner. Owen rooted around in his pack while we gave her a minute to recover.

"If you pull out a bag, I swear to god I'll chop your hand off," Bethany said under her breath.

Disappointment flashed across Owen's face, his hand seemed to walk its way to a different area of his pack, and he came up with a candy bar and a dazzling smile. "No worries."

Bethany turned away with a curt nod, and he immediately dove back into his pack.

"We're burning daylight, people. Onward!" I hated to press Lori, but I had few enough friends and no desire to explain to Ms. Eisner why Owen's body had been found at the bottom of a cliff.

"Feeling anything?" Bethany asked as we drew close to the entrance.

"Just a tingle. I don't think the monk's home today." Hopefully that wouldn't make it harder for Lori to figure out what was setting me off.

Although the interior was gloomy, sunlight angled through the doorway so we didn't need flashlights. With no magic flaring, I wasn't surprised to find the room empty. We took a few minutes to describe how the scene had played out. Lori kept interrupting to ask how that made me feel, more interested in where I'd been standing and my thoughts at the time than anything we'd seen. The discussion made me feel like I was in therapy.

"So there's a couple of different ways I can approach this." Excitement replaced Lori's prior weariness as she puzzled out our options. "Finding items is pretty straight forward if I have a clue about what I'm looking for. The more precise, the better attuned I'll be. For instance, let's say we knew a lost magic ring was the problem. Thinking of jewelry would be good, of a ring better, and of a gold band with silver crest surrounded by diamond chips best. And my best results end with 'oh here it is.'" She pantomimed picking up and holding out a small object. "Good results tend to be more like 'I sense it's in that direction.'" Lori waved vaguely off to the east.

"That's easy. Concentrate on a monk with a broken nose wearing a red robe," Owen said.

"I really don't think that vision, or whatever it was, will have much impact on my talent. I find *things*, physical items that I can hold." Lori pinched her thumb and fingers together as if grasping something tangible. "That being said, I have been known to dabble in more esoteric investigations. I key best on emotions so maybe you could share what you feel?"

Great, more touchy-feely stuff.

"It's a fluttering here." I touched my sternum and concentrated on the sensation. "Maybe mild nausea."

"Not exactly what I meant, and not something I need to hear about after the week I've had." Lori blew out a breath and pursed her lips. "Would you say this sensation makes you agitated, or maybe nervous?"

"Not exactly."

"Afraid of the unknown forces you face?" She raised an eyebrow.

"Not scared. Curious though, we all are." I thought that might be the ticket, but Lori looked like she'd bitten a sour grape.

"Objects it is," she declared after another round of questions didn't yield a clear emotion to focus on. "What's most likely to set off a magic resonance? Ideas, people."

I kind of liked applying the scientific method. Brainstorming a cause and having Lori do a seeking for that particular object felt nice and methodical. We worked through a lot of the standard tropes like magic wands, cursed rings, intelligent swords, and the like. Without a clear description of a specific artifact we wouldn't get a precise location, but the general category of item was enough for her to discount it as the source. The downside of using the process of elimination was that we'd never truly run out of options. But we did finally start to run out of ideas as we sat in a circle racking our brains.

"How about a dagger?" Owen said into one of the lengthening pauses as we all ran out of steam.

"Similar to a sword and already ruled out." Lori shook her head, looking tired.

"Golden fleece."

"Enchanted pen."

"Magic armor."

The collective ideas trickled out, but our magical detective assured us each had already been covered.

"I think we're back to the monk," Owen said, garnering a round of moans.

I was about to steer the conversation on, given Lori's flagging enthusiasm and the earlier head-butting between the two. But something made her brighten.

"Maybe, but not like you think." She nodded with increasing enthusiasm as she spoke. "A dead monk might work."

"Come again?" Bethany clearly didn't like the sound of that.

"Power often settles in bones or remains. Especially if this is a haunting of some sort." Lori climbed to her feet. "I think it's worth a shot."

Okay, now I might be nervous and a little scared. Were we about to summon the dead? Bethany, Owen, and I made space by backing to the wall. Lori opened herself to the universe at large, using her now-familiar pose of chin raised and eyes closed, turning slowly with arms spread wide. Her normal two rotations stretched to three, then four. This had to be it; something was coming through.

"Nothing." Lori dropped her hands, and we all deflated. "Guys, without a clear anchor, I just don't think this is going to work."

All that time and energy wasted, defeating the Shadow Master, chasing after a way to find the dean, fixing the guidance system, activating the portal, and getting so close I could taste it. And now we were at another dead end, blocked just shy of making that last leap to the monks who might hold the key. I was supposed to be this rare and powerful tinker. I should have been able to get the portal system working fully instead of just dumping us on the island. All I could think was…

"I am so stupid!" Heads jerked up as I mentally kicked myself. "The guidance cabinet is the best link we have. I mean, you're not going to find it, but the whole point of coming here has been to get it working and find the monks. Here, I'll show you."

I whipped out my cell phone and flipped through pictures of my project. The cabinet, basic schematics, close ups of the gemstone controls—it was all there.

Lori nodded as she took it all in. "That's more than enough detail. Make some room, and I'll give it a try."

"Dude, that's a serious engineering fetish," Owen said as we crowded back against the wall. "Like maybe you need professional help."

"Oh come on." I knew he had to be joking. "Tell me you don't have pics of that sacred project-bike you're always talking about."

Rather than answer, he focused on Lori. *Game, set, and match.* Feeling smug didn't last long thanks to Bethany's eye roll, which said clear as day that we both needed our heads examined.

"This has promise." Lori stopped turning, faced the back of the room, and followed her talent to the bronze hoop marking the rear doorway. "Somewhere in this area. It's not your well-documented device, obviously, but there's a similar feel."

She ran her hands over the stones, worked around the metal outline, and focused on the wall to the left of the door. We gathered around to help her search the stacked stones, pushing and prodding as if for a secret lever.

"These have been here a thousand years," I said after a while. "I doubt we're going to find any loose."

"What are these?" Being shorter, Bethany concentrated on the lower section of wall, where she found two round metal plates embedded in the stone. "They have hinges."

"Looks like door stops," I said. "Lori, anything?"

The disks were blackened by age and set near the floor about two feet apart.

"This is part of it." Lori traced her fingers around one of the medallions and pressed hard on the top edge.

The plate sank a fraction into the wall before pivoting out to form a small metal shelf with upright prongs. She did the same thing with the second, then found a third plate embedded in the floor two feet from the wall. Pressing on the last plate popped up a pronged pedestal that formed an ankle-high equilateral triangle with the other two.

Lori made one last circuit of the area. "That's the last one."

"So is this supposed to summon the ghost monk?" Owen stared at the back entrance as if willing the scene into existence. When nothing happened he turned to me. "Feel anything?"

"Same old tingling." I ran a hand over the cold metal at one corner of the triangle. The contact didn't make the prickling any worse, but it didn't make it any better either. "But know what?" I traced the tabs that extended up from the plate, trying to figure out where I'd seen the offset pattern of three before. "These are brackets. Hang on."

My phone was in my hand again, and it took a while to find the picture I wanted. Way back before the beginning of work on the guidance system, I'd snapped pics of the globe and portal. I finally found a good shot of the globe's framework.

"Bingo!" I zoomed in so the others could see. "These are the same brackets from the dean's globe, the ones that hold the guidance device in place and link it into the portal system." I swiped back and zoomed in on the fancy scrolled feet of my project, the ones that looked like violin necks. "Damn, it's fuzzy, but you get the idea. See how they'd fit nicely between these prongs. This triangle here is a docking station for the guidance unit I've been repairing."

"Well, these brackets aren't going anywhere soon." Owen pivoted one of the wall fittings up and down as he inspected the workmanship. "No visible screws or pins. I don't know what's holding these in place, but I'm betting you'd have to chisel them out."

I cringed at the thought. We'd been careful to respect the local ecosystem and not damage the ancient artifacts left by the monks. Even if the order had existed long past what historians believed, their heritage still belonged to the countrymen of this area. Plus, except for Lori dowsing out their location, none of us sensed magic coming off the brackets themselves. Tearing them up to take back to Attwater wouldn't be helpful.

"Let's review what we know," Bethany said. "The journal is pretty clear that the guidance system should link the portal to the Chrono-monks. Jason fixed the system, but all it did was set up a portal to where they'd been years ago. A bunch of hunting around found clues in the form of the monk apparition and these brackets. Jason, is it safe to assume your repairs are done correctly?"

"Yeah. There were a ton of severed spell connections, but those were straightforward to reconnect with my tinker talent. The hard part was finding the right ends to splice together. There is definitely still a void at the core of the spells though. Comes across as a blank spot, but I've triple checked and there's just nothing left to connect."

"Was it just time or something else that caused the spells to fail?" Bethany pressed on one of the oddities that kept rising to the forefront of my thoughts.

"The damage certainly wasn't normal spell decay. The cuts were clean, precise, and thorough. I figure the guidance system was deliberately sabotaged. There's a whole appendix in my final paper describing my theory."

"If someone wanted to cut off access to the monks, could they deliberately have removed whatever spell component is missing too? Maybe as a failsafe in case some upstart tinker came along and tried to fix it?"

"Possibly," I conceded. "If so, it must interface through induction or something because I've got no more loose ends to tie into." I ran a hand over the nearest wall bracket—sturdy, ageless, immovable. "If this is as far as the system could bring us and Bethany's failsafe hypothesis is correct, then all that's left to do is bring the guidance component in, mount it up, and see what happens. Maybe it has to be activated from here to reach all the way to the monks."

"Won't the portal back to the school collapse if you pop out its brains?" Owen didn't understand how the system worked.

"Nope. The mirror is perfectly stable once coordinates are fed in. It would be hard to reestablish without a guidance system, but the gateway will stay in place indefinitely until shut down. It honestly couldn't hurt to try. Ten minutes to hoof the box over." I reached my right hand out to grab the middle mount. "Plug it into these bad boys and—yow!" Touching my fingers to the second bracket closed a circuit, and the background tingling I'd been ignoring blossomed and shot through my chest.

"Are you okay?" Bethany stood over me with Lori right behind her, which made no sense.

"Whoa, that's a live wire!" I think I yelled, hard to tell with my ears ringing. "I'm fine. That just caught me off guard. What the…"

I was lying on the floor several feet away, having been knocked back from the triangle mounts. The energy hadn't been the throbbing that preceded the monk visions, nor had it been directed at me. But it still packed a wallop. Yet I'd sensed something important, important enough that I wanted to give it another go.

"What the hell do you think you're doing?" Bethany's legs blocked my path as I crawled back over.

"The brackets tap into a spell that's…down." I didn't know how to better describe the brief flash of insight. "I need another look. Now that I know what to expect, I can handle it better. Promise."

I tried one of Owen's charming smiles, but it probably came out looking like I had gas. The women weren't at all inclined to step aside and let me "get myself fried" as they put it. Owen, on the other hand, seemed ready to batter-dip my butt and send me on my way. Some unpleasant yelling and constructive brainstorming led to a compromise.

"Ready?" I asked over my shoulder after grasping the first bracket.

"Got ya." Owen tugged from behind, and my belt buckle dug into my stomach."

If I looked like I was in trouble, Owen promised—a bit too gleefully—to yank my butt out of there by my belt. As an added precaution, he had one of the magic-cancelling pouches we used to contain nasty enchanted artifacts. Owen wore the velvety black bag like a glove on the hand holding my belt. Theoretically, the bag would break the flow of power should it try to jump from me to him.

I wore a lower-grade pouch on my left hand, the hand I was about to use to grab the second bracket. Hopefully the pouch would mute the power while still letting me get a read on where it came from. If the pouch insulated the flow too much, I could always slip a finger or two out and test the water that way.

"Here goes nothing."

27. A Betrayal

G INA DIDN'T MIND the waiting—at first. Playing guard on this side of the portal hadn't been too bad. With her new job and the department being short staffed, there was an endless supply of reports and administrative minutia to keep her busy. But now that she'd been to Skellig Michael herself, something had changed.

She smiled at the thought. Things had definitely changed—for the better—there under the blazing stars. She missed more than just the ocean breezes and salty air. Perching at Jason's workbench and scrolling through mind-numbing paperwork just didn't seem as exciting. She should be out there helping solve this mystery.

Of course there were plenty of other strange things afoot. Gina turned back to her work, checking and rechecking the daily reports. Something big was definitely brewing. The department just didn't know what, or when it would break. Demon lairs continued to empty out and enemy scouts roamed the woods beyond the school's grounds. Too many coincidences.

"Will you please stop?" She swatted Mel's dustpan away from her feet for the third time.

Having a robot hovering and constantly swooping in to clean up specs of dust too small for the human eye didn't exactly help the time fly by either. Jason was clearly trying to impress her, but she'd take a little action over fastidious robots any day. Speaking of which—she checked the time, waved Mel back into his corner, and turned to the door.

After a short wait, the handle rattled, turned a fraction, and fell still. It had happened like clockwork for the past hour, almost as if someone wanted to be caught. Gina fired off the text she had queued up, crept to the door, and yanked it open. Nothing.

The pattern was baffling. This person either had severe OCD or was deliberately baiting her. But why the dance? Why not just get the confrontation over with?

The portal would keep without her for a few minutes. This time when she relocked the door, Gina stayed in the shadowed alcove outside.

Before long, light footfalls came down the corridor. She resisted the urge to look, forcing herself to remain hidden as she fired off another text. A shadow fell across the doorway just before the approaching woman stepped into view.

"Why am I not surprised?" Gina's rhetorical question made Roxy smile, a dazzling white smile showing too many teeth for her petite features.

"Hey there, Gina. Stalking your boy-toy, I see."

Roxy hadn't so much as batted an eye at finding someone crouched in the entry alcove. This was what the woman had expected, had wanted. *Why?*

"Classy as always, but I'm more interested in hearing why you've been snooping around." Gina waited for a reply. When none was forthcoming, she ushered the woman down the hall. "Then I guess we'll go have a chat with Ms. Murdock."

"You don't seem to understand how this works." Roxy' smile turned worried as she reached out and grabbed Gina's hand. "I need your help with a...problem."

An electric jolt jumped between their fingers and raced up her arm. Roxy's eyes grew huge, and a quiet sob escaped her. She cast a frightened look over one shoulder before turning back with pleading eyes. Gina had seen victims, knew when a woman needed help. Roxy was scared and vulnerable. The woman's smile returned, tentative at first then radiant and...fierce.

A prickling like pins and needles spread through her chest, reminding Gina of the flutter of anticipation she'd felt when Jason took her to the island. That flutter had blossomed into electrifying excitement and left her heart wrapped in a warm cocoon. The ugly prickling sensation probed the edges of that warm place—and winked out along with any thought of helping Roxy. Gina yanked her hand back and rubbed her numb fingers. Why on Earth had she thought the woman leering at her needed help?

"OMG, you love that twerp!" Roxy dropped her act with a huff of indignation. "Fine. We'll do this the hard way."

"Little bitch." Gina threw out a shield just in time to block a blast of magic. "You tried to charm me!"

Roxy reached for another spell, but Gina had no intention of continuing a hallway duel. She swept air currents across the floor and cut Roxy's legs out from under her, sending the woman sprawling and her next spell flying wide. By the time Roxy scrambled to her feet, backup had arrived.

"Don't do it!" Power flared between Melissa Murdock's hands, her magic aimed straight at the blond bimbo.

"I'd listen to the lady if I were you," Gina said. "That spell could take down a full magus."

The security chief had access to specialty magic. The spell she trained on Roxy used a spirit-heavy blend of elements to bind and incapacitate. The magic penetrated most shields and seeped into its target at a cellular level to induce a walking paralysis. Once struck, the only movement possible would be what the caster permitted.

"I assume this young lady is the one you've been trying to catch?" Her boss backed Roxy up to the wall and joined Gina.

"Looks like it." Gina caught a hint of magic drifting from Roxy, but it cut off as soon as she rounded on the woman. "Reach for one more spell. I dare you."

Roxy pouted and held up her hands. Good; the paperwork for unleashing that particular security spell would be a nightmare. Gina was about to suggest grabbing an empty room for a quick interrogation when the distinctive hiss-crackle of the school's announcement system came from speakers along the ceiling, followed by…music?

Mellow bass plucked out a slow back rhythm. Staccato piano and horns preceded an echoing refrain: "why don't you do right." The singer took a sultry breath.

"Like I said." Roxy's grin held no warmth as the song drifted on, lazy and seductive. "You don't understand how this works."

Pain slammed the back of Gina's head. Her world exploded into sharp, brilliant light. Every fiber of her being burned. She must have pitched forward and smacked into the stone floor, but couldn't struggle to her feet. Every attempt to move was met with numb throbbing that locked her muscles—legs and arms, hands and feet. Even her head refused to turn as Gina drifted through a white haze. And still the music played on.

* * *

"Time to wake up, girl." Roxy's voice pierced the haze.

The blinding white light faded, and Gina blinked at shiny metal. Her head wouldn't turn, but Melissa Murdock stood just within her peripheral vision off to the left. Roxy had a casual arm draped around the security chief's shoulder.

"Melissa, do something." Gina was surprised to find she could speak, less so that the woman who'd paralyzed her didn't help.

How could the head of security be in league with Roxy? But Ms. Murdock's slack face and dead eyes told the truth. The woman was under a spell, the same coercion Roxy had tried on Gina. The hypnotic music cut off abruptly, replaced by wailing alarms.

"I believe my other loyal subjects are hard at work on their own tasks." Roxy caressed Melissa under the chin. "Be a dear and make her open it."

Melissa nodded, sickening adoration and a willingness to oblige shining in her dark eyes. Power flowed within Gina, and she found her hand rising until her palm was flat on the metal before her. She recognized that hum of energy and the whisper of metal on metal as the bolts securing the vault retracted. Melissa made her step back to allow the giant door to swing open.

"Wait here. I'll just be a minute," Roxy said, as if Gina had a choice in the matter—although she may have been talking to Melissa.

"Ms. Murdock, snap out of it," Gina hissed as Roxy disappeared inside, but no amount of coaxing or cajoling made the slightest bit of difference.

Roxy returned clutching Jason's football device in her arms and wearing a truly terrifying smile. Murdock's spell forced Gina to lock up the vault and follow along helplessly as the three headed back toward Jason's workshop. Gina again tried to talk sense into her boss only to find she was no longer allowed the luxury of speech.

The audible alarms went silent as the system settled into visual warning mode. The flashing pattern, three long followed by two short, repeating, meant a physical security breech. Something or someone had gained direct access to the outer ring. Gina kept track of the lights, watching for and dreading the shift that would indicate the next ring in had been compromised.

Feet pounded down the halls to either side as they crossed an intersection by the stairs—salvation. But the students scurrying for safety had no interest in holding up the head of Attwater's defenses. Black-clad security personnel weren't any better, exchanging terse updates with their boss before moving on while Gina screamed inside, trying to break the compulsion.

Even at half capacity, the school should muster an excellent response. In dire situations like this, the auxiliary units that trained in the special talents wing would also step up to help quell whatever Roxy had put in motion. The outlook improved considerably when they rounded the last corner to find Ms. Eisner and a handful of senior personnel blocked the workshop door.

Impossibly, Roxy fired off commands to the small group. The acting dean and the others nodded, turned away, and headed off to do her bidding.

Not Dean Eisner! Gina railed against the spell, nerves convulsing with effort, but the magic didn't so much as let her twitch. How could Roxy possibly have gotten control of so many?

A flash of insight took her thoughts back to the talent show and Roxy's unexpected performance—the music, her dance, the strange flickers of almost-magic. That had been the same music drifting through the halls before Ms. Murdock attacked. During her performance, Roxy had draped herself over several people in the audience, including the security chief, the dean, and others in important positions. Attwater's core personnel were compromised.

Gina's role seemed obvious as the spell walked her to the workshop door and made her open the magical lock. Murdock could have gotten Roxy into the vault, but only Gina and Jason had their biometrics keyed to his workshop. That Roxy hadn't just activated her control over the security chief to get the football meant she'd had other plans in mind. Gina took what satisfaction she could in the fact the trap she and her boss had sprung was forcing Roxy's hand. Hopefully accelerating the woman's schedule would play in Attwater's favor.

"I'd love to stay and chat, but this lovely device has work to do." Roxy closed the door on the turmoil in the hall.

Gina glared as she marched over to stand in the corner next to Mel.

"Oh, that's it, slay me with your thoughts. Many have tried over the centuries, I assure you. We'll save the gory details for later, shall we?" Her implied threat wasn't lost on Gina.

Roxy set Ms. Murdock on guard duty, swept through the swirling mirror portal, and disappeared with the football. Melissa blinked and tilted her head a fraction when the other woman winked out of sight. The tell was miniscule and lasted only a moment. Spells didn't travel through portals. Perhaps Roxy's influence had been weakened by her departure. Unfortunately, Ms. Murdock had cast the paralysis spell, so that bit of magic still held strong.

28. Slam the Door

THE INSULATING BAG prevented the magic from blowing me across the room. But plenty of power came through to get a rise out of my talent. That gave me something to work with.

"Doing good," I assured the others as my own power threaded its way into the contacts I held.

Filaments of energy coursed underneath the triangle between brackets, underneath the hut. This was a reservoir, deep and timeless. The magic didn't flow through me, it simply existed. My consciousness sank deeper, trying to plumb the depths.

Down, down, down.

Still no end in sight. The energy could well extend to the center of the Earth. Panic rose, swift and unexpected. I was drowning, running out of air. With nothing in need of repair and no avenue to follow, my talent floundered.

Yet a faint echo grounded me, a sense that this vastness was somehow part of the whole that was the guidance device. My rational mind argued the reverse was more likely; the artifact I'd repaired must be designed to tap into this primordial magic. Either way, I had found what I'd come for and began the long journey back.

I broke the surface and gasped for air, sucking down a great lungful of salty dampness as I released the mounts. I tried to push to my feet, but my knees refused to unbend. Violent shakes took hold, and I curled onto my side to let them pass.

"All good," I managed through chattering teeth. "Magic shock or something. It's letting up now." I sat up, giving my body more time to recover. "The guidance device definitely belongs here. I'm betting that even without the silver mirror, it'll find the Chrono-monks."

I told the group what I'd discovered—or, more accurately, the roughest outline of my experience. Much of the encounter came through impressions and sensory inputs I couldn't put a name to, much less describe.

"Then we've done it," Owen said after I'd finished. "Let's get your project and finish this."

For once there was no dissent. Since we'd be back shortly, we left the brackets open and headed outside. Cold wind and a dark sky greeted us.

"How long was I in there?" I'd expected to step out into sunshine.

"Two solid hours." Owen shrugged. "We were discussing pulling you away when you came back on your own."

"No wonder my muscles rebelled."

"Ooh, the northern lights." Lori had just reached the rocky point with Bethany.

The stars shimmered beyond the outcropping, fading into a spectacular display of wispy blue-green streamers that snaked across the sky. We crossed over to the little field and stood on the path between cliffs and portal, taking in the sight.

I'd never seen the aurora borealis in person. The phenomenon appeared unbelievably close, as though the lights came right down to the edge of the island. They seemed to gather behind the oratory, whose pillars rose in solemn shadows against the spectacle.

"Something's moving up there!" Bethany was right, though it hardly warranted her note of panic.

"I think it's Gina." I squinted at the figure in the oratory as we walked closer, but instead of my girlfriend's denim jacket, the woman wore fuzzy pink. "Roxy? What the heck are you doing here?"

"Hey, lover-boy." Roxy hunched over the stone surface, her hands moving across the center of the altar. "Love to chat, but I'm a bit busy."

Her hair was a dark mass against the background lights, but a glow rose from beneath her hands. I took the steps two at a time and slammed into a wall of power surrounding the oratory. The energy felt familiar, and for good reason.

The football device sat above the stone bowl. Roxy had a hand on each end. With deft twists, she spun the hemispheres, pressed them closer together, and then spun them again. Roxy entered a precise combination with rapid adjustments that brought the device ever closer to forming a single sphere.

"What do you think you're doing?" I beat a fist against the barrier, but dropped it when she finally looked up. "What the hell?"

The voice had been Roxy's, but in the glow of the football her hair whipped about, wild and alive. Her narrow face had grown longer, her cheekbones sharper, and her eyes blazed as they reflected the energy spilling between her hands.

"Aren't you full of questions?" she hissed around a darting tongue that pushed too far out of her mouth and tested the air like a snake's.

I stumbled off the top step. Diving into the magic reservoir had fried my brain, was making me hallucinate. I palmed my eyes and stepped back up. The wall of energy still blocked me. The football still flared. And Roxy was still…wrong.

"Jason, you need to see this." Bethany had stayed put with the others still gaping at the northern lights.

"I've got a more important issue here." I worked my way along the barrier like a mime looking for the door.

"No, I really doubt you do." Bethany's voice took on a quiet urgency and she bit off each word with a crack of command. "Look…at…the…sky!"

Was everyone going nuts?

I stepped back and looked over the oratory roof. The aurora glowed even brighter now, with purple and yellow melding into the earlier streamers and forming a glowing wall. All very impressive, but we had to get the football away from Roxy before—

The stars visible behind the aurora shifted. I blinked and wiped my face, honestly worried that I'd sustained a magical concussion. The thought was comforting for about three second. Then the stars moved again, swirling, dancing, and sparking where they intersected with the glowing wall in the sky.

The points of light formed outlines, living, three-dimensional constellations like glittering titans that threw themselves against the lights, against the barrier at the world's edge—the barrier the monks had constructed.

Demons.

But those weren't shadows, lurkers, or even mimics. These were something else, indistinct creatures of cosmic proportions—or at least that's how they appeared through the barrier. My mind flashed back to the scrolls we'd studied, back to the space reserved for uncategorized terrors above the mimics in the demon hierarchy.

The barrier that we'd assumed to be the northern lights did more than just *appear* to swirl down to the oratory. Those trailing ribbons of energy snaked through the columns and converged on the wave of power flowing from the football. Roxy finished her adjustments and placed the sphere in the stone bowl.

At full power the waves of magic snapped to the channels carved in the stone table, flowing out to all the cardinal points before sweeping into the sky and merging with the world barrier. Now I got it. Roxy was attempting to bolster the ancient shield. The barrier, the reservoir, the football—they all held the same power, were all part of the monks' mechanism for keeping the demons from our world. The football had massive power. But was it enough to reinforce the barrier?

Lori's shriek had me pivoting to see a massive clawed hand pushing through the shimmering wall that stretched and strained attempting to hold back the apparition. Fiery talons as long as swords pierced through, but Bethany and Owen called wet, icy wind to drive the hand back. The football wasn't working. If anything, the barrier grew weaker.

I turned to Roxy. Power ran freely through the channels, but in the wrong direction. Energy flowed *from* instead of *to* the barrier.

"Roxy, you've got the polarity reversed." I clawed at the invisible wall, which seemed to be a side node originating from the football as it sucked down energy. "Let me help."

"Adorable," Roxy looked up, gaze ferocious and even less human than a moment ago. "You still think I'm here to help."

"We have to go!" Owen grabbed my arm and hauled me away from the oratory steps. "Roxy duped us all. She's a mimic. We need reinforcements."

Roxy raised a hand, clutching the air with long pointed fingers as my friend dragged me back. Her eyes widened, and she tensed as though ready to chase us. But she kept her focus on the energy pouring into the football, unable to leave its vicinity without disrupting the flow. A wave of her hand sent the shield around the oratory rushing outward in a sparkling blue wave. We ran down the path to the head of the steps.

A glance back before plunging through the portal showed the wall of light blanketing the sky was dimmer. More creatures crowded the other side, raking and goring each other with claws and horns for the privilege of throwing themselves against the monks' power.

The barrier still held. But for how long?

29. Under Siege

F LASHING LIGHTS AND the zing of magic met us when we emerged from the mirror and crashed into Melissa Murdock. Feet pounded outside as people rushed past, but we had more immediate concerns than whatever had the school in an uproar.

"Watch out!" Bethany pushed Lori to the side as a fireball splashed against the wall behind her, just missing Mel's recharge station.

Gina stood next to my pint-sized bot as if she didn't have a care in the world while her boss called up another spell. Fire was a terrible thing to use in such close quarters. The room's temperature had already jumped to uncomfortable. More fire spells would broil us all.

I went for Air, the fastest element at my command, intending to keep Ms. Murdock off balance until we could figure out why she'd gone berserk. The blast I sent out hit much harder than I'd anticipated, slamming the security chief into the back wall. She crashed through my supply shelf, thudded against the stone, and crumpled into a heap.

"Way to go, Team Air-bender." Owen scanned the room for more threats before dropping his hand.

Residual wisps of air magic curled up from his and Bethany's fingers. We'd all had the same idea and hit the woman simultaneously. Lori rush over and checked on Ms. Murdock.

"Out cold, but still breathing." Lori ran her hand through Ms. Murdock's hair. "No bleeding, just a huge lump. Do we tie her up or what?"

"Gina, what the hell's going on?" I turned to our two placid spectators, making yet another mental note to program my robot with a watchdog mode.

Instead of explaining Gina just rolled her eyes. I stepped closer to demand answers and noticed her eyes still moving, repeatedly cutting left to the fallen woman. I touched Gina's shoulder, shook it, but she didn't even flinch.

"You'll find duct tape and zip ties in the top drawer of the workbench," I told the others. "I think Ms. Murdock put a spell on Gina."

This time Gina's eyes did roll up, then back down, then up again—the best nod she could manage. While the other two turned Ms. Murdock into a living cocoon, Bethany and I played twenty questions. Gina answered with her eyes, up and down for yes, left and right for no.

It took longer than I would have liked, but we managed to get the gist of what occurred. The next logical question was what to do about the situation.

"Can anyone in the school counter a spell like this?" I asked the others.

We'd formed a semicircle around Gina, who still stood rigid with arms by her sides. She tracked the conversation and could even comment after a fashion with some well-timed eye movement. Ms. Murdock came to, but refused to say word, no doubt thanks to the magic compelling her.

"Help from security seems to be out of the question," Owen said with a nod at the trussed up woman. "Maybe the nurse?"

"The infirmary's more for handling accidents on the job, but let's keep it as plan B," I said.

"Things this severe are usually handled by the front office." Lori looked to be fading fast, but had refused to grab a spot on the floor to rest. "I'm sure Dean Gladstone would have known what to do. He was always bringing consulting experts."

"Ms. Eisner's got to have the same contacts." I nodded, warming to the idea. "She's probably our best choice."

"Then again, maybe not." Owen pointed at our silent member.

Gina's eyes darted left and right as though watching a tennis match on fast forward. A few more yes-no questions teased out that our acting dean was also bewitched. Roxy had been a busy girl while I'd delved into the power under Skellig Michael. Gina's optic nod when asked if others had been compromised severely limited our options.

"There *is* one other group that might help." Bethany was oddly cautious and chose her words carefully. "Some of our talent teachers—" She stopped mid-sentence and huffed out an annoyed breath. "There's a group—" Her eyes found the ceiling for a few seconds as if she counted to ten. "Mon and I might know someone, but…it's a long shot."

We waited for more, but she only offered a shrug of apology—as if things weren't already strange enough. Roxy had stolen an object of ridiculous power from its safe little nook in the vault. Our own people had given demons access to the school while evil Roxy tried to destroy the world barrier with said artifact. And topping the charts of unbelievability, Bethany was unable to string ten coherent words together. How on Earth were we going to put everything right and get the football safely back under wraps?

"No stellar options, but I've got an idea." I huddled everyone in close. "Check my logic on this. Attwater's vault has magic dampening similar to those pouches we use. Wouldn't entering the vault nullify these controlling spells?"

We kicked it around with much enthusiasm and little actual information. Minor spells for necessities like emergency lighting still functioned beyond the big circular door. That meant the dampening spell had design limitations as to what magic it suppressed. None of us were experts on compulsions, but the consensus was that it just might work.

"Except none of us are on the vault's access list," Owen pointed out.

"But we do have a human key and a hand-truck." I pointed at Gina who for some reason stared daggers at me.

* * *

"If that stupid football device is really syphoning off the world's protective barrier, this is the worst threat in ages." Bethany ran ahead as we carted our incapacitated passengers through the halls. "The schools have dealt with mimics before, but never one with an artifact like that."

"Maybe she's just being controlled too." I ducked low as muted explosions sent chunks of debris raining down.

My hand truck's left tire bounced over a broken stone, and I threw out an arm to steady Gina as she lurched sideways. The web belts strapping her to the metal rails held, and my hand dropped back to the handle before I lost control.

Gina stood on the cart's metal plate with her back against the uprights, strapped in as I pushed her down the hall Hannibal-Lecter-style. Ms. Murdock trundled along on my left, similarly trussed up and standing on the hand truck Owen pushed. We'd left Lori and Mel on guard outside the portal.

"Come on, man!" Owen's curse was directed half at me and half at the crumpled light fixture he swerved around. "You saw her hair and claws. She's a demon for sure."

"They'll have to assemble the equivalent of a magical swat team to take her down." Bethany slowed and raised her arm at ninety degrees with fist closed, bringing us to a stop. "And it's got to be fast before those new monsters come through."

"Roxy could just be possessed." I paused to let Bethany check the intersection ahead.

Possession was pretty rare and only marginally better. Mr. Gonzales had gone through physical changes under demon influence, and it took a herculean effort to free him. But deep down I knew Owen was right. I'd been a sucker from that day in the alley when Roxy had conveniently shown up with her seductive smile and killer robots. I'd never stood a chance, but it was hard to admit I'd been so stupid.

"Clear all the way to the stairwell." Bethany waved us forward.

Damn, I forgot about the stairs.

I tugged on each of the three dangling straps, cinching them tight around Gina. Owen did the same for Ms. Murdock. The woman hadn't said a word for the entire ride. She didn't even look upset, just leaned back quietly as Owen pushed her along.

Gina seemed secure, but I'd stopped asking if she was comfortable on account of the holes her glare kept burning in my favorite shirt. As we pushed through the double doors onto the landing, I briefly toyed with the idea of having Bethany be the one to roll Gina into the vault. Waiting outside with the demon hordes might be safer for me. I sighed, dismissed the thought, and spun the cart around to attack the first step. It was going to be a bumpy ride.

We reached the lower level without losing either of our charges and spilled into the inner hallway under rapidly flashing lights. The strobe effect was giving me a headache. I was trying to remember what triple flashes followed by a single long flash meant when Bethany pulled up short. I nearly crashed into her.

She'd stopped alongside the security door to her special training wing. None of us knew what went on down there. It was a secretive place where the more interesting talents were trained. That's why it was so weird to see the door standing wide open. Lights down the center of the hallway showed classroom doors to either side, same any other corridor. But the passage was so long that we couldn't see the far end.

As we gawked, a burly bearded man and a slim teenage girl rounded the corner pushing the kind of cart you see in posh hotels. But instead of being piled with luggage, it held two dead lurkers. Two was a guess given the tangle of furry arms, jutting tusks, and dripping ichor. A chest-high cage sat in front of the bodies and held one more demon. The caged demon gripped the bars with a clawed hand and clamped the other over its bleeding stomach, a stoic figurehead as the cart sailed by.

The big guy nodded and steered toward the door. I returned the gesture, both hands on the handles of my own cart—a surreal moment like two delivery men waving good morning as they continued on with their living parcels.

"I'm sorry, guys." Bethany looked like she might be sick. "The vault's not far. Follow the hall around to the left past two more intersections and you're home free. I've got to go check on Mon. I'll meet you back at the workshop as soon as I can."

"Bethany, wait!" Too late; she was already dashing down the hall after the demon wagon.

"Who needs her?" Owen patted Ms. Murdock's head as if she was a toddler. "We've got our own women. Onward!"

He forged on, oblivious to the sizzling of spellfire from up ahead and the daggers thrust at his back by a certain mobility-challenged woman. I could almost feel the heat radiating from Gina's glare. In her current state, Ms. Murdock hadn't seemed to mind Owen's antics, but I pitied him if she remembered after the enchantment was lifted.

Two intersections was one too many.

The small troop of lurkers plodding down the left-hand passageway spotted us immediately. They resembled turtles or giant beetles with mud-colored shells. All six rushed us, running on two legs and slicing the air ahead of them with wicked talons.

Owen blasted them with a fireball before I'd even decided on a spell. He knocked Ms. Murdock over in the process, and she landed with a grunt. Fire was Owen's go-to element. Sometimes it was the wrong choice.

"Damn!" Owen's second shot was already blazing down the hall. "Fire resistant."

I'd been sucked in by peer pressure and took precious moments to ground the Fire I'd called and reach for Air. I should have led with what I do best. A whirlwind formed between my fingers, but it was going to be too late. I threw myself in front of Gina to put something between her and the charge.

Blue-white lightning sizzled down from above and turned the lead lurker into a charred lump. The blast scattered the rest of the pack and nearly blew Gina and I over. Dark gray clouds billowed along the ceiling, covering the exposed piping and roiling above the regrouping demons. Another energy bolt lanced down and a second turtle-demon dropped.

"Yee-haw!"

My ears were already ringing, and the high-pitched cry had me clamping my hands over them as Chad strode down the hall. His raised hand glowed with power that was visible even without using magic sight. Two more bolts speared down and sent the last of the demons into full retreat.

This was no common core spell, but Chad had thrown lightning once before. The power was special magic born of his bond with the living building that was Attwater School.

"Just in time." My nose and eyes weren't doing too well, and I snorted to clear the stench of scorched demon from my nostrils.

"You're welcome." Chad tipped his hat at the women, but a dangerous glint shone in his eyes when he turned to me. "Any particular reason you're kidnapping these fine ladies?"

"It's complicated." For some stupid reason my brain focused on how naturally he pulled off wearing his cowboy hat instead of the power gathering around his fist. "They've been hexed."

As Owen and I filled him in on the basics, the suspicion drained from his eyes. Chad nodded, saying he'd run across other faculty members acting against Attwater's interests.

"She's hurting and violated," he said, referring to the school. "Imagine open wounds and insects crawling over you. I'd love to help you guys take down Roxy, but I have to take care of this."

Guided by his bond with the building, Chad had been working his way through the lower levels, channeling Attwater's power to eradicate the demon infestation. It was a losing battle because they just kept pouring in.

"Take point and get us to the vault," I said when he was about to rush after the fleeing demons. "Ms. Murdock will need your intel and can muster people to seal those breaches."

"That makes sense." He gazed wistfully down the hallway past the charred lurkers. For a minute I thought he'd give in to Attwater's siren call. But Chad squared his shoulders and tipped his hat at Ms. Murdock. "Lead on."

Damn his cowboy genes.

That was the kind of smooth confidence I'd been going for with my own headwear. Chad's fit his face well, slim and stylish instead of the super-wide, obnoxious exaggerations from the movies. The old leather bush hat I'd found was equally attractive. But my short-lived attempt at rocking it had been quickly nixed by Gina and Bethany. Both women assured me that I looked silly.

Under cover of Chad's superpowers, we made the vault without further incident. I sheepishly pulled Gina's arm free and pushed her hand against the door to activate the lock. Then we wheeled our passengers inside and parked both women amidst the medieval weapons collection.

"So how long are we supposed to sit here?" Chad started pacing in front of the sealed door the minute we got situated.

"Until the spells weaken." If Chad didn't bolt in the first five minutes, I'd eat my hat.

"We might want to take a couple of weapons with us back to the island." Owen ran his hand over a long-handled halberd and let out a low whistle.

"Think twice about that one." I'd examined many of the items when hunting for a project. "It's got a nasty curse that's currently broken, but you wouldn't want to take it outside of the vault."

"How about this?" He picked up a morning star with an iron ball connected to the wooden haft by thick chain.

"Attwater says demons are pouring in through the garage entrance." Chad's anxiety was palpable. "I'll dash down, crack a few heads, and come right back. Promise."

"Or maybe you could all focus on the reason you're here." Gina's voice was harsh from disuse—not because we'd been ignoring her. "Can anyone reach the damned buckles?"

She clawed at the strap around her middle, but the buckle connected back near the support bar.

"Sorry, had to keep those tight so you didn't fall." I hurried over and loosened the straps at her chest, waist, and knees. "Wait, take my hand."

Gina leaned on me as she stepped off the hand truck and flexed her knees. She worked through all her joints, checking that everything still functioned and working feeling back into her extremities.

"You okay?" I couldn't read her expression. "No residual effects?"

"I think I'm good. Murdock hit me with a top-notch restraining spell. Good plan bringing us here. It's shattered completely." Gina rolled her neck and bent to touch her toes, but shot back up with a grimace. "I've got to go!"

She darted around me, past Chad and slammed her hand onto the door, bouncing on her heels as the mechanism cranked the bolts back.

"The enemy's roaming the halls out there." I couldn't let her go after Roxy alone, but we had to get Ms. Murdock back on her feet too. "We need a plan!"

"Yep, you work on that. I'll be right back." She tried to push past the door before it had opened wide enough and let out a string of blistering curses.

"Something's still wrong." I pointed from Chad to Gina. "Grab her."

"Grab her? Seriously?" Gina's look stopped our demon-blasting cowboy dead in his tracks. "The only thing still wrong is lots of morning coffee and zero rest stops along my hijacked-by-a-mimic day." Her weight shifted as she danced in place. "Chad, by all means tag along, but *do not* get in my way."

She spun and ran out. Chad gave a shrug and followed.

"We'll just wait here then," I said to the empty doorway.

30. Skellig Again

"**O**W, MY HEAD," were the first words Ms. Murdock uttered since we'd come back through the portal.

"How do you feel?" I waved Owen over.

"Like I'm just coming off of a three-day bender." Her arm jerked against the duct tape. "Why am I tied up?" She rolled her head taking in the room. "And in the vault?"

"Sorry, you went kind of nuts." I wasn't ready to untie her just yet. "What's the last thing you remember?"

"Helping Gina bring someone in for questioning, that blonde with all the hair."

A bit of back and forth convinced us that Ms. Murdock was no longer under Roxy's spell. Her memory of the day's events remained spotty, with fleeting impressions surfacing as we filled her in. Untying her took a lot of cutting and cursing that left chunks of silvery tape stuck in odd places. Gina returned with Chad in tow, looking much more relaxed, and rushed over to help with her boss.

"Can this ability of yours find Ms. Eisner and the others being controlled?" Ms. Murdock asked Chad after our recap of the situation.

"Never tried to find specific people before." Chad slid his hand over the stonework behind him as he considered. "But I think we could do that."

"Then I'll need Mr. Stillman with me," Ms. Murdock declared.

"I've wasted too much time already," Chad said. "Attwater's hurting. She'll die if they find the heartstone."

"We'll bring the bad actors down here to break those spells. *Then* we can focus on sealing the school and mopping up the attackers." The security chief's tone allowed no room for argument, but her face softened at the pain in Chad's eyes. "The demons were well prepared and probably have an endless supply of foot soldiers. Help me close those wounds to stop the bleeding first. After that, I can focus all our resources on making the school safe again."

Chad nodded. He understood, but didn't like the idea of letting the demons run loose for a second longer than necessary. Ms. Murdock agreed that we also couldn't afford to ignore Roxy and the threat to the world barrier. As much as she wanted Gina's help with Attwater, Ms. Murdock agreed to let her second in command handle the assault on Skellig Michael.

Contacting the lost monks would have to take a back seat while we dealt with the immediate threats. And, unfortunately, we'd have to take on Roxy ad hoc until the situation allowed a cohesive strike force to be assembled.

"Don't you have some secret weapon that takes down mimics?" I asked.

"Thought you'd never ask." Ms. Murdock led us to the back of the vault, keyed open a storage locker, and handed over three silver disks the size of dinner plates. "These are inhibitors. Get a mimic to step on one, and the device should incapacitated them for a short time. We only have these three, and they take forever to make. Let's dig up a couple of other items. I'm not sure how to handle the apparitions you saw behind the barrier. So stop her from bringing it down."

The rest was typical gear like flash-bang grenades and the magical equivalent of cattle prods. But I couldn't discourage Owen from taking a magic weapon. At least he picked a short sword, which was less likely to bite an untrained wielder. I shuddered to think what he'd do to himself with that morning star.

"Can we *please* go now?" Chad was bursting at the seams despite the fact we'd only spent a scant fifteen minutes formulating our plans.

"There's one more important detail." Ms. Murdock led Owen by the arm to a corner near the weapons rack.

She probably was as worried as I was about him waving around medieval weapons. Urgent whispers passed between the two. Owen nodded and grinned as if hearing a raunchy joke. Quick as a snake, Ms. Murdock's hand shot up, grabbed Owen by the ear, and pulled his head down to her level. His cavalier smile vanished as he visibly gulped and gave the woman the most earnest nod the grip on his earlobe allowed. They exchanged a few more words before she released him, and the pair walked back to join us. Owen followed meekly and reclaimed his spot next to Gina.

"I think we're all set." The security chief's tone said it was go time. "Be careful. I'll send backup as soon as it can be spared."

Owen, Gina, and I made our way back toward my workshop, while Chad went with Ms. Murdock. Pockets of fighting sounded in the distance, and the occasional shuddering boom had me wondering if it was invaders or defenders blowing things up.

"Looks like you got schooled by the boss," Gina said to Owen as we climbed the stairs.

Rather than answer, he fumbled with his belt and adjusted the leather scabbard holding his new sword. I'd given the weapon a quick once over with my talent. There was nothing technically wrong with it, but the Earth enchantment that kept the blade extra sharp had a couple of twists to the magic that I couldn't follow. I'd recommended Owen pick something else, then warned him to watch for unexpected side effects when he'd insisted the sword was perfect.

Gina no doubt referred to the ear-tweaking Owen had gotten from Ms. Murdock. Knowing Owen, the guy probably still didn't know what he'd done wrong. I felt for him a little, but was also glad to have Ms. Murdock's ire focused on someone else.

It was a relief to round the corner and find my workshop door shut tight. I'd been half afraid the invading demons would converge on my little corner of Attwater while we were off reviving the women. Slightly less worrisome had been the thought of Roxy unleashing nightmares through the silver portal and finding the door smashed open from the inside—less likely since the beings we'd seen would be too big to fit through the mirror.

"Lori, it's just us." I knocked before unlocking the door.

Bethany had beat us back. She and Mon guarded the portal while Lori snoozed in the corner. Disconnecting the guidance system from the globe only took a few minutes. Deciding on our exact plan of action took longer. The school went to great lengths to pound home its message of never taking on a mimic without professional backup. So much for doing things the smart way.

"What do we know about Roxy that can be exploited?" Gina asked.

"She's tops with magic," Owen said. "So everyone keep on their toes."

"Don't let her touch you." Bethany's eyes slid my way. "That's how she gets control."

"I suspect I'm immune now." I thought back to the last time I'd run into Roxy. "But I don't plan on getting that close anyway. I'm not sure this one's a weakness, but Roxy's over the top competitive and doesn't like to lose. Maybe we can goad her into a mistake."

"Do we all agree that the first priority is getting your guidance unit in place?" Gina's question garnered a round of nods. "If she's still busy working with the football, we might be able to slip around the rocks and get to the hut without her noticing. Everyone stay sharp. Roxy's been acting different from the norm, but I've never heard of a mimic caught alone without minions. Owen and I will run interference on any lurkers. Bethany and Mon, you handle shadow demons."

"Right." Bethany patted the oversized sketchpad she'd picked up on her way back, the one housing her nastiest drawings.

"Just a reminder, I don't know for sure what'll happen after I activate this thing." I ran a hand over the wooden device tucked under my left arm. "Best case would be that we've suddenly got a bunch of helpful Chrono-monks on our side. Alternatively, it could just give me coordinates for resetting the portal. Or a thousand other things could happen. I just don't know."

I growled in frustration. Taking on Roxy ourselves seemed foolish, but we might be pressed into doing just that. The others each carried one of the immobilizing disks from the vault. Lori was in no condition to do much of anything and would stay with Mel to watch our backs. She'd also send reinforcements through the mirror if and when they arrived. On a scale of one to five, our plan was a solid two; not very encouraging. There were just too many unknowns, but we had to press ahead. What else could we do?

We weren't going to get any more ready, so everyone gathered close, I stepped through the portal, and…bounced off the shimmering surface.

"What the hell?" I tried again with similar results. After rechecking twice and experimenting with the mid-island and coastal landing spots, I figured I knew what was happening. "Roxy expanded that magic shield to cover all three portal locations. We're locked out."

"How the hell does she know about the other two sites?" Bethany threw both hands in the air.

"It's a small school. People talk. That's not important right now." Owen waved the question away with a suspiciously nervous laugh. "What's important is getting this device where it needs to be to find those monks." He put his shoulder against the portal surface and tried to force his way through like the mirror was a jammed door. Owen's feet slipped as he shifted and strained, but he stopped after noticing us all gaping at him. "Okay, fine. I might have told Roxy about our trips to the island, including how we avoided all the stair climbing. So sue me. The information wasn't exactly secret, and she was dying to hear how things were going."

I wanted to ask him what the hell he was thinking, to rail against the mess he'd caused. Bethany looked like she'd slap him upside the head. But I'd been on the receiving end of Roxy's curiosity. Who knew what she'd done with the tidbits of information gleaned from *our* conversations over the past year? Hell, I'd probably jeopardized the school more than anyone.

"Owen's right," I said to forestall the brewing argument. "Let's focus on how to get back to Skellig Michael."

"How about using another portal from a specialty classroom?" Mon suggested.

"Those are totally different systems." I'd figured out the silver mirror with hints from the dean and lots of time, which was a luxury we didn't have. "We'd have to find a teacher to program one of those."

"And our coordinates would still be blocked," Bethany said. "We'd need a new landing point."

"No problem there." Gina whipped open an app on her phone to pull up a satellite map. She poked at the screen for a while, her brow furrowing. "That's too weird. The public databases have placeholders for that region instead of true coordinates. Let me try your laptop." She went to my workbench, but gave up after five minutes of searching. "Same thing. With good distance measurements and relative directions we could back off to a known location and work it out, but the calculations would need to be precise."

"Wait, I might have alternate coordinates." I dug out my phone and pulled up my GPS app. In addition to the portal locations, I'd snapped coordinates at the overlook where Gina and I had stargazed. "Yes! But these could be too close to Roxy and still blocked—heck, the whole island might be. This is a spot near the hut where we need to install the guidance device."

"Aren't you the romantic?" Gina snatched my phone and jotted down the coordinates.

"I wanted to look up what constellations are visible this time of year," I stammered as another thought occurred to me. "No need to even look for another portal. I can try these right here."

Doing so involved reconnecting the guidance system and inserting a new offset into its spells. Everyone grabbed a seat to wait. The portal took the new setting just fine and was up and running in under an hour.

"Seems clear, but we need a test," I announced when my hand pushed easily through the glowing surface of the mirror.

As usual, Mel got to be our test dummy. That wonderful little patch of grass sat extremely close to the edge, so I took the simple added precaution of tying a rope around his waist. Video from Mel's camera was great, but wouldn't stop him from plummeting over the edge if something went wrong. Ironically, I trusted the portal safety mechanisms to kick in for humans more than I trusted it to protect a robot.

Mel nodded as I explained what to do, then plunged through the gateway. The video feed showed him landing farther back from the cliff than expected, a ringing endorsement of those built-in safety measures. Pale light filled the sky, a mixture of breaking dawn and maybe some residual visible energy from the barrier. Mel's camera didn't have the focal length for that kind of distance, but there was definitely movement in the wispy clouds.

My robot trotted along the rock outcropping and peeked around the point, trying to give us a look at the oratory. A wall of gray crisscrossed with creases filled the screen as though a wrinkly sheet had been thrown over Mel.

"Crap!" The rope zipped through Owen's hand. "Something's got him." He clamped down on the rope and lurched toward the portal. "Little help?"

Everyone grabbed a section and heaved. The line went taught for a split second as we strained. Then the rope started coming back in. With so many hands on the line it was hard to tell, but it felt like we were dragging Mel back on his butt. Even with his shiny new outerwear, I'd have repairs to make. But it was better than losing my robotic pal.

"Just about there." The knot connecting the last few feet of rope broke the mirror surface. I grabbed it and hauled in a frayed end.

31. A New Breed

MEL WAS GONE. I blinked at the frayed strands curling from where the rope had parted. The fact that I hadn't felt the debilitating backlash of my creation being destroyed gave me hope. But then again, I'd never lost a robot on the other side of a portal.

"Now what?" Owen had his sword in hand.

"We proceed with extreme caution." I shrugged and gripped the guidance device tight. It wasn't like we had a plan B. "Take point and roll left. We'll follow at five second intervals."

"After we're through, put this at the base of the portal as a last line of defense." Gina handed Lori her capture disk and turned to the five of us that were about to leave. "Everyone take an extra-long stride on the return trip to avoid triggering the disk. Murdock didn't give us an antidote spell."

Owen's knuckles whitened around the sword hilt. He called Fire to his left hand before diving through the mirror. Bethany went next, followed by Mon. Gina and I brought up the rear.

We hit the ground ready for action, fanning out into a tense line with weapons and spells at the ready. But only raucous seagulls and the distant roar of surf met us. Pre-dawn washed across the bluff. My eyes snapped to the lightening sky, finding only drifting clouds. The rock promontory that hid us from the oratory stood tall enough to also block our view of the world barrier—or we were too late and it had already fallen.

The portal sat well back from the cliff and next to the beehive hut. With no one in sight, the first part of our mission would be a breeze. The others stood guard while I ducked through the doorway. Gina took up station in the entrance to monitor my progress and also keep an eye on the team.

Nighttime cold had crept into the stones, but nothing else had changed since our prior visit. I lined the guidance cabinet's feet up with the three brackets and gently lowered it into place. The last thing I wanted was to sink down through that disorienting reservoir of magic. I'd brought dampening bags to use as insulating gloves, but set them aside because they made securing the latches next to impossible. As long as I didn't touch more than one mount at a time, I'd be fine.

"All set," I called to Gina as the last foot locked into place. "I'm activating the spell now."

I set the gemstones ringing the top of the box to their neutral positions and triggered the web of magic at the heart of the device. I left the bits of new magic I'd added turned off, relying on interplay between the guidance system and that reservoir below to self-calibrate. There was little else for me to do but watch.

"Here we go." I keyed the final sequence and pulled my perception back far enough to feel safe while still being magically attuned.

Minutes ticked by. I risked peeking at the spell web to make sure I hadn't missed anything. The internal magic cranked away, but the massive surge that had hit me didn't flow through the feet. The only change was the barest glow of power in the curious void at the center of the spells.

"It's taking its sweet time." I touched one foot to get a read.

Not closing the circuit put me in control, and I snaked my perception down through the surface layer, past the cold stone and bedrock, and to the warmth of the magic. Tendrils of power snaked up like steam from a simmering cauldron, working its way toward the surface and the guidance system. The surface of the vast magic that stretched down into the earth bulged and rose slowly, glacially slow. I withdrew and sat back on my heels.

"What's the verdict?" Gina clipped off the question with her command voice.

"I'm sensing movement. We just have to wait."

"Any chance you can hurry things along?" She kept shooting looks outside.

Instead of brightening, the sky beyond the doorway grew darker. I shook my head, hurried over, and wished I hadn't. Clouds billowed over the top of the rocky ridge that hid us from view. Flashes of lightning lit the underside, painting the sky with dark silhouettes that shifted and stretched without settling on any specific form.

"That isn't a natural storm." I felt power rise each time the clouds lit up, each time the things beyond the veil attacked the thinning barrier.

"On the bright side, the monks' defenses are still up," Gina said.

"But for how long? The football must still be draining off power. I can feel the barrier weakening."

My talent was attuned to the energy signature. The sky resonated with the same energy I'd found deep underground. Before I could delve further into the thought, Mon and Bethany ran over, out of breath from more than just the short sprint.

"Something's coming around the point." Bethany waved her restraining disk at the long shadows gliding over the ground near the drop off.

"Several somethings." We could always retreat through the portal, but I was loath to leave the guidance unit unattended. Five of us could handle a few lurkers, but the commotion would draw Roxy's attention. "What the hell's Owen doing?"

Instead of falling back, Owen crept forward with shining sword in hand, looking entirely too eager. The lead demon stepped into view, and my blood ran cold.

"Is that—" Mon swallowed hard and tried again. "Is that a lurker?"

If so, it had been hitting the gym, and taking steroids— and possibly eating magic beans. The creature looked like a crocodile walking upright, except its face was pushed in so that the needle teeth crowded the space below its nose. Thick cords ran under the pebbly green hide of its tree-trunk arms and sequoia legs. The monster was the size of a two-story building and looked as though it could chomp us all down and still want dessert.

"I think that's something new." Lurkers came in a variety of shapes and sizes, but I figured there had to be limits.

The ground literally shook as a second monster worked its way around the rocks. The things were so big that negotiating the rocky point took all their attention to keep from falling. But the pair was sure to spot us soon. We needed to come up with a plan of attack fast, maybe find a reptilian weakness we could exploit.

"Have at you, foul beasts!" Owen shouted at the top of his lungs and ran at the first monster with sword raised high.

We didn't even have time to react. The demon spotted his charge and slapped a massive webbed hand down at the idiot. Even without the hooked claws, the hand was big enough to flatten a cow.

"He's going to die," Mon looked away just as the strike landed.

But somehow it missed our friend. Owen dodged left, swiped his sword across the leg, and shot a fireball straight up into the gaping maw. The beast stumbled, and Owen used the precious seconds to dance and parry, scoring hit after hit. He could only reach knee-high. The magically-sharp sword bit deep, but didn't inflict much damage. The sheer ferocious glee and audacity of the attack had the monstrosity dancing back and unable to land a return blow. Owen handled the sword amazingly well, even switching hands to take advantage of an opening. He whooped like a maniac the entire time.

"Let's get in there before the idiot gets himself killed." I hoisted a pair of flash bang grenades and rushed forward.

The women flanked me, firing off spells as the second creature tried to come at Owen from behind. My first grenade hit the new demon in the chest, doing little good. I flung the second as hard as I could and nodded in satisfaction when it blew right in the creature's face.

Ice formed on the rocks near the edge as Mon, Bethany, or both went after the coldblooded angle. The original demon snapped and lunged at Owen, caught a sword point in its snout, and backed onto a patch of ice. Its foot slipped off the edge, and the beast followed with a mighty roar as it dropped out of sight.

"One down!" I grinned, a little of Owen's cavalier attitude rubbing off.

"This is *so* not a good day." Gina lanced out with fire at the remaining gator, but her eyes were locked on something behind me.

A shadow fell over us as a third creature worked its way around the rocks. This one wasn't likely to lose its footing at the cliff edge because it looked like the kraken and King Kong had a baby. But they shaved junior and gave it horns, and momma must have been two-timing with a megalodon because baby ape-squid also looked a little sharky around the edges.

The newcomer wasn't quite as tall as the gators, but it filled the path and then some with thick octopus coils clinging to the cliff edge on one side and slithering over the twenty-foot high outcropping on the other. We had to fall back to the hut to keep from getting hemmed in between the two monsters.

"Ahoy, beasty, prepare to be boarded!" Unbelievably— idiotically—Owen charged.

"This isn't normal." Gina growled deep in her throat.

"He's got nowhere to go." But I was wrong.

Owen hacked at the white underbelly of the roiling tentacles, again dancing away from the massive fists that tried to pound him to pulp. Our avenue of retreat closed and the gator pushed us forward. For the moment we were still out of both monsters' reach and threw everything we had at the ape-squid in an attempt to keep our friend alive for a few more seconds.

But this new creature ignored the barrage. Tentacles looped around boulders to either side, and it hunkered down low forming a living wall across the path. It still flailed at Owen and took the occasional swipe at anyone who got too close, but clearly planned to let the gator move in and finish us off. We were trapped.

"Where's Owen?" I'd lost track of him.

"You're not going to believe this." Gina pointed off to our left beyond the edge of the cliff.

Owen stood on a fricking tentacle, skewered it with his sword, and leapt to the next. He ran along the undulating flesh out beyond the cliff's edge as if the thousand-foot drop didn't exist. The only problem with his strategy—aside from being certifiably insane—was that there was no way to avoid the ape torso. Once he was out of tentacle stepping-stones, he was done for. Gina saw it too.

"Son of a bitch!" Gina grabbed Mon's restraining disk and hurled it like a Frisbee.

The magical device flew true and straight, gliding to the ground beneath the ape torso where the tentacles merged. A wave of power blew up from the disk, washing the squid portion in crackling blue energy. The field spread quickly across the massive creature. Slithering tentacles stilled, and the ape froze mid swipe with mouth agape and blackened fangs gleaming in the dim light.

"Gator, gator, gator!" Bethany pushed us into a stumbling run toward the frozen ape.

Owen continued to dance his way across the upper half of the demon. Some of the spring had gone out of his steps as though he was disappointed at the lack of challenge.

Frozen or not, there was no way the women and I would be climbing out over the abyss. A dark opening sat at the base of the rock wall beneath dripping suction cups.

"That looks like a way through." I steered the others to the narrow gap, passing beneath the giant hand that had been poised to swat Owen.

I slowed, seeing something familiar in the flat expanse between the massive fingers and over-long thumb, the rough gray skin crisscrossed with clefts and creases under the crackling immobilization spell. That massive palm was the last thing we'd seen on Mel's video feed.

"Come on, there's daylight." Gina tugged my arm, pulling me into the fleshy tunnel.

I didn't need much encouragement. The ground shuddered and a whoosh of flames splashed over the spot where I'd been gawking. The gator sucked in another big breath, embers glowing deep in its gullet. I pushed Gina into a crouching run as the demon let loose a burst of flame that sizzled and crackled as it cooked tentacles. No wonder Fire had little effect on the gator.

We popped out the far side covered in clear slime and smelling like sushi. One last tentacle curled around in front of us, blocking our view to the oratory. The gator-demon wasn't equipped for climbing, and we could just make out the ridges along its head bobbing back and forth as it paced on the far side. The ape-squid made an excellent roadblock.

"That's going to make getting back to the portal problematic," Bethany said.

Owen swept down from above, sliding the last few feet along the slimy coil and landing nearby. He experimentally poked the rubbery skin with his sword and shook his head at the lack of response.

"Such a worthy opponent." Owen scanned the shadowy field ahead. "Where's the she-demon?"

I hauled him back by the collar when he started off on his own. The sword's magic burned bright, and a quick inspection confirmed what I'd feared.

"Let's get the lay of the land before charging in," I said. "Put the sword away for a minute and help us plan."

"But we have the element of surprise." He waved the weapon in circles as if to rouse us to action. "Let us press the advantage."

"You could have gotten yourself killed out there." Bethany stopped him this time, her fear and anger breaking through Owen's cavalier attitude as she waved out over the cliff. "What were you thinking?"

"Hey, demons are the bad guys here." Owen blinked and looked at our scowling faces like *we* were the crazy ones. "And the bigger they are…" He jabbed the air with his sword.

"Put away the sword, and we can debate if dancing across thin air on squid tentacles makes good sense." He raised the weapon higher and opened his mouth to reply, but I didn't give him the chance. "Humor me."

"Fine, but we're wasting time." Owen slammed the sword into its scabbard and turned on me with an angry glare. "Now, if you have a better way to fight, I—" He laid a hand on the tentacle he'd slid in on and fingered the slimy skin. The condescending look slid off his face as his eyes traveled up to where the coil looped out over the cliff. The color drained from his face, and his eyes widened into saucers. "Dear god."

"Now you get it." I pointed at the scabbard. "That gives you a boost but also takes away your fear."

"And what little common sense you have," Bethany added.

Owen's easy agreement to stick with grenades and spells actually made planning a little trickier. A glance into the clearing showed open ground all the way to the oratory. Power flowed down in colorful streams and disappeared under the stone roof. I hadn't gotten a good look, but Roxy must still be up there with the football. Even without a gauntlet of mega-demons to run, the problem of how to sneak up and subdue a mimic remained.

"We've got one more of these." Bethany held up the last of Ms. Murdock's disks. "But Roxy's not going to just let us in close to freeze her."

"We need a distraction." That was the thing sword-wielding Owen would have been good for. "And to hit her from all sides."

Her shield formed an arc in front of the steps, blocking the site of our original portals. But we were already within its boundaries. By necessity the plan fell into place quickly, and there really wasn't much to it. We only came up with three simple steps: split up, draw fire off each other, and slap the immobilizing disk on her. Then I could deal with the football, hopefully before the storm overhead broke and released more nightmares.

We dashed out into the eerie glow of morning sun trying to shine through the fractured barrier and encroaching shadows that assaulted it. Intellectually, we'd all known what to expect, but everyone paused under the tapestry playing out. Black, spidery cracks splintered the pale aurora filling the sky to the north. A blood-red tentacle the size of an oak tree snaked from a hole in a badly shattered section, suckers raking at our side of the barrier as another ape-squid tried to work its way through. Dark shadows with glowing eyes hovered in the background and dwarfed the massive hybrid that was itself a hundred times bigger than normal lurker demons.

We spread out and crossed the field, keeping low and quiet. The gator-demon caught sight of us, bellowed Godzilla-style, and let loose with more bursts of flame. The Ape-squid's bulk protected us, and jets of fire burned away its left shoulder. In its attempt to reach us, the enraged super-gator pounded and clawed at the helpless thing blocking its path.

Stealth was definitely out of the question. We hurried on, scanning for traps. The small field was clear of magic except for a hint of power coming from the steps where the shield had blocked our return portal.

The oratory, on the other hand, positively blazed with energy. I hit the steps from the right, Owen took the left, and Bethany came up the middle, while the other two watched our collective backs. And still Roxy hadn't made a move to stop us. I stepped onto the oratory's stone floor, expecting a trap. Roxy stood on the far side, hunched low over the football.

32. Titans Battle

T HERE'D BEEN NO need to creep up slowly. All of Roxy's attention was on the device, all her energy focused on the silver and gold sphere that screamed with power. Too much power as more of the world barrier's magic poured into the seam between the halves, flowing from the channels carved in the altar. Yet she forced more into the device.

The power tasted of cold bedrock and molten lava, of ocean depths and mountain crags. This was the flavor of the reservoir of magic deep beneath Skellig Michael. The power of the Earth itself had protected mankind all these centuries, but now that magic was draining away.

The barrier was failing fast. The sky held only a faint echo of the ancient power that had been in place. Soon the fragile shell that remained would shatter completely.

"You cannot stop this!" Roxy bared her teeth, straining to raise a glowing hand from the streams flowing through the stone.

Owen and I hit her with spells from both sides, elemental magic that would have flattened any lurker. Our magic bounced off. Energy split out from her shaking hand to slam each of us back against the oratory pillars. I blinked away stars, scrambling to my feet before she struck again.

"The old gods are coming." Roxy's voice took on a strange reverence. "The time of man and demons alike is at an end. For ours is the—no!"

Crackling blue energy crept up her waist, rising from the silver disk Bethany slid across the table. Roxy batted at the restraining magic, but her hand froze as the spell touched it and spread on.

"You cannot stop what's in motion, Jason." She sounded sad. "Glorious days are—"

The crackling aura snapped into place, freezing her solid.

"She does like to talk," Bethany said. "You boys okay?"

"I'll live." Owen winced as he patted the smoking patch on the front of his jacket.

I'd been rubbing the back of my head where it had slammed the stone column; there was a lump, but nothing debilitating. The hand I ran over my chest came away damp. My jacket hadn't even been scorched. The demon slime must have acted as an insulator. Then again, Roxy had redirected barrier energy at us. My talent resonated with those energy flows and had likely spared me the brunt of her attack.

Now that Roxy wasn't guiding the power, energy spilled from the overloaded sphere, clashing with the influx draining off the barrier. With nowhere to go, the ribbons of power flowing down from the sky thrashed blindly across the stone altar. I soothed the nearest with an outstretched palm, letting the magic sense my intent and then coaxing it back toward the barrier.

My tinker skill kicked into overdrive, stretching further than intended. I felt the damage above, the cracks in the sky, as invisible wounds on my arms. The magic that had been torn away flowed into the sundered barrier and eased the phantom pain on my skin. Returning the adrift magic only strengthened the world barrier by a fraction, but gave me one less variable to deal with. The sphere whined with power.

"The football's going critical." I'd seen this happen with Mr. Gonzales and reached for the device.

The last time I'd deactivated the football to keep it from exploding, the device had been set to release its stored energy. I'd needed Roxy's help to decipher the power readings and work through the combination that stepped the football down safely. This time the sphere was set to absorb magic, and Roxy's help was certainly out of the question. I needed to reverse the polarity fast and guide all that energy back into the barrier.

"It's already melting down." I twisted the hemispheres counterclockwise hoping to reverse the polarity, but they only moved a fraction. "She's forced too much energy in."

I struggled to pull the halves apart, feeling for the next notch with touch and magic. I imagined this was how safe-crackers used to open mechanical locks, spinning the dial a fraction, sensing a minute catch in the tumblers, and then moving on to the next number in the sequence. After an agonizing thirty seconds, I hit that first spot, and the hemispheres separated by the thickness of a penny. I fumbled and twisted, searching for the next point, shaking my head because there was no way I could work through the entire sequence in time.

"Throw it off the edge!" Gina jabbed her finger out at the choppy ocean, out under the cracking shell that barely contained the demon overlords—or old gods as Roxy called them.

"No good. It'll blow the barrier." I knew it in my gut.

The sphere contained the barrier's power, magic drawn from the reservoir deep below the island. But an explosion would release too much energy over too short a time, like plugging a delicate computer straight into an industrial power station. If the football exploded anywhere near the island, the barrier was toast.

"Can you disarm it back at the school like last time?" Bethany asked.

"We only have minutes." I shook my head. "Not enough time, but at least that's far enough away to save the barrier."

"If it even holds." Bethany eyed the growing cracks overhead with a doubtful frown. "The school or the world. Not much of a choice."

"Maybe a portal hop?" Gina keyed something into her phone. "I'll try to get Murdock to set up a portal out into the desert."

"Might work." I managed to back the device down another notch, then had an idea. "Let's get it back to the vault. The dampening spell will shut the sphere off and give us time to figure out a safe way to deal with it. Either way, we have to move. I'm not making enough progress to stop the overload."

"We've got another problem." Mon pointed past Bethany.

The blue glow on Roxy's skin had dimmed to a faint nimbus as the crackling power of the disk faded. Her gaze darted to the sphere, and she strained to break free.

We dashed down the oratory stairs and broke into a run. The restraining spell had dropped away from the demon blocking our path, but it didn't matter. The ape portion sagged above its blackened squid torso, a sightless, filmy eye gazing skyward. Between the left half of its face being smashed to a pulp, the bone protruding from its charred shoulder, and the fact that three tentacles had been burned away, it was easy to see the ape-squid was dead.

"Gap's still there, and the gator's wandered off." I shoved Owen, Bethany, and Mon ahead of me, while Gina brought up the rear.

Roxy's scream split the air as power flared behind us. This wasn't the quiet, steady magic of the barrier and reservoir. Fire licked out from the oratory on a wave of dark elemental rage as if every core spell I'd ever seen had been released at once. There was no mistaking the blazing form that stepped onto the bluff, with wild eyes and hair flowing on updrafts of magic, as human. This was a demon mimic, and she was beyond angry.

Gina tossed grenades and spells in our wake to slow Roxy, then dove into the gap right on my heels. The sphere whined with power, not exactly painful, but the vibration numbed my arm and made it difficult to hold.

We emerged from the slimy tunnel, dashed around the rock outcropping, and came face to face with the gator-demon. Or more accurately, we came face to shin with it. Mon was already down. Bethany had her propped up against the rocks and stood protectively over her panting girlfriend. Owen eyed the portal and stone hut as if gauging his chances of making it before the massive gator could squash him.

As if the screaming magic of the sphere wasn't enough, a familiar unease speared through my stomach, setting my talent on edge. My gaze shot to the beehive entrance, which should have been dark. Light streamed from the square doorway. I doubled over, clutching my middle, the pain much worse than last time. The pure, radiant energy that shone from inside the hut was no flickering candle. The magic had risen.

We skidded to a stop alongside Owen, who scooped the football out of my hands as I convulsed around another wave of agony and lost my grip.

"What'd she hit you with?" he asked.

"Nothing." *Yet.* I stabbed a finger at the glowing doorway. "Guidance system's online. There's a portal in there."

"So the Chrono-monks are coming." Owen nodded like a maniac. "They can make this all right."

"No." I shook my head and pushed upright, getting a handle on the intense reaction my tinker talent had to the power in the hut.

The painful tingling was different from when the vison of the monk manifested. There was a polarity, a singularity of flow involved, as if the power was pulling every cell of my body toward the source, irresistible as the gravity of a black hole. Things did not escape from that kind of phenomena.

"No, it's a one-way gate. We can go to them, but they can't return." My magic was certain of that much.

"Worry about the bomb first," Gina suggested. "Can we make it to our Attwater doorway without Godzilla crushing us?"

"Why isn't it spitting flame?" Owen looked from portal, to hut, to gator. The monster had its head cocked so it could watch us with one eye.

"Out of fuel." I figured that was more likely than it being scared of our awesome powers.

"Or it doesn't want to hit *her*!" Gina pushed us toward the rocks as Roxy emerged from under the squid and launched a bolt of energy.

The ground exploded as her spell struck a few feet beyond where we'd been huddled. Gina returned fire, and so did Bethany. Instead of dodging, Roxy blocked both attacks with a shield that leapt into existence with a wave of her arm. I tried to dredge up a whirlwind, but my jangling tinker magic interfered. Mon rocked back and forth as if in pain while Bethany used an Earth spell to open a fissure that at least slowed Roxy.

"This thing's getting hot, really hot!" Owen looked down at the sphere as if just realizing he basically held a bomb.

"It can't contain that much magic." My abused senses screamed that we were rapidly running out of time. "Use your sword. Get to the vault. Gina will open the door. If you lose her, find Ms. Murdock."

"The sword?" Owen gaped. "You saw what I did last time. I could get us all killed."

The gator moved closer. The ground rumbled gently. I supposed it was trying to sneak up on us. That should have been impossible, but to be honest we'd been so focused on Roxy—the mimic—that its ploy had worked. Roxy picked her way over the cracks Bethany kept laying down.

The gator no longer needed fire breath. It was close enough to step on us or start an avalanche on the rocky wall we sheltered against. Even Owen saw we were out of options.

"Fine, I'll used the bloody sword." Owen's hand closed over the hilt, and a confident smirk replaced his scowl.

But he didn't draw the weapon, just stared up as a shadow passed above us. A long row of white suction cups streamed over our heads like the windows of a passenger train. The massive tentacle shot past and wrapped around the gator's arm. Another whipped out to snake around the thick green neck. This tentacle had been charred down one side, but that didn't slow it down one bit.

We scattered as rocks tumbled down and the ape-squid we'd left for dead flowed around us to engage the gator. Muzzled by one giant arm, the gator couldn't use its deadly breath, not that fire had done the job last time. The ape pounded the other demon with its good arm and clamped onto the gator's shoulder with its ruined mouth until that arm fell limp.

The ape-squid hauled its opponent toward the cliff edge, opening our avenue to the portal. Owen dashed onward, Gina close on his heels. We could make it out while the demons fought. I turned to give Bethany a hand with Mon when a crushing weight slammed me to the ground.

Hair and eyes wild, the mimic stalked toward me with a glowing fist held high, ignoring her battling titans as her magic crushed me into the rocky soil. Something in my back cracked, and new pain lanced through my side.

Triumph shone in her eyes. She may have lost the sphere, but the damage was done. The small amount of power I'd managed to redirect into the barrier wouldn't last long. The beings Roxy had paved the way for sensed it. Massive blows boomed like thunder as they struck the failing protection, and more fractures shot across the aurora curtain.

"Leave us alone and go to hell!" I gasped out my curse.

Bethany raised her hand to unleash a spell, only to be blasted off her feet. The gator-demon roared and toppled in the background as the ape pulled it over the edge of the cliff. Both titans fell in the slow motion trick caused by scale and perspective.

Roxy never looked, never blinked, never broke eye contact as she ground the life out of me. My joints creaked and popped. Her singular focus meant she also never saw the tentacle shoot across the ground as the monsters disappeared over the edge.

"You don't—" Roxy's reply cut off as the tip of the questing arm cupped around her face.

Heavy coils enveloped the startled demon and slammed her to the ground. The tentacle zipped away clutching its angry catch as the ape-squid plummeted. Magic flared between fleshy seams, blowing away chunks of squid arm as Roxy fought to escape. Just as she got a hand free, tentacle and mimic slipped over the edge and were gone.

Ten seconds later, the ground lurched with a thunderous crash. The pressure that had been driving me flat winked out, and I struggled to my knees. Mon cried out as rocks tumbled from the wall to my right. Bethany was at her side in an instant, cradling and reassuring the girl, though I didn't see any obvious wounds.

Thirty yards away, Owen climbed to his feet and looked from portal to hut as though the quake had rattled his senses. Gina had beat him to the portal and was waving him toward her.

"Let's get out of here." I started over to help with Mon.

"We'll be right behind you. Go!" Bethany waved me off.

Thunder still raged in the sky overhead, and for all I knew that second ape-squid had broken through. The barrier would hold the truly nasty things off for a while longer, maybe long enough for us to come back with a solution.

"Be quick, okay?" I broke into a stumbling run, holding my side against what felt like cracked ribs and the flaring magic from the hut.

I'd almost forgotten about the guidance system. Stopping the explosion was still job one, but the monks' magic called.

33. Cavalry

I NSTEAD OF HEADING to Gina and the school portal, Owen backpedaled, darted to the beehive structure, and ducked inside. Damn, we didn't have time for side-trips.

"Owen, get to the vault!" I changed course and entered the hut a few seconds behind him to the sound of two men in a heated exchange.

Pain again flared as my magic roiled. I fought through the doorway and the worst of the discomfort to find the furniture had returned. Our monkly apparition was already on his feet, but instead of arguing with thin air, he confronted Owen, who leaned on the edge of the desk and held out the football.

Wait—that wasn't right. The scene had no substance before. How could our friend be sitting on the desk? The power in the room felt different too, more acute. Everything down to the monk's flying hands looked the same, except more solid. And the doorway at the back of the room flared with the energy of a dozen portals. That was the one-way ticket to wherever the Chrono-monks had gone.

"But you can take care of *this*, right?" Owen shook the vibrating sphere at the monk.

The hooded figure nodded reluctantly. "Only one may pass through."

Owen caught sight of me in the doorway and gave an apologetic smile. "Sorry, Jason. I need this for my mom."

The monk cursed when Owen dashed around him and disappeared through the glowing doorway. Then the hooded figure slumped and turned, the same motions he'd made every time this scene played out—except this time he gazed right at *me*. The monk looked me up and down as if taking my measure.

"Tinkers mend." He spun away, hurried after Owen, and slammed the door shut behind him.

Just like always, the contents of the room faded from sight. The power and gateway went with it, and the guidance system spell powered down.

"He left?" Gina came up behind me.

Before I could answer, a disorienting wave of energy blew back through the doorway. For a second I thought the gate was reopening, but this wasn't barrier magic, or the portal, or even the guidance system. This was new, a rending force that tore at me until something gave—as though a bit of my soul had been cleaved off. The wave of energy rolled on, the odd sensation passed, and the energy coming through the door again faded, leaving only stacked stone.

"That wasn't the sphere exploding." I answered Gina's next question before she asked. "Totally different magic. But yes, Owen's gone. And it's a one-way trip. I think I know why, but for now let's just get back to Attwater and find help."

I unhooked the guidance system, being careful of the ancient power that still bubbled just below the floor. Bethany and Mon waited outside, the goth-girl looking marginally better as she leaned on her girlfriend.

"As if this day could get any weirder." Bethany must have been referring to the strange blast of power, except she was looking off to her left.

When the Attwater portal came into view, I saw what she meant. The rippling green surface usually resembled a scummy pond. But peaks formed as a shadowy figure tried to push through. Transit by portal could be disorienting, but there wasn't any resistance. Yet the surface of the magic stretched like a balloon as a hand holding a black cane finally broke through. The arm was followed by a shoulder and then a white-haired man with a pencil-thin moustache.

"Dean?" Another shadow pushed at the portal while I gaped at the man we'd been searching for since last semester.

"That was quite the trip." Dean Gladstone pulled down the lapels of his train-conductor jacket and took in the scene. "Salt air, rocky terrain, and beehive architecture. I haven't been to Skellig Michael in a very long time." He turned to Gina and me. "Ah, Jason, Ms. Williams, and friends. Wonderful to see you all, but please step back. We've got more coming through."

Twenty men and women pushed through the portal over the next few minutes. All wore the same black tactical gear as Gina, although their clothes had faded to dark gray and were patched and threadbare. On top of that, they all looked…shaggy, as if barbers were in short supply where they'd been. This had to be the lost security contingent that had disappeared with the dean.

"How'd you get back to Attwater?" I couldn't recall the exact number that went missing, but it looked as though everyone had returned.

"We haven't been to the school yet. I assume this portal leads to the silver mirror?" The dean continued at my nod. "We've been…elsewhere, and having a bugger of a time getting back even after I found the right path. Had to come at the portal somewhat sideways. There is a lock on the time-stream that finally opened just moments ago. I've no doubt you'll be able to shed light on what's changed. Our location tells me that at least one of my messages got through. But by the look of that barrier, I'd say we have some work to do before catching up."

He jabbed his cane skyward at the cracked curtain of protective light and the monsters assaulting it. Roxy and her mega-demons might be gone, but the situation remained dire. I quickly outlined how Roxy had used the football device to drain power from the barrier and that the sphere was now lost.

"I had concerns about that young woman," Dean Gladstone said when I finished. "Mimics are too damned hard to identify unless they use dark magic. Regrettably, the person watching Ms. Debove while we figured out her powers ended up on my little excursion. Now we've lost a precious opportunity. I would very much have liked to speak with the monastery. On a brighter note, I *do* know a thing or two about the barrier. Let's see if we can set things right."

He deployed his team along the ridgeline to guard against whatever might cross into our world. A half-dozen took on the second ape-squid. A concentrated barrage from the team couldn't force it to retreat. The flailing magic I'd sent back into the barrier seemed to have trapped the demon halfway through. After a quick debate, they decided to save their spells and just put a watch on the creature.

Gina and I followed Dean Gladstone to the oratory. He placed both hands on the stone altar as if trying to divine what had happened. After a time, one hand found its way to the shallow bowl that had held the sphere.

"I would have liked to study that device you found." His shoulders slumped. "It must act as battery and transformer to meter magic into the barrier. That sphere or one like it would have been part of the regular replenishment of the barrier, but of course the monks haven't been around lately." He began a circuit of the oratory, touching each of the four pillars with subtle magic. "I've been saving this reserve power for an emergency. The current situation certainly seems to qualify."

"So you *are* a Chrono-monk." I marveled as his touch released four flows of power that curled up to bolster the aurora.

"An honorary member at best. If they'd trusted me more, perhaps I'd have known the power of that sphere and been able to keep their defenses at full strength." His smile was sad as he patted the last column. "These only hold a limited amount of energy. Let's see what else can be done while the pillars discharge."

Over the next half an hour, Dean Gladstone led his security team's repair efforts. These were the cream of Attwater's force. Each person quickly grasped the complex Spirit spell he taught on the fly. Flows of magic reinforced the cracked areas as world magic from the oratory slowly thickened the barrier.

Spirit was the element of belief and conviction, and acted as a kind of bug repellant to the monstrosities trying to gain access to our realm. Thunderclaps grew infrequent, but shadowed faces with flaming eyes glared down at the defenders who dared thwart their entry. Yet, like any treatment for vermin, the elemental energy wouldn't last forever.

The last of the magic drained from the pillars. It hadn't been enough to make the repairs permanent. At best we'd put up temporary patches. More of the world magic held in that unfathomable reservoir was needed, much more. And for that we needed the sphere.

I wandered back over to the oratory and reached out to a pillar. The faint tingle of power told me it was indeed drained. I'd grown attuned to that energy and would have sensed it earlier if not for the spell the monks used to lock it away. The mysterious order was quite adept at hiding not only themselves, but the powers they'd wielded to protect mankind. Even though we stood on what might be the biggest magical repository on the planet, it had taken the guidance system to unlock the magic and make a gateway to the monks.

I thought back to when I delved into the midst of that energy. The reservoir had been insanely deep. The magic had risen to the guidance system's call with slow reluctance. And the power had still been there just below the surface when I'd removed the device.

"What are you thinking?" Gina must have seen the wheels turning in my head.

"The magic the monks used to make the barrier is still here below the surface." I pointed off toward the stone hut then down at my feet. "It'll sink out of reach soon, but there's more than enough to fix this thing right."

"And you need the missing sphere for that."

"Maybe not." I stepped up to the altar, ran my hands along the smooth interior of the bowl, and nodded. "It's close. We've gotten to…know each other."

The pathways through the stone of Skellig Michael were cold from disuse, but my consciousness flowed down, following routes of less resistance. The magic had retreated farther over the past hour, but I soon touched the familiar surface. The power halted its slow withdraw as if curious to see what I'd do.

I didn't thrust myself fully into the pool. Without the anchoring mounts in the hut I could easily get lost down there. Instead, I looked to the sky, pushing my tinker magic out like I had when redirecting the magic Roxy had been draining. The fact that I stood where the mimic had wasn't lost on me.

But I was a tinker. Even the monk had recognized that. *Tinkers mend.* And the barrier was broken.

The breath whooshed out of me as the vastness of the problem engaged my talent. The barrier lacked power, we'd known that. But countless points holding it in place around our plane of existence had pulled free too. The demons had been playing the long game, working those anchors loose over the years. And even bolstered by the Dean's people, the cracks were of course still a problem.

It was all too much. My mind stretched, trying to encompass the enormity of it, the vastness. I drifted, growing diffuse. Hot air currents breathed through a tear in the barrier like a sucking chest wound; fetid dank wind pulled me toward the gap. Eyes leered from beyond the opening, all too eager to welcome me to what lay on the other side. I jerked to a stop just shy of the opening.

"Jason!" Gina's hand was clamped around my upper arm, her voice urgent. "Whatever you're doing, stay focused. I'm not letting you go."

Her touch, her voice pulled me back to my body. I stood where I had been, one hand in the bowl reaching down to the power below, the other stretching out to the skies. The tinker talent extended my reach, marking, cataloguing, and flowing along the endless protection the monks had constructed. My talent would do the work. I would be the conduit.

Flow.

The thought invited the power, let it stream up from the depths, into my body, and then out to where it was needed. White filled the world, followed by earth tones and watery blue as the energies of the world filled me. They flowed out just as quickly in a beautiful rushing river. I held tight to my talent. Without the tinker magic directing the current, I'd burn out in an instant. I held hard to the reservoir too. Vast as the resource beneath us seemed, the power I siphoned off took its toll, and the level dropped.

Gina held tight, a rock and anchor that kept me from being swept away on a tide I could only direct, never control.

And the barrier mended. Its old anchor points snapped into place. An anguished howl rose from the other side. The aurora thickened, its black cracks knitting shut. With a massive crunch, the fissure holding the ape-squid healed over. Severed tentacles and a gray hand tumbled to the rocky shore far below. And still the barrier thickened.

I had no concept of how long it was before I collapsed onto the altar. Gina cushioned my head as it hit the blessedly cool stone. My arms were too heavy to move, my body an aching heap, but it was done. I didn't use all the magic, not by a long shot. The barrier had design limits. It had returned to something close to its initial power.

Of course that damned tinker magic hadn't been satisfied with the monks' blueprint. I vaguely recalled my power adding more anchor points. Denser weaves of power narrowed the inherent gaps that let shadows, lurker, and mimics through—the lesser demons, if you could believe that.

"That's all I've got." I gave Gina a smile that hurt my face.

People stood behind her, the dean in front of his team. Gina ran a cool hand over my forehead and rocked me—much the way Bethany had done for Mon earlier. I would have laughed if it didn't hurt so badly.

34. Clean Up

"WE CAN'T LET them get those." Mon was talking to Bethany as the two gazed over the cliff.

"Let who get what?" I asked as Gina and I joined them.

After a brief nap on my comfy stone table, walking around the bluff make me feel human again. Dean Gladstone came up behind us with his second in command, while the rest of his people scoured the island to take care of any nasty surprises that had slipped past.

"Just can't." Mon mumbled a few more words as if suddenly shy, something I hadn't seen since first semester.

"Bad," Bethany added with a nod to the rocks far below.

I lifted an eyebrow waiting for more, then peeked out over the edge. If you didn't look too closely, the mists down there fooled the eyes. You could easily mistake the massive carcasses for rocky coastline. The pile of severed tentacles were a little harder to miss because two had flipped over and waved white suckers as they undulated in the crashing surf.

I exchanged a confused look with Gina, who still refused to leave my side even though I was walking pretty darn well on my own. She simply shrugged and gripped my arm tighter. Apparently we'd both missed the memo about cryptic day.

"That sure is a lot of demon flesh to cover up. Somebody's going to have their hands full." I leaned into Gina, savoring the sunshine.

Since restoring the barrier, the sky had cleared. There wasn't a cloud or demon overlord in sight. The visible aurora also faded out, but not the power—that I sensed easily now.

"The rough seas will keep boats away for a few days." Dean Gladstone joined us near the edge. "I've already put in a call for help with cleanup."

Mon sucked in a sharp breath. Both she and Bethany looked as if they had something to say. The dean gave them a quizzical look, but the women returned their gazes to the ocean.

"And the school has things under control too." He gave the stones a brisk rap with the tip of his cane when one of his people called to him. "Duty calls. You've all done very well here today, even your friend Owen. Whatever his reasons, I'm confident the monks have welcomed him with open arms. We'll have plenty more chances to speak, but I wanted to express my gratitude. You should each be very proud." He sauntered away, exchanged a few words with his people, then called back to me. "It appears we've found a small robot that I expect you may know. Quite a shiny fellow, but his battery was depleted. My people took the liberty of returning him to your workshop."

"Mel's alive?" Okay, not the best choice of words. I didn't care.

I rushed over to shake hands and thank everyone. Knowing Mel was safe lifted a burden I hadn't realized I carried. I returned to the cliff's edge a few minutes later to find Mon and Bethany hadn't moved.

"You two okay?" I asked as the dean's people left. "Roxy certainly got her licks in. We should all see the nurse if the infirmary isn't overrun."

Bethany had scrapes and bruises like mine from being pounded flat by our not-so-friendly mimic. Mon had recovered from whatever debilitating magic laid her low during the battle of the titans. But something still bothered her, and it wasn't obvious from the outside what it was.

"We'll live." Bethany looked like she would jump back into the silent treatment, but relented with an expulsion of breath. "But maybe too much salt air is a thing. Let's gather up our stuff and head back. You can buy lunch and spill the beans about what went on at the oratory. It was quite the light show."

"Deal." I could eat.

* * *

Our estimate of how well Attwater had fared turned out to be grossly inaccurate. The demons had been purged from the school, but the building took a beating. Mr. Gonzales had his hands full and enlisted help from several departments.

Food preparation was not a focus for the administration, and thanks to a magical firefight, some major reconstruction was needed in the commons before students could again congregate.

After a quick report to Ms. Murdock, who confirmed the staff was free of demon influence, we disassembled the mirror portal and returned its three components to the vault. Security would use their own portals to continue clean up.

"Can't you just use the guidance system again to open the portal in the hut?" Gina asked as we wheeled the mirror into its nook.

"I seriously doubt it." I'd looked inside the unit with my frayed tinker talent. "The magic inside was deliberately cut last time but still in place. Now it just feels dead and dark. I wouldn't know where to start."

Even though Gina was the one with official access, we'd come to feel at home among the dusty relics Attwater collected. The four of us lingered, poking around and drawing comfort from the company. No one was in a hurry to go home and be alone with the day's memories.

"Do you think the Dean's right, that the monks will take care of Owen?" Gina asked as we sat around a small dinette that may or may not have once held mystical powers.

"Come on, we're talking about Owen. The guy could make a place for himself anywhere. Plus, he wasn't really feeling like his talent fit in with the whole demon hunting business." He'd said as much in our one-on-one chats. Of course I'd admitted to having the same concern.

I thought back to his argument in the hut. *That* monk certainly hadn't been pleased, but then again, our impulsive friend had been waving a bomb under the guy's nose. "The weird surge after he went through the gateway wasn't the sphere exploding. The magic wasn't right, so somebody on the other end must have helped disarm the thing. Dean Gladstone says my football was what they used to refresh the barrier, so they would have known what to do. He might have made a better call than my idea of stuffing the sphere back in the vault. If the magic here hadn't been enough…" I shrugged and trailed off. They got the picture.

"It still feels weird, him not being here." Bethany had never been Owen's biggest fan, but the pressure of his absence weighed on us all.

"The boy ain't dead, just off partying monk-style," Gina reminded us.

"At least he got out." Bethany sat next to Mon, clutching the other girl's hand as if working up the nerve to say more. "Sometimes having special talents that are…in demand isn't fun. We need to be careful with them and things like those carcasses…dangerous."

"Mega-gator and ape-squid? Dean Gladstone will make sure they're gone before people notice. I bet he's got a way to keep the locals from even noticing before everything can be carted off." My reply didn't calm her. I thought back to the terse cliffside discussion and made an educated guess. "You're worried someone wants the bodies."

"They…they…" Bethany shook her head, angry now. "Damn it! I thought the vault's nullifying field would help more."

"You've been spelled!" Gina looked at their clasped hands and Mon's compressed lips. "Both of you. You want to tell us more, but can't."

Both women nodded.

"You need to warn the dean. There are people…" Bethany rushed her words, but they still petered out.

"…who want the demons we killed back on the island." I finished her sentence and got a frustrated nod in return. "Who wants them? And what are they going to do, boil down body parts to make essence of mega-demon?" She shook her head violently. "Oh, right one question at a time."

Hadn't we just been through this with Gina? Anyone who's ever played a good round of twenty questions has ended up cheating at some point, especially if the first few yes-or-no answers don't narrow things down. Without a verbal clue or two, the game gets boring fast.

Unfortunately, Bethany and Mon didn't have the ability to cheat. Some questions seemed to hit too close to home for them to even respond. That, or there was something else they didn't want us to know. Often a lack of response filled in a blank better than a yes, no, or shrug, helping build a picture of the problem.

"So is this group connected to the special studies wing?" It was the only logical conclusion that fit the first dozen answers, unless a faction had approached both women outside of school.

No response, which I took as a yes.

We didn't get very far on why a special group of teachers would want dead demons, let alone how they could possibly handle the giant ones we'd fought. A cadre of teachers within Attwater's walls with their own agenda sounded like trouble. It was clear they weren't demon controlled, but they didn't operate in line with the school's mission either.

As we broke up for the night, I promised to warn Dean Gladstone about a potential for abusing the carcasses. Bethany and Mon didn't think he was part of the questionable group.

"What do you make of that?" Gina asked as she locked up the vault after the other women left.

"They're both scared, but the picture's still pretty fuzzy. What the hell do you do with a hundred tons of dead demon? Aside from being fresh from the void and their size, those monsters didn't have special abilities—unless they want to know why one turned on the other or how the ape survived fatal wounds."

"More than just injuries." Gina pushed the massive steel door shut and shook her head. "That ape-thing was dead. It had to be."

"Then maybe this is all about regeneration and figuring out the secret of coming back from the dead. Scientists study animals all the time looking for ideas to solve human issues. Maybe finding answers in demon physiology is a new branch of study."

* * *

"I will certainly look into it." Dean Gladstone was tidying up his office, which had been rearranged several times in his absence. "The special talents wing is run by a board of instructors spanning all three schools. As such, it enjoys a certain level of autonomy. But they still operate under our roof."

"And the dead demons?" That seemed to be the thing that most worried Mon and Bethany.

"I've authorized the use of large-scale dissolution spells, which should leave nothing to be exploited. I promise to keep a close eye on the progress and the island. I find it distasteful that our opposition knew more than I did."

"I'm sorry about...everything." Roxy's admittance to school, the sphere, and pretty much everything I'd touched.

"No feeling sorry for yourself. A major assault was long overdue. Your knack for landing in the middle of things has benefits." He slapped my back. "Even if the monks didn't return, you proved they still exist somewhere out on the timeline."

"So why don't they just return?"

"They may not want to. Or perhaps they cannot." He shrugged and dragged one of the visitor chairs over to the hearth. "Despite my time with them, the order remains unpredictable. The gateway you described would convey people through time. Temporal gates can be temperamental—if you'll excuse the pun."

"You mean something could be blocking their return the way you were locked out."

During my debrief, the dean had pressed for details about activating the gate and the blast that came through after Owen left. I'd also dropped the bad news that the guidance system wouldn't be doing its thing again on the island. My descriptions had helped him formulate a theory, but I was vague on the specifics.

"Possibly." He grabbed the second chair, and I helped drag it over. "Even without tapping into the mirror portal, we should have been able to return to the present. But my magic couldn't bring us closer than eleven years ago. The fact that I was finally able to punch through after your temporal gateway collapsed is significant. The events in that hut may have anchored this end of the exclusion zone at a fixed point in time. Meaning that I could not have returned any sooner. Further experiments might pinpoint the earliest date and help me research a related event. It's good to document such things. There can be nasty side effects when forces disrupt our timeline."

That was all I got on the subject. I helped rearrange some of his beloved clocks, handing each up as the dean hung them on the wall. Some got grouped by size, others by consecutive time zones. How he kept track of which clock was set to which zone was a mystery, especially when I noted the hours on two clocks were offset by thirty minutes. Was there such a thing as a half-time-zone?

"Formal offers will be coming through the placement office soon for your class." He stepped back to admire the new arrangement. "Care for a little advanced insight?"

Without naming specific companies, he outlined the top three jobs I'd be offered. Two were in industrial manufacturing facilities, and the third was a mobile repair outfit that sounded like it might entail working on older structures and storage tanks. I must not have looked terribly enthused because he reminded me of the placement office's commitment to work with my desires.

"Keep in mind that as a graduate you'll have access to portal travel, which eases commuting concerns and makes visiting friends much easier. Portals redefine long-distance relationships too." He added that last with a sly smile.

But Gina was only part of the problem.

"That's a fair point, but there's got to be a job that uses my tinker abilities more. And I want to keep working on robots. Sure, my magic is difficult to integrate with technology, but you know how it is." I waved at his wall of clocks.

Mel had been an evolutionary step forward in my robotic design, and I wanted a job that let me pursue my passion. With corporate pressures and the Attwater mission of guarding against demons, it was hard to envision having time for my own projects.

"Your talent would help in any welding repair." He held up both hands when I sighed. "But I understand. To be honest, I've been pleasantly surprised at how well you've managed with your robots. And your achievements at Skellig Michael? Let's just say you're going to be on my speed-dial if we have further problems with the world barrier."

"Which is fine, but not a paying job." Money still mattered to me and my landlord.

"Some facilities still have in-house repair divisions, others outsource work. I'll set up a meeting with placement to discuss options and think outside the box. This could be an opportunity to break new ground."

35. Goodbyes & Graduation

C LASSES CONTINUED AND finals commenced. We'd started our Attwater adventure with Objective Evaluations to determine each of our magic talents. We completed our education with trade skill tests to get the shiny new certifications that led to gainful employment.

On the magic front, talent testing varied by individual instructor. I got a taste of higher education by defending the paper and conclusions about my repair project. Lars did some fancy magical gardening, and Chad drew out the precise path of a hurricane making landfall off the gulf. Thanks to Attwater pulling some strings with the southern weather service, several hundred people made it off a barrier island safely before their small town got swept clean. Owen would have had a grueling day at the office diagnosing and repairing vehicles, but of course had dodged that bullet.

Bethany and Mon weathered the traumas inflicted by their respective teachers, but the experience left the pair quiet and brooding. Neither had said more than a dozen words for days, so I was happy to hear they'd be attending our intimate little post-graduation ceremony. We'd agreed to meet for a little care and share. Offers had been made by placement weeks ago. Some of us had bounced pros and cons against others, but no one had the big picture of where we were all heading. The party would be the big reveal and the time to discuss how best to keep in touch.

Our actual certificates of completion had been handed out in the auditorium where a hundred-and-fifty students could reasonably march onto stage when their name was called. Unlike universities, the three schools of magic didn't hold open graduation ceremonies. Our class consisted largely of adults, some of whom had grown kids of their own already.

Our trades training was a professional milestone more than an academic one. And in general, you didn't bring family and friends into a magic school more than necessary, especially when said institution was still recovering from a demon uprising.

Now we all gathered in Attwater's basement, packed into a low-ceilinged foyer the size of a basketball court off the main corridor. A plaque on a stone pedestal stood in an alcove at the head of the space. Familiar stone walls surrounded the seating area, pipes and glow bulbs just out of reach above. Some might find the proceedings claustrophobic, but the students had grown comfortable with these conditions. This was the true commencement ceremony to launch our careers.

"Did you catch the table of water glasses behind the podium?" Lars leaned over Bethany's shoulder and pointed. "Bet he's going to do that music trick again."

"That was more than a trick." Bethany shook off his hand. "Chad talks to the heart of the school."

"I know! It's going to be awesome." Lars ignored the rebuke and bounced in his seat with barely contained excitement.

The ceremony was the closest most students ever got to the mystical heartstone that embodied the building's evolving consciousness. The tradition of gathering graduating classes down here gave us an opportunity to bask in the school's spirit, a kind of blessing to carry us through those darker days we were each sure to encounter.

Dean Gladstone opened with brief comments, thanking us all for our hard work and continued commitment to be the front line eyes, ears, and defense that kept the nation safe. He praised Ms. Eisner for stepping up to be dean for the semester and handed her the reins of the event.

To keep the mood light, Ms. Eisner passed out a few fun awards. Lars positively swooned over his plastic trophy for most improved study habits. Our temporary dean went on to convey her thanks to the entire staff, then had us all rise, raise our right hand, and repeat a pledge.

"I—state your name—promise to use what I've learned for the betterment of mankind."

The echo from the crowd started out disjointed but soon settled into one voice with a cadence.

"To watch and defend against demons and those who abet them."

The oath was a short, innocuous repetition of clauses from the contract we'd each signed. Bethany and Mon stood right next to me, but I couldn't hear them at all. Of course, than may have been because Lars shouted his oath so loud that my right ear hurt.

The school dedication plaque behind Ms. Eisner took on a gentle glow as we affirmed our future roles. By the end of the oath, the magic shone bright from the little alcove, and pure familiar tones drifted across the audience.

Ms. Eisner waved us to take our seats. Chad was already at the water goblets, his hands deftly gliding across their rims to form another haunting melody. As before, Attwater responded, this time forming a magical duet. Complementing segments of the tune snaked through the crowd offering us good fortune in our future endeavors and reassurance that our efforts would not be in vain. Pain lingered beneath the notes. Attwater had been injured by the attacks. But stronger was the promise that our character would be forged and bettered by adversity.

Many heads, including my own, nodded, accepting the school's gift. Quiet sobs rose from some, while others like Bethany were more stoic. A skeptical frown crossed my friend's face, but I didn't interrupt Chad's performance to comment.

As the last notes died away, Ms. Eisner sent us out into the world to do great things and prosper. Timing on that depended on our individual job start dates. Most would be hanging around the school for a few more days, possibly right up to the semester break.

"Party time!" Lars strode across the commons waving a six-pack, but apparently caught part of our conversation. "No more demon plots and portal hops. This is supposed to be about us."

I'd been asking Chad if Herman had any theories as to why the monks hadn't come back. More than just Owen's disappearance rubbed me wrong. The phantom scene with the monk he'd eventually argued with had to be a kind of time echo, but what triggered it remained a mystery.

"You win." I held my hands up in surrender, took a cold can, and popped the top. "Why not lead us off. What's on the horizon at Lars central?"

The table was already heaped with snacks. Kitchen and commons were back in full operation, and we weren't the only group holding a post-graduation gathering. Chad leaned against his favorite stone column, at such ease that I wondered how he'd manage away from the school. Mon and Bethany sat to his left, still not very talkative but more relaxed than I'd seen them in days. In fact, they looked excited, as if finally accepting what lay ahead.

"I scored big time!" Lars took a seat and scooped pizza bites onto a paper plate. "Staying with the homeboys. Say hello to the Philadelphia Zoo's newest botanical specialist."

"Congrats." Though I'd yet to catch a glimpse of any of the mythical people the guy supposedly hung out with, he seemed genuinely pleased with the new job. "Do demons target zoos?"

"Not so much, but there's been activity at museums along the river. I'll be watching the airport too. What about you?"

I'd wanted to go last because of the interesting bargain Dean Gladstone helped me strike with placement. "Something a little different. I'm setting up a repair shop near Norfolk. I'll get work from the shipyard, but also offer custom repair services."

"Not just welding then?" Chad asked.

"I wanted to use my talent more. The dean's calling it a pilot program so I'll have extra reporting to do back to placement. But if all goes well, I plan to branch out and offer consulting services on robotic designs too. There's been a lot of demon interest in the area's naval bases and industrial complex. I'll be spread pretty thin, but it's better than factory work. You?"

"I'm kind of staying put." Chad patted the stonework and gazed fondly into the sighing vents over our table. "With the school's portal network, I can get a read on the weather anywhere. And security wants me on a special project."

"Makes sense." I thought back the deadly bolts he threw with Attwater's help. "Sounds like you were the star demon slayer during the attack."

"We just did what needed doing," he said. "I suspect they'd like to tap into Attwater's senses and be able to use her as an early warning system even if I'm not around. She's okay with the idea, but the devil will be in the details."

"Bethany and Mon?" I didn't know if they'd be able to share, but had to at least offer the chance.

"We're going away," Bethany said after glancing at Mon.

Cryptic as usual. I took a sip, and was about to float the idea of a three-month reunion.

"Can't say where. We'll keep in touch, but don't speak to anyone about either of us. Okay?"

"It almost sounds like you're not taking Attwater jobs," Lars said. "The placement office really does work with you if you give them the chance."

"Placement isn't involved with *our* job…offers." Bethany snorted in disgust and looked around to ensure no one else was listening in. "Our assignments aren't negotiable. So we've found other work, low-profile jobs to stay off the radar. Neither of us want our talents to be…used, not by…them." She forced the words out past the magic that constrained her, then bit her lip. "If the dean asks, let him know we're sorry and will pay the school back when we can.

And tell him thanks. I think he tried to help, but it only made things worse."

"Don't worry about us." Mon slipped an arm around Bethany's shoulders. "This is what we want."

As difficult as the topic was to talk about, they both seemed at ease with their decision. Taking control of the situation had chased away their haunted expressions. I shivered to think of what assignments had been selected in the dark recesses of the special talent wing. Dean Gladstone would understand why they broke their contracts. Hopefully the school wouldn't demand that their scholarships be repaid. Bethany and Mon had already paid enough.

With formalities out of the way, we turned to some serious eating and reminiscing. In eighteen short months, Attwater had become a second home. That we could laugh and reminisce despite all the trauma spoke to the oddities of the human psyche. A world of magic had been opened to us, friends were found and lost, and the path ahead was sure to be fraught with danger. But the future promised excitement and interesting careers. We'd survive.

Epilogue: A Visit to Skellig Michael

S URF CRASHED AGAINST the rocks far below on a coastline clear of massive demon carcasses.

"The cleanup seems to have gone well." Gina peered out over the edge, her curls dancing wildly on an updraft of salt air. "How's the barrier looking? I just see clouds."

She shaded her eyes and scanned the sky. The dean wanted me to check on the shield one last time before leaving to set up shop in Norfolk. With the mirror portal still locked away, his request gave me a convenient excuse to use a security portal and ask Gina along. We'd come at midday because the daily high seemed unable to struggle above fifty as winter began in earnest.

"Still nice and strong, which should make for spectacular northern lights this winter." I exhaled through my teeth as I studied nuances in the magic flickering between anchor points, several of which let off a faint spark in my tinker sight.

I'd made a circuit of the upper bluff and oratory, reaching out to inspect the net of protective magic. The energy wasn't in the sky, but imagining it was helped my mind cope. In truth, the barrier stretched around our world at a seam between realities. Physics might call them dimensions, but that term didn't quite fit—not with magic involved. It was the same with the aurora borealis. Underlying scientific principles of charged solar particles and atmospheric composition caused the phenomena, but the intensity and duration were heavily influenced by the magical force shielding us from the demons' domain. People worldwide that had never before witnessed the wondrous lights would be in for a treat in the coming months.

"I sense a big but." Gina's rubbed my upper arm, and gave me her best cynical smile.

"*But,* I think the power's still eroding," I admitted. "Hardly noticeable, but magic does bleed out at several key points. I don't see any way to fix it."

"You probably can't." She hurried on at my scowl. "There's still a little thing called entropy. The monks regularly replenished their spell, so leaking power is probably part of the original design."

"The dean did say he'd need my help maintaining the barrier."

"There you go." She bumped shoulders and slipped her hand inside my leather jacket, where it settled, warm on my chest. "Think of it as job security."

"Speaking of which, they've authorized a portal for my repair shop. Once I get the materials in and tooling set up, I can pop back over to see how you're doing. Heck, I don't even technically have to live in Virginia."

"That might raise some eyebrows on your tax returns." She laughed at my expression and kissed my chin. "We'll make the long-distance thing work. I'll miss you while you're getting organized, but I'm going to be swamped too. The school's still a shambles. Ms. Murdock wants me to stay on through summer, but I bet she's going to try to make my job permanent. The dean's team members are still reintegrating, so we'll have to see."

"Is that what you want, to stay at Attwater?" I knew she missed using her talent.

"Not forever. I've still got my sights set on underwater welding, and if I don't bring my salamanders out to play once in a while, the little hotties are going to revolt." She snuggled in close under my arm. "I'm impressed that you got placement to try a new approach, maybe a little jealous."

"It was something Owen and I discussed." I wished he'd gotten the same chance. "Neither of us was seeing a good fit for our magic. I'd suffocate on a factory line."

"Well, I'm proud you stood up for yourself. It's good for the school to evolve. Too bad Mon and Bethany weren't able to work something out."

"It's high school all over again," I said. "We were the misfit lunch table. I buck the system, the girls duck out of their contracts, and Owen doesn't even graduate."

The sun broke through the clouds, and I walked her around the rocky point under the pretext of inspecting the barrier from a different angle. Except for the fallen rocks and broken cliff edge, you'd never know two titans had blocked the narrow trail and battled to the death. Massive feet and tentacles had stripped away the thin layer of topsoil in front of the beehive hut, but the old red sandstone making up the island had weathered the abuse intact. Beyond the rocky bluff, our flat little oasis of wild grasses had survived unscathed.

When we cleared the trickier section of path, I snuck a kiss that Gina returned with warm enthusiasm. I couldn't help letting my hands rove, sliding down over her hips then back up beneath her puffy coat. My eyes must have darted over to the patch of grass.

"Well, that was yummy." She pushed back and patted my chest, smooth vapor clouds puffing into the wind as she caught her breath. "I get the feeling you're done with inspecting the barrier, but" —she held up a finger, arched an eyebrow, and pointed to our special place— "*that* is not happening, not in this weather. You can take me somewhere nice and warm tonight. There's this nifty thing they just invented called the mattress. Got it?"

So much for impulsive and romantic. Wasn't a guy supposed to emotionally connect with relationship milestones? You couldn't get more formative than that night under the stars and shimmering magic—our little patch of grass at the top of Skellig Michael.

Maybe my hormones were talking, but I still felt the pull of that wonderful memory, the throbbing energies overhead. I frowned because the tingling sensation wasn't just coming from the blue horizon.

"I think we need to go check something out." I turned inland, and Gina dropped her hand with a startled huff.

"Fool a girl once…" She hurried to catch up and saw where I was heading. "You're *not* getting past second base on a cold stone floor either, mister."

"What? No." Throbbing in my chest called to my talent. "It's the magic."

We ducked into the hut at the same time the monk swept through the non-existent back door—except it was there, as were the books, desk, and flickering candle.

"Still?" Gina tried to pull me back, but I gently shook her off.

I crossed the small room and waved a hand through the surface of the desk. No resistance. The monk sat, opened his ledger, and dipped his quill just like always. The power of the echo had my stomach buzzing, but I'd become familiar with the world magic and energy of the vision. The scene no longer caused intense pain.

"Owen's already gone through, so why are we still seeing this?" I scooted around to look over the hooded figure's shoulder, but didn't recognize the language he wrote in.

"It's like a distress beacon that just keeps repeating a broadcast." Gina made a grab for the candle and when that failed studied the flame closely. "I can't reach the flame with pyromancy either. Fire's ethereal properties are thought to cross planes of existence. But I might as well be reaching into a movie with my talent. Crap!"

The monk's head jerked up, his glare sending Gina stumbling back.

"Deep breaths." I covered my laugh with a cough. "It's just the scene playing out again. Owen must have stepped into the room. Now they'll argue and storm through the gateway."

I stepped around the desk to join Gina, stupid because it wasn't really there. The monk pushed to his feet, hood still shadowing all but his eyes, eyes that softened and crinkled at the corners as if he smiled. Instead of shouting and throwing up his hands, the monk circled the desk and stretched out both arms in greeting. We stepped aside as he welcomed an invisible newcomer and dropped into sedate conversation with occasional gestures at his desk and the back door.

"This isn't like before," Gina whispered into the silence.

The red-robed monk walked to the wooden door, held it open for his invisible guest, and then passed into the gateway and vanished. The furniture followed suit, fading from sight and leaving us standing in the empty stone room.

"What's changed?" I knelt and touched one of the brackets we'd used, carefully probing to the reservoir far below. "The world magic is quiet. This was just another echo."

"The monks must have a second visitor coming."

"Except with the dead guidance unit there's no way to activate the gateway to the Chrono-monks' time bubble." I caught her raised eyebrow. "It's the dean's theory. He thinks the catastrophic event that keeps his talent from accessing the past decade also threw the monastery into a pocket reality sitting outside our timeline." I jabbed a finger at the empty doorway. "Unlike a normal portal, that gateway had a temporal shift."

"Great, on top of everything else, Owen's lost in time."

"You know, I think that's what he wanted." I thought back to our friend's last words. "He went through for his mom."

"But his mother died in a car crash when Owen was just a kid."

"Yep, over ten years ago." The math was pretty simple and supported my suspicion. "The dean had to go back more than eleven years to break into the timeline, and was only able to push back into the present after Owen went through to the monks."

"So Owen's the key?"

"Or something he did. Dean Gladstone's going to keep experimenting to pinpoint the exact date where the blockage starts. Then he can search for a correlating event. I'm willing to bet that date is the day of the accident, the day Owen's mom died."

"That's why he went all gaga over the Chrono-monks." She looked to the sealed doorway and nodded.

"Must be." There was nothing we could do about it now even if we wanted to. "I think the monks helped him go back to save her."

"No wonder the timeline's gone sideways. Do you think he succeeded, that she's alive?"

"Figuring that out would take some detective work. I think he grew up in Virginia, and there's got to be a zillion Jones."

"Even harder if she kept her maiden name." Wheels were definitely turning behind those brown eyes.

"Don't worry." I figured I better head her off at the pass. "The dean's being a duck."

"A...duck?"

"You know, calm and serene as he glides along." I bobbed my head like said waterfowl and paddled my hands to illustrate. "But below the surface he's paddling like crazy to get a handle on the time disruption. He'll soon have the Chrono-monk equivalent of crime-scene tape stretched around the locked section of timeline. Yep, the dean will figure out what happened. But I don't think changing the past worked." A headache settled behind my left eye as I followed the logic. "If Owen saved his mom we wouldn't be having this conversation. We'd never know about her accident because he would have never mentioned a car crash that didn't happen."

"Unless we're immune or your linear-time assumption is wrong." Gina might not have been *trying* to make my head explode, but she was certainly standing in the splash zone. "What if Owen's mom is alive? What then?"

"No idea." My breath billowed out as I shook my head. "Telling his folks about magic isn't an option. Plus, it wouldn't do any good."

"But at least they'd know how much their son sacrificed."

"True, but Owen wasn't looking for accolades. He just wanted to undo what happened."

After learning about the monks, Owen and I had chewed over the idea of time travel. I hadn't understood his enthusiasm at the time, but he'd come to accept the fact that we'd never know if someone changed our past. Cocky as he was, if Owen *had* managed to go back, he'd be at peace with no one ever knowing.

We basically agreed to disagree on that point and did our best to refrain from speaking of Owen in the past tense. An afternoon chill settled over the island as though Skellig Michael was urging us to be on our way. We talked about the days to come and took one last stroll along the cliffs, drawing out our final moments on the island before turning back to the portal and whatever the future might hold.

~

Loved it, hated it, somewhere in between? Let people know!
I'd be eternally grateful if you'd share your opinion of *The Forgotten Isle* or any other books on my Amazon author page.
https://amazon.com/author/steinjim
Your review need not be long, only takes a minute, and is super helpful to new authors. – Jim

About the Author

Jim Stein hungers for stories that transport readers to extraordinary realms. Despite sailing five of the seven seas and visiting abroad, he's fundamentally a geeky homebody who enjoys reading, nature, and rescuing old pinball machines. Jim grew up on a steady diet of science fiction and fantasy plucked from bookstore and library shelves. After writing short stories in school, two degrees in computer science, and three decades in the Navy, Jim has returned to his first passion. His speculative fiction often pits protagonists with strong morals against supernatural elements or quirky aliens. Jim lives in northwestern Pennsylvania with his wife Claudia, a grandcat with a perpetually runny nose, and the memory of Marley the Greatest of Danes.

Visit **https://JimSteinBooks.com/subscribe** to get a free ebook, join my reader community, and sign up for my infrequent newsletter.

Made in the USA
Middletown, DE
08 November 2023

42225119R00177